MURDER
BEGETS
MURDER

MURDER BEGETS MURDER

by

JAMES CORBETT

Introduction by

HOWARD PEARLSTEIN

RAMBLE HOUSE
2014

CORBETT BEGETS CORBETT

It's easy—too easy—for modern writers to get all smarmy and critical and nitpicky and make sport of James Corbett. For those who enjoy that sort of thing, I recommend William F. Deeck's book: *The Complete Deeck on Corbett*—he's as nitpicky as it gets, and he's quite funny doing it.

To be honest, Corbett's not the greatest genre writer of his era. But pulling silly or funny or incomprehensible quotes from any of his 43 novels and using that to ridicule him may tell more about the writer who does that than Mr. Corbett himself. He published 43 novels in 22 years. As might be expected, he didn't do a lot of going back and editing—nor, apparently—did his editors. (An example: One paragraph about the murder of a man made to look as if it had been suicide was written, from a different viewpoint, but with the same specific points repeated on the next page.)

I decided to try to find the context and underlying factors that made him appear so idiosyncratically awful to we modern folk. I admit some trepidation, though, after reading Mr. Deeck's book, the feeling of being in the same sort of danger that faced detectives such as Kurt Russell in *The Mean Season* or Matthew McConaughey in *True Detective* who, in looking too closely at the mind of a serial killer, were sucked down into the monstrous miasma of the disease, resulting in total mental breakdown.

But I pressed on, hoping the mind of a serial murder mystery writer wouldn't harbor such infectious ruin. And a serial murder mystery writer he was—43 novels published in 22 years! Definitely—according to his critics—a "Stop Me Before I Write Again" compulsion.

But let's put it in context. Corbett was born in 1887. Victoria was Queen, Robert Cecil was PM, and the Irish Crimes Act had just been passed—suspending trial by jury in Ireland. The Thin Red Line had finally settled Shaka Zulu's hash with rifles and cannon against spears and shield and made Zululand a British Colony. And Glenfiddich single malt Scotch whiskey was distilled for the first time on Christmas Day of that year.

This—his last of the 43 novels—was published in 1951. In his native England that year, Winston Churchill was re-elected as Prime Minister, and the British National Health Service was still listing Mental Diseases of Negroes such as *drapetomania*—"the irrational desire of slaves to attempt to escape," and *dysaesthesia aethiopica*—"the disease that causes slaves' laziness and free negroes to engage in rascality."

In the USA, Harry Truman was obliged to remind Dugout Doug MacArthur of the US Constitution and the Chain of Command, Remington Rand delivered the first Univac, and the Rosenbergs were tried and executed.

Around the world, there was a blue sun seen all over Europe, the result of forest fires in Canada, and there was a State of Emergency declared in Egypt because of riots. Okay—some things are the same.

In his time, before the word took on any sexual meaning, Corbett was what they would call: "A queer fellow." (Jan Morris once wrote about how unfortunate for the language it was—turning a most useful and descriptive word into a sexual derogatory.)

"Queer" in a sense of "Odd," but more intensely so.

A house I once rented could be called "queer" in that meaning. It was charming and attractive, all redwood on the outside with clever rustic touches inside. And also inside, something was not quite what it should be. It took a while to realize why. There wasn't an actual right angle in the place. Not a single corner was 90 degrees. Every one was just a bit off—93 degrees or 87. As I said, charming and attractive, but also a bit disturbing.

So with James Corbett (not to be confused with the boxer, "Gentleman Jim" Corbett nor the rifle-toting Jim Corbett, author of *Man-eaters of Kumaon*).

He was a James, never a Jim. James Corbett was structurally sound and had many excellent features, charming, interesting, but all were—by usual standards—just slightly out of plumb.

Sometimes it seems, as Mr. Deeck pointed out, that English wasn't his first language, and he had no idea what language it might have been. Actually, there is one I know of, in which both syntax and reality are so mutable as to change willy-nilly. That is the one spoken by the Siberian Chukchi people—an Amanita-using shamanistic reindeer-herding tribe who, in their stories make Mr. Corbett's tales sound like a Dick and Jane Reader. Of course, I only read them in translation.

Maybe it's not the syntax. Noam Chomsky created this sentence as an example: *"Colorless green ideas sleep furiously."* Syntactically perfect but also incomprehensible. And to say that ideas may be both colorless and green strikes me as somewhat Corbett-esque.

Some of the queerness is due to the way language has changed over the years. He uses words that are either archaisms or local jargon or humorous versions of both.

He often over-describes, filling a sentence all chock-a-block with adjectives, but more, it seems, from a sense that his readers—1930's and 1940's—weren't familiar with police procedures nor medical ones.

But when he gets to something all English schoolboys know, say, a portion of turbulent English history, his narrative is purely as spare and referential as that of a minimalist poet.

The murder has taken place in Castelton House, a 15th century mansion still in possession of the original family, but one which is supposedly under a curse. And Detective-Inspector Croft has been sent to investigate and he regards his destination's history on arrival at the stately home:

*History . . . Here it was, surging invisibly around him.
Birth, death, pain, laughter, tragedy, tears, quarrels, love,
hate. 1432—Henry VI, Joan of Arc, the Wars of the
Roses . . . The Casteltons building and settling in the midst of
feudal upheaval—a great Catholic family bringing the
Church into the home.*

*The Reformation . . . Mary, Elizabeth. Protestantism . . .
the pursuivants . . . the crude political pressure . . . persecution . . . loyalty to the Crown . . . the grim holding on to an
untenable position . . . forced abjuration of an ancient faith,
never to be restored. It was all here.*

Made me think of the abstract artist of the same era having to justify his art, showing that he could paint portraits
quite well, but preferred the way he was doing it.

And of course, the villain telling the captive of his clev-
erness, is, today, the stuff of standup comics, even though in
this case it doesn't end with the Flying Squad crashing
through the door. But that's a matter of a style being repeated so often it no longer has meaning.

So, if you're looking for the nitpicks and the howlers,
again, I recommend checking online for Mr. Deeck—there
are several sites with transcriptions of his address to mystery
writers, listing all the Corbett incomprehensibles, but there is
one supposedly high on the WTF list that I find delightful,
and even use it as a sig from time to time.

It makes me realize that perhaps none of his critics have
noticed the man had a very British, very dry sense of humor.

The phrase I love is: *Like searching for an ostrich in a
forest of monkeys.*

If you know that ostriches are open plains desert birds
and wouldn't be found in any forest, with or without monkeys, then it makes perfect sense. It's about what we might
call a snipe hunt.

"So I asked the Commander of the company looking
for WMD's in Saddam Hussein's Iraq. 'Were you able to
find any?' "

"Get real. It was like searching for an ostrich in a forest of monkeys. Of course not."

So read on—let yourself enjoy it. It's quite a tale, actually. Quite satisfying.

Howard Pearlstein
Oakland CA
June 2014

CHAPTER I

TERROR BY NIGHT

SHE HAD MANAGED to fall off into an uneasy doze when the queer sound came from somewhere downstairs. Marjorie Castleton opened her eyes with a start, and for a moment or two lay blinking at a long shaft of moonlight, broken into a fantastic pattern by an ancient leaded window. The pale bar lay across the floor, plucked like a ghostly finger at the hem of the silk bedspread near her feet, touched in its passing the corner of an oak chest, so that the worn black iron of its fastenings seemed to shimmer. On her bedside table the insistent tick of a small clock was urging her back to full consciousness.

In the semi-darkness she set her teeth, body tensed against a repetition of the noise. Then it came—a scuffling, bumping sound that made her throat constrict and her heart beat faster. A moment more she lay, fighting against the terror of the unknown, then suddenly nerved herself to put up a hand to the pendant switch of the light above her bed. She flung back the coverlet, got out of bed to slide her feet into a pair of lacy mules and her arms into a quilted dressing-gown. The thin rustle of her movements merged into a renewal of the greater noise from below—the echoing scrape of laboured movement, the thud of quick footsteps; then suddenly a muffled cry, a slumping noise—and a brief interval when it seemed that all had gone strangely hushed and dead. Marjorie Castleton took in a deep intake of breath, and put the back of a hand to her tumbling mouth. Nearer at hand, it seemed, a door clicked abruptly. Then silence again.

Suddenly she became aware of the little clock once more in the scheme of existence. Time beat on; she clung blindly to the high courage that had already brought her so far and forbidden her to give in to that which was unknown, unpredictable—the shadow across her young life. She strained her ears for what might come next, then caught it as a far-away noise—the rapid shuttle of feet repeated. It terminated abruptly in the distance and she breathed again, her slim hand falling to her side and rustling against her gown. The blanketing silence of the small hours was again over all.

She stood there undecided. She felt that she should go on, but her slim body seemed to be immobile by the bedside. The girl looked around helplessly, then forced herself into movement once more. A step forward . . . And then she froze anew. The footsteps were repeated, but closer now. Closer, more frightening—outside her very room. The little distance between her and that which she feared no longer existed. It was upon her; there was a low, insistent knocking at her bedroom door.

While the seconds ticked off she reviewed the situation, almost like one in a state of mental abstraction. Tonight . . . other nights . . . tragedy stalking her, brooding over all . . . the gradual undermining of her easy confidence . . . the forced, subconscious acknowledgment of that which demanded recognition and refused to be put aside. Her lips were trembling now, and her breathing shallower and more rapid. The knock came again—urgent, more insistent. At that, she nerved herself somehow to meet the challenge. She forced herself into movement; forced herself to approach the heavy old oak door of her room, to put out a hand to swing it open towards her, and dreading all that while that which might be waiting on the other side.

A man, shadowy in the semi-darkness. She peered at him, uncertain of his identity, fearful of his presence, until he spoke. His voice was urgent, deliberately kept low for her sake. "Miss Castleton, don't be alarmed—"

"Oh!" she said. "Oh! It's you!"

"I didn't call out," he said, "because I didn't want to frighten you and make things worse. But I woke up suddenly—"

"Then—you heard it? That awful noise—"

Unbidden, Tony Scott stepped into the room and stood at her side. "I did. I'm not a light sleeper, as a rule, but after what you told me, and the fact that this is my first night in a strange house, I didn't get down to it very well, I'm afraid. Miss Castleton, I feel that I should investigate. But I called in to ask you to stay where you are, in safety. Leave this to me."

There was quiet confidence in his deep voice that she found good to hear, but she nevertheless laid restraining fingers on his arm. "Don't go, Mr. Scott."

He shook his slightly tousled head. "Why? Because I'm your guest and you somehow feel responsible for me? Sorry. Miss Castleton. To me, that seems to be all the more reason why I should help you. Good job there is a man in the house at present. Keep your door closed and let me have a stooge around. There must be a perfectly rational explanation for all this."

But she clutched at his arm more firmly. "There's something—horrible, beastly. I just can't explain it, but I feel . . ."

"Don't let it get you down." Tony Scott hesitated, and then found impulse irresistible. His own strong fingers closed over hers, and he pressed them reassuringly. And although this man was a comparative stranger to her, she did not object. There was comfort in his strength—that, and something more that even in this time of mystery and peril was attractive to her feminine instincts. "Look," he said, "we're wasting time, Miss Castleton. You've got trouble, and I'm the only man in the house. Stay here."

He released her fingers gently. His own tingled for the feel of some sort of a weapon—anything. His favourite niblick, a hefty spanner—at least something to help even up the mysterious odds below. He was a little above the average height, but of medium build, young and healthy. He had his fists, anyhow, and he meant to use them, if need be. It was ghostly, here in this upstairs gallery with its many shadows among the old carvings. The flooring creaked softly beneath his weight as he went forward. Some little distance away his ear caught the sudden babble of female voices, and he nod-

ded to himself sombrely. He could account for those, anyway. The servants . . .

His descent of the wide oaken stairway was accomplished resolutely, but with caution. At the turn of the stairs
an old, long-cased clock greeted him with a low, creaking
tick. It was serene, undisturbed, as it had been for generations. Serene in the presence of intrigue and mystery, of unexpected happenings, mirth, tragedy. Scott took breath as he
paused there. He tried to peer over the twisted banister rails,
but found himself baulked by the turn of the landing.

There was dead silence from below. Silence and a great
patch of chequered moonlight, sweeping across the shadowy
expanse of the Great Hall as he gained the bottom of the
stairs. Good enough for him to stop worrying about the advisability of finding a light-switch. He saw chairs, shadowy
pictures, the great bulk of the long refectory table that stood
as centre-piece. The chill of the stone floor, broken here and
there by rugs, seemed to strike upwards through his thin
slippers.

Nothing here, he decided, as he stood peering about uncertainly. His square jaw was thrust upwards aggressively,
his teeth set, fists clenched. Yet he told himself that he might
relax. He would make a cautious tour of the rest of this old
rambling house, then get back to bed and see what had best
be done in the morning. But as he moved forward anew he
caught a slight rustling sound at his back and swung around.
"Really, Miss Castleton, I told you—"

"I'm no coward," she said firmly. "What is it?"

"Nothing," Scott answered, and moved forward a pace or
two, his eyes trying to pierce the shadows. "After all the
trouble you've had, this place is probably getting on your
nerves, although I won't deny that there seemed to be a dickens of a shindy down here a short time ago." He was moving
forward as he spoke, skirting furniture. "I think—Good
God!" he said suddenly, and stopped.

She was at his side instantly. He heard her quick but restrained breathing. She was wordless with horror. Scott gently put her away from him and dropped to his knees.

The huddled mass that had once been a man lay crumpled face downwards by a shadowed door. The fingers of his left hand seemed to be scrabbling at its lower panels; his right arm was bent beneath him. As if from a great intervening distance Scott heard the creak of footsteps and the sharp burr of an elderly woman's voice. He lifted his head. "Lights!" he said urgently.

The housekeeper negotiated the last four stairs, turned right sharply and hurried across to the wall. Switches clicked beneath her fingers. Scott found himself blinking in the sudden radiance as he stared down at the dead man.

Marjorie Castleton bit desperately at her lip to restrain a scream, then turned her head away. She felt herself to be reeling, and Scott looked up just in time. He sprang up, moved across to catch her.

"Steady, now—steady!" he urged, and felt her slimness relax in his arms. "Give me a hand, Miss McCracken."

The grey, hard-bitten housekeeper came forward. She averted her eyes from the floor by the exercise of a resolute will-power. The girl fluttered her eyelids, struggled to stand alone. "I'm—all right . . ."

"Sit ye down, Miss Castleton." The housekeeper's angular shoulder turned Scott dexterously aside. The woman scraped a high-backed chair forward, and exhibited surprising strength in turning it so that it faced away. She guided the girl into it and forced her gently downwards. And suddenly Marjorie Castleton gave a deep sob of sheer horror.

"The—the Blue Room!"

"Nonsense, Miss Castleton," Scott growled. "Take it easy, now."

"Outside the Blue Room . . ." the girl went on dully. "I've tried to fight this thing. I've tried not to believe—"

"Go on being that way," he urged her. "There's no sense in giving in now. Won't you take her back to her room, Miss McCracken? Please—"

He looked at the elderly housekeeper appealingly. She was massaging the girl's left wrist, almost automatically. "I'm no' a believer in skelpies an' such like mysel'," she said slowly, ignoring Scott's request, "but this goes beyont a body's reckoning. First the mistress, then the Colonel, and now—"

She half-turned, and Scott saw her haggard, lined face. "This hoose, Mr. Scott—"

"Is like all other ordinary houses," he snapped back, holding grimly onto his own nerves. "And after all this man's a stranger."

"Have ye looked at his face then?" she queried, her strong, veined hand still on Marjorie's shoulder; and Scott went down to his knees again. There was blood unavoidably on his hands as he strove to raise the dead weight and turn it over sufficiently for the terrible shattered back of the head to be momentarily hidden and so that the cold, agonised have might be brought to the light. "Take a look, Miss McCracken," he invited harshly. "Know him?"

The old housekeeper's own features were like granite as she turned from the girl and forced herself to look down-wards. Scott sensed the struggle to conquer revulsion and keep her voice steady. "No."

The young man hesitated. He could not force the girl to face this thing. At all costs she must be got back to bed. He went to stand beside her.

Gently he said: "I intend to contact the police without further delay, Miss Castleton. You must do as I say, now. You'll be only hampering things to stay here. Trust me to do the best I can in the circumstances."

"Very well," she said numbly, and got to her feet, sway-ing. Scott put out a hand and again found himself check-mated by the housekeeper.

"Leave her to me," she said, almost roughly.

The guest stood back and watched the pair go slowly up-stairs. The girl's shoulders were bowed, but on the landing she suddenly straightened up and looked down at him. Then she turned away, urged gently on by the woman who had mothered her for most of her young life and who was still proving to be a source of strength in this further ordeal that had now come upon her. Scott turned on his slippered heel, searched for and found cigarettes on a side table, and lit up. He felt that he needed it. The action recalled to him the state of his hands.

He took a handkerchief from the breast pocket of his pyjamas and wiped his fingers. Blood—too much of it. Blood on the dead man's shoulders, and the bright glint of it on the stone-flagged floor. A hell of a mess to walk into.

Scott breathed out smoke, and felt his nerves to be the better for it. From where he stood, he looked across the famed Great Hall of Castleton House, and for the first time saw a casement window swinging open, and unsecured by the wrought-iron bar. It hung down, the hole clear of its peg. The cigarette between his fingers, Scott made his way across to it, found it to be of convenient height, and leaned head and shoulders out into the night. It was clear and windless—not even the faint rustle of nearby trees coming to his straining ears. He looked down, as he drew his head in again, at the white scratches on the stone of the deep window-ledge.

Ingress and exit for the killer, most likely. How else?

The sound of female voices upstairs had ceased. Scott drew on his cigarette again, glad of the little occupation it provided—a civilised convention in an otherwise strange world of the antique. The ghostly centuries seemed to be pressing in upon him, the dead weight of the atmosphere of the strange old house was upon his shoulders. His was an alert, fresh young mind and a stout heart to grapple with problems that were not of his seeking, yet which cried aloud for solution. He had come down here to do a job, and blundered into the inexplicable . . .

The old and the new. He let ash drop to the floor. A knotted girdle in the Blue Room, blood from a dagger wound spilling down on to an upset dice-board, the point of a fine Italian rapier plunged into a man's chest, the sudden choke of an apoplectic seizure, a bullet in the head when far from home, a trailing hem of a gown and a loose board on the stairs, another bullet—but nearer to the ill-fated house, this time—and now—this.

It was Scott's job to know and remember these things.

"Poor kid-poor kid!" he said to himself grimly, and moved sharply forward, his slippers making a little clicking sound on the stone floor. Here was something else that was modern, thank God! He slipped open the flap of a carved oak cover that housed a telephone on a wall table, lifted the instrument and grimly dialled "999." He had not long to wait for an answer.

CHAPTER II

QUIET WEEK-END

AT 3 A.M. the man in Room 14 of the "George Hotel," near Harlingham, Sussex, was stretched out luxuriously on his back and snoring rhythmically. Detective-Inspector Philip Croft, C.I.D., New Scotland Yard, he might be, but he was as human as the next fellow in the more prosaic aspects of life. And he had had a long day.

The afternoon had been too glorious for anything else but a walk of two solid hours' duration. Croft called it "loosening up" to get the grime and noise of London out of his system for a bit. And it enabled him to renew the old associations that appealed to him so strongly.

This was the quiet week-end to which he always looked forward so much. No family ties now remained to him; but in Harlingham and its surroundings, the sizable but not yet overrun resort situated pleasantly between Hastings and Pevensey, was much to remind him of his boyhood. He liked to revisit the old place where he had friends and space to move about, precious little to do and long hours to do it in. The last observation had become stock to him by now; he said much the same thing year after year when he wangled the time off.

The walk, extended until he had had his fill and his eyes had begun to ache a little from the glare of a July sun on dancing water, streets, lawns, the long white promenade, had done him a power of good, apart from the cool of the evening and a cold tub followed by dinner at the house of his old friend Barry Emerson. It was no wonder that Croft was sleeping soundly now. He did not hear a deferential tap at his door; grunted a little when it was repeated more loudly; and turned over grumblingly when it became an imperious rap. At the same time the voice of the middle-aged night porter of the "George" was raised in urgent supplication.

"Mr. Croft! Mr. Croft, are you awake?"

Croft slid back to consciousness with a start and sat up violently. "All right. You can come in."

The night porter cleared his throat. "Sorry to disturb you. Mr. Croft, but it's urgent. The telephone."

The man in bed rubbed his unshaven chin and looked at the other morosely. "Tell 'em I'm dead."

"I said that I'd fetch you, Inspector. It's Harlingham Police Headquarters on the line. Mr. Emerson himself. He said I was to pull you out, if necessary."

"The Chief Constable?" Croft peered around. "Chuck me my overcoat from over there. I didn't think it worth while to pack a dressing-gown and slippers. Where are my shoes?" He groped downwards. "Hum—here we are. I must say it's a hell of a time to rout anyone out. I only left him a few hours ago."

Croft padded out in the wake of the porter and downstairs to the lounge. He was yawning as he leaned an elbow on the little reception desk and picked up the phone left lying on its polished surface. "Croft speaking," he said. "That you, Emerson?"

The brisk voice of the Chief Constable came to him over the wire. "Sorry to haul you out of bed like this, Inspector, but there's a job for you—a local job."

"But I'm having a break, sir—a holiday—off duty."

"You wouldn't thank me if I passed you up on this thing," Emerson retorted. "There's a murder just broken. You know Castleton House, of course?"

"About five miles from here," Croft said, and felt his interest roused and his tiredness dropping from him. "I've never actually been inside the place, although I was at a fête affair held in the grounds when I was a kid. Isn't that the place that looks like changing hands?"

"The same. Another of the stately homes of England due to pass into the safe keeping of the National Trust. You know how the Press has been playing it up lately, following the death of the Colonel. That's what makes it so important to me now."

"And to me," Croft said. "*You* know how dead keen I am on anything in this area. I've been reading a lot about it recently in the illustrated magazines. *Country Life* had a four-page spread about the place and the *Sketch* did it rather well. Um, I see what you mean. Eyes of the country focused on it sort of thing. Rum old place. What are the details?"

He listened tensely as Emerson spoke in almost staccato fashion, his quick brain absorbing facts and storing them away in his alert mind. Then he posed a question and reached inside his pyjama jacket to absently scratch at his chest. "How do I stand in this thing if I take it on? You know what I mean."

"Your Assistant-Commissioner was working late," said the Chief Constable glibly. "He was able to deal with my trunk call on the spot, a short time ago. Like me, he was very reluctant to spoil your week-end, but he feels that you're too good a man to have around not to invite you to take a crack at this case. He feels, as I do, that if only by reason of the recent publicity accorded Castleton House, it would be far better it I called in the Yard now, at the outset."

Croft was silent for a moment; then: "I think I agree there."

"Glad to hear you say so. And I know that you'll take it in the spirit intended when I say that I think you're a sound man. It's fortuitous, of course, that you're on the spot; but you know the district and you're interested in it. Your A.-C. was glad to give you a completely free hand, and has author-ised me to tell you as much."

Croft grunted. "How can I refuse? I know it isn't an or-der, strictly speaking; but, of course, he'd know how I'd feel about it. Thanks for your interest."

"But I shan't be with you—at least not just now," Emer-son pointed out. "You'll excuse my presence on the—er—scene of the crime, but I'm tied to my desk here. Get dressed. and I'll send a car to pick you up right away. It'll take you on to the house; and Inspector Paynter will look after you when you get there. He's on the spot now. You'll like him, and he'll have orders to give you absolute authority throughout. He's at your disposal. 'Bye."

Short and sweet, yet Croft knew enough to be going on with, at any rate. Not an easy nut to crack, by the sound of it. He went purposefully back to his room while the essentials of the case milled around in his mind. He continued to ponder them grimly, a little later, from the back seat of a police car that ate up the distance to Castleton House, situated in isolation well outside the town.

It was his business to have an encyclopaedic mind, just like Tony Scott, who had thankfully hailed the appearance of Inspector Paynter so that he might get into some clothes. Castleton House—building commenced about 1432, *vide* the daily Press and the glossy magazines. Family gradually dying out since the middle of the eighteenth century. Last of the line, Miss Marjorie Castleton, young, pretty, motherless. Father killed in shooting accident only three months ago. His wife fell downstairs years before. No other children, and few by way of close relatives. The Colonel left very little but the property. Crippling death duties; girl trying to meet them but being forced into a course of action all too common nowadays. Either unwilling or unable to sell the huge old house and grounds, she was negotiating to turn it over to the National Trust on proviso that she be allowed to retain private accommodation in one wing upstairs.

The house would then become a show place for all and sundry, but she would not be turned out of it altogether. In favour of the arrangement, too, was the fact, tentatively announced, that the entire fabric, inside and outside, would be thoroughly renovated by experts—a course of treatment that had never yet been accorded to the ancient structure.

Croft stared at the back of the uniformed driver, as the car turned into huge iron gates by a lodge, and with a long tree-lined driveway leading up to Castleton House itself. The dead man, as Emerson had been quick to point out over the telephone, was not a local resident. Preliminary investigation by Paynter, who had reported back immediately, had already established the existence of a return half-ticket by rail to London in the waistcoat pocket of the man with the fractured skull. It appeared to be all there was to go on at present, but it seemed to present added justification for Scotland Yard being brought into the scheme of things.

The crunch of the driveway gravel beneath the tyres of the speeding car provided accompaniment to the Inspector's thoughts. From being a small boy he had always had an interest in the old place and its extensive, park-like grounds. He had supplemented, in later years, the vague idea of its extent and importance that he had gained from previous hearsay. Wide reading, particularly lately, had given him a better knowledge. Strangely enough, he'd always wanted to get closer to the place but had never had an adequate chance to fulfil such ambition. His family had removed from Harlingham. Croft had found himself in London—and, some time later on, in the Metropolitan Police.

Boyhood dreams are seldom realised. The embryo engine-drivers, gallant firefighters and would-be prime ministers so often end as fat stockbrokers, wholesale grocers or mere clerks. Croft pursued a logical train of thought. The wish to sometime inspect Castleton House fully and at his leisure was subsidiary to the greater desire of early youth. And like that, it would now be fulfilled in no uncertain measure.

The greater desire. Croft smiled reminiscently. Barry Emerson's uncle had been a resplendent, but stout, sergeant of police in Harlingham. Perhaps he had fostered the dream in the first place. Certainly they had stuck to it as boys— Philip Croft and Barry Emerson in class, surreptitiously reading the exploits of Nick Carter and Sherlock Holmes under cover of desk-lids; Philip Croft and Barry Emerson trying to gain admission to the gallery of the local police court on Saturday mornings; saving up for a microscope; smearing themselves all over with a horrible concoction of lampblack, vinegar, shoe-polish and blacklead in their attempts to fingerprint all and sundry; or trying desperately to brush off the hardening smears of plaster of Paris from their clothes after making casts of footprints in the mud of a lane.

Even though the doughty pair had finally been divided by circumstance, the ambition to take up police work had come true for both. And both had hoisted themselves from the uniformed ranks—the one to the exalted position of Chief Constable in his own home town, the other to a trusted, quick-thinking and acting detective-inspector of the most famous police force in the world. Croft smiled grimly to himself at the thought. Although he had remained such a life-long friend of Emerson, he had never really thought that he would be one day "working his parish."

The police phrase, however, seemed to be a little inapplicable in presence of the sensed, rather than seen, surroundings as the car stopped in front of Castleton House and a uniformed constable jerked open the door and put his head inside. By the light of the lamp at the man's belt, Croft got out and stretched, then followed the constable up four broad stone steps and so into a double porch where one of a pair of huge, arched, studded oak doors stood slightly open. Almost immediately he was in the famed Great Hall of Castleton House, and Inspector Paynter, a tall young man in plain clothes, was hurrying over to meet him. He returned Croft's greeting with a handshake that almost made him wince.

A keen man, this Paynter. Youngish, pleasant-faced, with a calm, well-modulated voice. Croft sized him up swiftly on the spot, as he sized all men up at a first meeting and was suitably impressed. "Where are the other people?" he asked bluntly.

"I've got them all together in a small sitting-room over there, Inspector." Paynter indicated a door guarded by a stolid constable. "I thought it best to keep them away from the body."

"Still in position?" Croft asked.

"It hasn't been moved except for the attentions of our surgeon, who's gone back with the rest to write his report, sir."

"The rest?" Croft queried. "You mean—"

"Photographers, fingerprint men, Inspector. They didn't find much. There's no trace of a weapon, either."

"I see. What's the doctor's opinion—on the spot, I mean?"

Paynter considered. "He was able to give the time of death at roughly 12.15 A.M. That coincides with the time of the upset and Mr. Scott's coming downstairs. He says he noticed the time by the clock on the stairs, even though it was a bit dark. A silvered dial. I suppose that you'll be taking over completely now, sir?"

"As per your instructions from the Chief Constable," Croft said. "Between the lot of you, you seem to have kept the night telephone service fairly busy. But I compliment you. You appear to have done a great deal in a remarkably short time." Croft looked around at his surroundings.

Life, he told himself, is full of coincidences, some of them more fortuitous than the rest. He had been reading up about Castleton House out of pure interest—sentimental interest, if one cared to put it that way. And now behold—he was planked right down in the middle of it, with a murder to boot. But he was not completely strange to its topography. He knew, for instance, that the big door almost opposite him on the other side of the hall, led into the famous Long Gallery. The A.-C., that astute superior of his in a secluded office in the grey pile of New Scotland Yard, had known all about Detective-Inspector Croft's private requisitioning of Press material about this place. It provided another cogent reason—if it were necessary to cite one—why Croft had been deemed, on the quickest of telephoned decisions, to be the man for the job.

History . . . Here it was, surging invisibly around him. Birth, death, pain, laughter, tragedy, tears, quarrels, love, hate. 1432—Henry VI, Joan of Arc, the Wars of the Roses . . . The Castletons building and settling in in the midst of feudal upheaval—a great Catholic family bringing the Church into the home.

The Reformation . . . Mary, Elizabeth. Protestantism . . . the pursuivants . . . the crude political pressure . . . persecution . . . loyalty to the Crown . . . the grim holding on to an untenable position . . . forced abjuration of an ancient faith, never to be restored. It was all here. It seemed to impinge on the mind that was groping for it subconsciously. And then the later centuries—the fall and rise, the holding on, of a family that had never sought the notoriety of courts or councils but had preferred to remain secluded in its heritage.

Croft shook himself out of it. With Inspector Paynter he moved across to where the huddled figure of the dead man lay underneath a blanket.

Croft took a long look and then straightened up. "You say you've not found anything like a weapon yet?"

"Nothing, Inspector. There's a lot of stuff that could be used in a pinch, of course—old brass and such like; but I've been over all that with the others and there seems to be nothing missing and nothing out of place."

"Identification?"

Paynter shook his head again. "His clothes might tell us something, sir, but I don't know about the rest. It's queer to me, apart from the railway ticket I found."

"How so?" Croft raised his eyebrows a little, and Paynter produced a small official notebook.

"Like this, Inspector. I listed all the stuff and put it back, temporarily. A trifle of money, a fountain-pen and stub of a pencil, a comb in a case, a pocket-watch with no sort of a number or inscription to help us, box of matches, three cigarettes in a packet and an odd collar stud. Whether he toted it along for emergencies or whether it's one of those things you find and pop into a pocket automatically, I can't say."

Croft had been listening intently. "Exactly how much money?"

"Three and fourpence ha'penny, sir."

"To take him out and back to London? I see what you mean by 'something queer.' No wallet, no handkerchief, no letters addressed to himself."

Detective-Inspector Croft was speaking softly, musingly. "This poor devil who copped it wore fairly heavy shoes.

Quite sufficient to make those scratches on the window-ledge. Which one is it?"

He went over to look at the spot indicated by Paynter. "Hard to tell," he said, after a brief examination. "As easy for the marks to have been made by two men scrambling through as one."

"I've been outside," Paynter said. "Too dark to do much, even with a torch. It's dry weather and it's paved all around the house. Couldn't pick up a thing."

Croft nodded and went back to stare down at the body. "Age, forty-five to fifty," he said. "Shortish, thick-set, not too well-dressed. Sandy, going bald—as near as you can tell for that terrific wallop that caved most of his head in and must have produced almost instantaneous death. Looks a doubtful customer by his face and appearance. Perhaps Records may tell us something."

He was groping desperately at some sort of a reconstruction. "Two men. The getting-in not accomplished very skilfully from what I already know—bumpings and scufflings. Motive I just don't know. Robbery?"

He gestured with his strong hands. "Perhaps the second man followed the first one in after a short interval. The pair seem to have contacted, quarrelled, struggled. God knows why. But one gets a hell of a slug from the other—maybe a gun butt was used. The killer hasn't much time then. I think it's pretty certain that he must have heard people stirring upstairs, and he realises that he must beat it, p.d.q. But even so he deems one factor to be of vital importance to his safety. He must look after it, even though the seconds are precious. There's just time enough to snatch wallet, handkerchief and what-have-you else that's ready accessible in the dead man's pockets. But he hasn't got time to attend to other probable clues of identity. He can't stop to look for laundry-marks on underwear, for instance. He can only take pot-luck with the little he's able to grab and get out by the same way he came."

Croft sighed. "Thank you for leaving things *in situ*, as regards the body, Inspector. I think I've seen all I want to of it—for the present, anyway. I'll ring through to headquarters, tell them that I've arrived and so forth, and arrange for an ambulance to collect the remains. Then I'd like to see the people of the house."

Inspector Paynter pointed out the same telephone used by Tony Scott some time before to make his emergency call, and Croft found a chair near to it and sat down. There was little he could say to Emerson at this stage of the proceedings.

When he got up, he stood thinking; then walked across to the window again, scrutinised the floor in the vicinity of the body, looked curiously at the still-closed door of what he judged from its position to be the ill-fated Blue Room that he had read so much about. He could understand, by reason of the stone floor, how sound would carry upwards and how eerie the effect would be during hours of darkness; but beyond that there was little he cared to venture upon with confidence.

No fingerprints on or near the window, according to Paynter who had checked up with the quick-working police crew before it left for headquarters with the doctor. Precious little to go on at all, in fact. And, in common courtesy, Detective-Inspector Croft could not well defer the questioning of the little group of people who were awaiting his appearance so patiently in the small sitting-room that led off the hall.

None of them was suspect—as yet. He saw no valid reason why they should not be questioned together, in each other's presence. Croft turned to Paynter.

"Who did you say is in that room? Miss Castleton—"

"And a Mr. Anthony Scott—"

"Representing the National Trust," said Croft. "I've seen his name in the newspapers. Who else?"

Inspector Paynter shuddered visibly. "An elderly woman, tough as they make 'em. A Miss Elspeth McCracken, Inspector; a—a dragon, if ever I met one."

"I smell singeing," Croft said sympathetically. "What's she to do with things, anyway?"

"Housekeeper and old nurse to Miss Castleton, sir. She has a tongue like barbed wire. Then there's a couple of maids." Paynter referred again to his unobtrusive notebook. "They seem to be the only ones who offered to stay on here, but I gather that even that was a struggle. There's a giggling little thing by the name of Millie Smith—general maid to Miss Castleton. Then there's an Elsie Wright—older, plumper, the conventional idea of a cook." The local man tapped at the sitting-room door and opened it for Croft to enter.

Scott got up at his appearance. The women remained sitting, although Millie Smith half rose and appeared to be decidedly uncomfortable by reason of her sheer nervousness. The angular-looking Miss Elspeth McCracken surveyed the man from Scotland Yard coolly—and disapprovingly— enough from beneath her grey, craggy eyebrows. Paynter made a general introduction, and Croft spoke. "I'm sorry for the inconvenience and your enforced wait," he said, "but I can't help it. I'd like to ask a few questions, and I'll try not to detain you long."

He heard the heavy breathing of the cook, and the high-pitched, nervous giggle of Millie Smith, the maid. Better get them cleared out of the way first. Both had very simple stories. They, too, had been wakened by the unwonted noises of the night, had heard Mr. Scott and the mistress moving about. In the denuded servants' quarters on the top floor of all, where they had adjoining bedrooms for fellow-feeling and security, the maid and cook had joined forces in eager but hushed inquiry as to what might be afoot. To them had come the gaunt Scots housekeeper, to scold them into quietude; and they had remained crouching in the gallery when she had gone downstairs in pursuit of her mistress and they had followed to the foot of the short upper staircase. It took Croft a second or two to sort this out.

The galleried first storey of the house, of course, from which the bedrooms led off. In a corner of this was a door behind which were narrow stairs leading, in an awkward bend, the short distance up to the cramped little servants' rooms with their tiny dormer windows. That was the particular spot in this queer old house they were talking about. Croft put a few questions, compassionate towards their nervousness. Had they seen possible intruders around the house at any time? No. Had they heard noises in the night before? A frightened shake of the head from Millie. Was there anything they thought he should know?

The cook glanced across at her young mistress, sitting despondently. The old housekeeper turned her head sharply. "There'll be no need for romancing, Elsie."

"She means the—the Blue Room," said Marjorie Castleton in a low voice. And Tony Scott cut in upon her.

"Stuff and nonsense, Inspector. I keep telling her so. Absolute rubbish."

"One at a time, please," Croft said pleasantly. "I'm sure that you'll agree with me that it's best we dispense with these—er—ladies. I think they have had very little to do with the situation."

"You can go too," said Marjorie Castleton without looking up. She was twisting a small handkerchief between nervous fingers, and spoke directly to the housekeeper.

"Are you sure you'll no' be needing me?" Miss McCracken answered a trifle rebelliously. "To have these strangers clumping and blethering aboot the place—" She got up, and swung around on Croft belligerently. "It's well ye should know that there's nothing I can tell you, either. I tellt the maids to haud their whist upstairs and then I came down to see to the mistress."

"Perhaps you'll grant me a word with you later," Croft said diplomatically, and held the door open. "Inspector Paynter will see you to your room." There was a little devil of malicious humour in the words.

"Indeed he will not," she shot back at him. "I'll thank him to mind his ain business and I'll mind mine. Ye'll excuse me, sir."

She swept past Croft and the outraged Inspector Paynter with a stiff rustle of her old-fashioned brocaded dress. Croft closed the door gently behind her. He looked across at the man beside Marjorie Castleton's chair.

"You're Mr. Scott, aren't you?"

"That's right." The young man smiled disarmingly. "Down here for the week-end."

"Just like me, in fact." Croft smiled back in return. "Anything you'd care to tell me?"

"I don't see that there's much I can say," Scott replied. "You probably know why I'm here. As representative of the National Trust, I came to talk things over with Miss Castleton, following her inquiries with us and her expression of a desire to see the house in safe hands. Like Miss Castleton and the servants, I was awakened by the dickens of a noise from downstairs. I heard Miss Castleton moving about her room—mine's fairly close by. Naturally, I went to her to see if all was well, tried to make her stay in her room, and came downstairs to investigate."

"It was plucky of you, Mr. Scott," the girl said, lifting her eyes for the first time.

And now Detective-Inspector Croft saw her face clearly. Young, lovely, hair a mass of ordered fair curls, skin the product of youth and outdoor exercise, eyes of a startling—almost childlike but decidedly attractive—blue. Yet it was easy to see that they held strain, that there was an emotional disturbance that was threatening to rack the girl through and through to the very core of her being. Croft noted Scott's modest reply to her words, and framed further questions for the young man to deal with.

He seemed to be very quick and capable in his replies, taking as much as he could upon himself in order to avoid further distress to the girl. Croft gained a very good idea of how things stood, solely by reason of such intelligent and excellent co-operation. But with all this, he found that there was, after all, very little indeed to be learned.

No one knew who the dead man might be. No intruder had been found, nor weapon discovered. There were no actual suspicious circumstances to provide a lead-up to the crime.

The window? Marjorie Castleton corroborated that her questioning of the Scots housekeeper had elicited the fact that the latter had confessed to having left it slightly open. So little had disturbance been thought about in a secluded place like Castleton House that such an action was perfectly understandable and, in fact, could be overlooked. It was, after all, July and the weather was inclined to be sultry. Nothing easier than for an intruder to guess at such a fact and go looking for just such a window. Nothing easier than for him to find it, to put a hand in and thrust the iron bar off its peg so that the window would swing open.

All perfectly straightforward, yet Detective-Inspector Croft felt himself to be baffled. Not only by the actual, physical fact of murder. There was something else, he felt—something deep and mysterious that he could not shape up to—something he could not describe, but nevertheless felt deep in his bones. Quiet week-end, eh? Good God—no! But at least he'd swapped it for something interesting . . .

CHAPTER III

LADY IN THE BLUE ROOM

IT seemed to Detective-Inspector Croft, as he stood facing Marjorie Castleton and her companion, Tony Scott, that there were really two considerations claiming his attention. There was the murder of an unknown man, and there was a mystery—or so it seemed from the attitude of the girl— inherent to Castleton House itself.

As to the first, he had done all that might be reasonably expected for the moment. He had realised as much upon his replacement of the telephone in the hall. As to the second matter—he just didn't know. Perhaps this was conditioned by the murder itself. Without that grim happening, Marjorie Castleton's vague fears and forebodings might have been brushed aside lightly enough. But taken in conjunction with the killing—especially as he seemed to have no sort of a lead on it yet—they should be worth investigation. What else could he do? He could not hope to adequately guess at motive for the crime; and, lacking that, it seemed only logical to try to get to the bottom of what was disturbing the girl's mind. From her distraught manner it argued that in some mysterious way she regarded the murder as some sort of culmination. As such it might only prove to be a train of fanciful imagination.

On the other hand, there might be some sort of a link, however tenuous.

Of course, Croft said to himself, as he mentally took stock of the situation, he had a rough idea of the legend of the Blue Room. But he didn't know the details. He was a practical sort of a cuss himself—as practical as the attractive

young Tony Scott. Like him, he had a wholesome contempt
for old women's stories. Hauntings and hobgoblins he didn't
hold with—not in this enlightened modern world. But it was
inevitable, he supposed, that in a house of such antiquity as
this something would be in evidence that savoured of the su-
pernatural. Such was only to be expected.

What troubled him was the fact that Marjorie Castleton
was letting it so obviously disturb her equanimity. In the
giggling, inferiority-complexed Millie Smith or the fey old
cook—yes. But not in an expensively educated, highly intelligent young woman of the calibre of the mistress of the
house. That was what aroused Croft's curiosity. Therefore,
let the girl talk.

But she refused to talk, as soon as the Inspector engineered the conversation into channels he hoped were favour-
able to himself. Whether it was that, in spite of all his diplo-
macy and gentleness, she developed a feeling that she might
be thought gauche and unreasonable if she let him have his
way, he didn't know. She stood up abruptly.

"You must forgive me, Inspector, but I don't think that
such matters personal to me will help at all in clearing up
this horrible affair. I've told you all I know about it, and the
servants and Mr. Scott have corroborated the details. May I
be excused?"

"Certainly." Croft bent his head in submission. "You
must be very tired and overwrought, and you're missing your
rest. I'm afraid that I must stay here for a while yet. I want to
take a look around by daylight, if you don't mind."

"Of course," she replied, and hesitated. "Shall I send the
housekeeper to you? I mean if you'd like a cup of tea, or
anything—?"

"Thank you—no," Croft said.

"And I've such a headache, Inspector. Perhaps I'll be
able to talk to you better in the morning."

Scott was quick to go to her side. "Let me help you." But
she summoned up a wan little smile of refusal. "I can manage. If there's anything you want, do help yourselves."

The Scotland Yard man watched the door close behind her, and found a chair. "Sit down, Mr. Scott."

Scott had found cigarettes. "Thanks. Mind if we talk, Inspector?"

"I'd be glad of it," Croft said, reaching for an ash-tray. "Miss Castleton doesn't seem to be in a very co-operative mood, anyway. Of course, we can understand that, I think. She seems to have had a dickens of a lot to put up with lately. Er—might I ask if she's confided in you at all? I mean, to a man in your position . . ."

Croft removed a shred of tobacco from his tongue—". . . and she seems to like you well enough."

"We've got along very well together," Scott answered. "I've seen her a couple of times at our offices in Town; and we both thought it a very good idea that I should come down here over the week-end and try to tie the ends up on the spot." He frowned. "That's what makes me so anxious to talk to you."

Croft began to see daylight. "You mean that this murder is liable to upset your particular applecart, Mr. Scott? Don't mind me being blunt."

"I'm grateful for it. While we waited for you to put in an appearance, Miss Castleton started to talk to me. What she had to say seemed to be the result of an intense struggle with herself, but she had the courage to bring it out at last. She said: 'I'm sorry, Mr. Scott, but I just can't go on like this. I think that this finishes everything for me. I can't go through with our arrangements.' "

"And you were naturally surprised?" Croft queried.

"Surprised, Inspector? I was thunderstruck. She's committed nothing to writing yet, of course, and was perfectly entitled to say what she did. But it meant my falling down on the job. I felt that she at least owed me an explanation. There was nothing acrimonious in what we both had to say, of course. Like you've just done, I rather pitied her for the succession of ordeals she's had to face."

"*I* tried to treat her gently," Croft said. "Look here, Mr. Scott, I'd like to get things straight. Suppose we start at the beginning? You tell me that you enjoyed Miss Castleton's confidence, so I presume that you'll have a fairly general idea of how things stand with her. I don't think that you'll be violating that confidence if you speak to me freely."

Croft paused, as though to give added weight to his argument. "Of course, you know what I'm looking for," he said quietly. "Something—anything—that might possibly help me to get a line on this murder business. I'm not saying that Miss Castleton is directly involved, but surely you can see what I'm driving at? Anyone with half an eye can see that the lady's struggling with some mysterious influence. Right. Then isn't it natural to somehow couple it with a further mystery—tonight's baffling affair?"

"Spooks don't bat people over the head," Scott said, a trifle cynically.

"I'm inclined to agree with you there. But we're also faced with the fact that sane people of Miss Castleton's calibre don't usually take account of such hooey. That's what's worrying me. And, naturally, because of my position and her own dispirited feeling she won't speak to me with any sort of freedom. I can quite understand that."

Croft looked squarely at the young man. "But if I know how things stand with her, I might be able to do *you* a good turn. If there's anything in this strange mix-up for me, then the fact of my perhaps being able to sort it out might operate in your favour. Miss Castleton may see things in their right perspective after all, and let her deal with you go through. See what I mean?"

He spoke carefully, and Scott was quick to seize upon the implication in his words. "I do see what you mean, Inspector. That's just what I've been thinking myself. That's why I said that I'd like to talk to you. Look here—"

He stopped and looked down at his hands. Croft sat patiently on, smoking. Then Scott raised his head. "I haven't known her for very long."

"But you're already beginning to think quite a lot about her," Croft finished for him. "That's what you're trying to tell me, isn't it? Put me down for a meddling old fool, if you like, but I'm only trying to help. Believe me, Mr. Scott, I sincerely understand."

"Thank you for that, Inspector. Odd, perhaps, that a fellow like me should find something more than the strictly business angle in my dealings with her. I know her so little, you see; but I already admire her so much."

"And I think," Croft said placidly, "that she's not altogether averse to you. Hence the week-end and the confidence she's shown. Shall I be putting my foot in it altogether if I say that I hope it keeps fine for you in that direction?" And, catching Scott's friendly grin, "We can't expect too much at once, of course. Your feelings towards the lady may be reciprocated, but they're not sufficiently established yet for you to try to batter her troubles down by main force. Suppose we get back to the point, then?"

Scott was decisive now, as he felt that they were about to jointly get to grips with the problem. "I hope you're a good listener, Inspector. It's been my job to study Castleton House pretty thoroughly. I can give you some sort of a foundation for what we both classify as utter nonsense, and if I couple it with what Miss Castleton has told me, you can get a fairly good idea of what it's all about.

"Centre of all this is the Blue Room."

Croft nodded. "Some sort of a legend attached to that, isn't there?" he asked. "I've never been able to get the details."

"Like to see inside it?" Scott asked, rising.

"I should, seeing that Miss Castleton has asked us to make ourselves at home," Croft answered. "Don't worry. The police ambulance will probably have been by now and carted the remains away. That's why I came in here in the first place, to keep you all busy for a minute or two. It enabled Inspector Paynter and his men to shift the body to the front entrance and await the ambulance's arrival. Lead on, Mr. Scott."

"Right," Scott said, and went on speaking as they gained the hall. "There's the library over there on the right. There's what used to be a sewing-room on the other side of that outside door. Ahead of you, in the Long Gallery, there's the music-room on the right, and on the left there's the study, both opening off it."

Croft moved forward a little and looked to the left. "Where does this little passageway lead to, then?" he asked. He was now standing near the stairs.

"The kitchen and dining-room, with the third outside door to this place," Scott explained. "But I'll show you the Blue Room."

He went back to the door adjoining the room they had just quitted. Gently he turned the handle, reached up and found a light-switch. "It's quite celebrated."

"So I hear," Croft said, and looked around as he stood still for a moment or two, trying to let the atmosphere sink into his consciousness. "Why do they always call the haunted room 'blue'? I thought it was a mere convention of fiction."

Scott laughed. "Not in this instance. These tapestries are worth quite a bit, although somehow the successive owners of Castleton have never entertained the idea of selling them—any more than they'd dream of letting any of the furniture go. The family's always thought too much of every stick and stone here, you see. No matter what the pinch, they'd sooner have died than sell as much as a chair. The late Colonel went over the line a little. He was so desperately in need of the ready that he sold several items from the library some years ago. Miss Castleton tells me that he was not a bookish man, and deemed such a course to be the lesser of two evils, if you see what I mean."

"Better than furniture," Croft nodded. "By the way, didn't Miss Castleton think of disposing of some of the contents of the house to enable her to hold on?"

"I discussed that point with her," Scott said. "She assured me that the idea had occurred to her, but she had abandoned it because she was appalled at the thought of things being broken up like that. All or nothing with her, you see. These tapestries, for instance."

Scott put out a hand to touch the nearest, and the movement was almost reverent.

"These are possibly priceless; but you see, it's pride embedded in long ancestry. I agreed with Miss Castleton when she told me, in a terribly earnest way, that she couldn't think of letting them go to a museum—even at a whacking good figure. You see, these *make* the Blue Room."

Even by the glow of electric light Detective-Inspector Croft could see that the rich blue colouring was largely undimmed by time. It was predominant in the fine embroidery, and he felt himself sharing Scott's quiet enthusiasm. The pieces were of fair size, almost covering each wall, with the exception of the farther end of the room where a small mullioned window was high set. Long-dead hands were responsible for their careful preservation over the centuries.

"Blanche de Castleton," Tony Scott said in a hushed voice. "Fifteen hundred and sixty. She hanged herself in here by her own girdle from the middle beam." He pointed upwards dramatically, and then relaxed.

"Sorry for talking like the proverbial guide, Inspector."

"Carry on," Croft said. "The hour is appropriate for giving me the creeps, although I don't scare easily. Let's have the story."

Tony Scott smiled. "Well, it goes like this. Blanche was a daughter of the house at the time. She had a paralysed arm."

"I see."

"She was almost an extremist in devotion," Scott went on. "There was a holy well in the vicinity of Canterbury, and she went there for a cure. She vowed that if this were accomplished she would employ her released fingers in making a set of the finest, most delicate tapestries in return. The miracle worked for her, and she left the well of the Blessed Virgin and came home to work for eight solid years at the things. The theme is the Annunciation, and, of course, that's where the celestial colour comes in.

"But during that time things were happening. You know your history, Inspector. Mary and Elizabeth. It's known that the Castletons did their best to withstand the growing incursion of Protestantism. They hid their priests and endeavoured to dig their toes in and hold on. But inevitably there came a day when they could resist no longer. The pressure had become political, as well as religious. You'll remember what I told you about the Castletons holding on to their heritage through thick and thin."

"I get it," Inspector Croft said slowly. "Hang on to the place at any cost." He was thinking of Marjorie Castleton and the proviso about the upstairs wing.

Scott's thoughts were slightly different. "The hanging on in this instance," he said, "only meant one thing. Change your religion or go under altogether. There was no possible question of evasion. Refusal meant not only imprisonment or the block, but also confiscation of the estate and the razing of Castleton House to the ground."

"So that even martyrdom wouldn't have availed the family? Nice times to live in."

"That's about the size of it, Inspector. The Castletons saw that it would be utter suicide to persist in their recusancy and gave in. All but Blanche.

"She couldn't or wouldn't understand—wouldn't accept the inevitable. To her, her faith was her very existence. I expect that everybody in the family had a go at talking her out of it, but it was no use. The cure she had experienced seemed to have made her faith stronger than in any of the others—or, if you like, it had made her less level-headed. There are times when surrender is the only policy to adopt, if one's to live to fight another day."

Detective-Inspector Croft grinned. His liking for Tony Scott was increasing. "So Blanche determined to stick it out?" he said.

"She did. Nothing would move her. She even went so far as to say that all should be sacrificed—house, estate, the lives of everyone—that there should, if need be, be a complete wiping out of the entire family and Castleton Hall itself rather than abjuration. The family tried to be sensible about this. They tried to quieten her down, when it became clear that no one could hope to reason with her. They confined her to the Blue Room. It wasn't called so then. The name was bestowed on it later, when the tapestries were hung here in perpetuity."

Scott touched the old fabric again. "The fact that she was so confined proved the last straw to poor Blanche. She thought now, you see, that the apparent unreasonableness of the family amounted to a callous betrayal of her and her beliefs. Like all seriously ill-balanced neurotics, she either couldn't or wouldn't see that there was anything wrong with her. This was open imprisonment by the men of the house who were deliberately going over to the other side from choice instead of compulsion."

"I should think," said Croft, almost to himself, "that eight years of needlework in here, alone, would be enough to drive anyone semi-balmy. What then?"

"She went off the deep end completely. Blanche finished the tapestries one day, waited for her room to be unlocked so that she could be brought out into the Great Hall to dine with the family, as usual, and when she was at the table suddenly got to her feet and cursed the lot of them."

"The curse of the Castletons." Detective-Inspector Croft almost whispered the words. "A lot of tommy-rot, of course . . ."

"She cursed the entire family," Scott said. "With especial reference to the male side. She seemed to have it in for the men most of all. I should think she ended in a fit off hysterics, because it seems that, as gently as possible, they led her back to this room and locked her in after quietening her down a bit. It's easy to picture the scene. They'd return to the Great Hall to determine what had best be done in this fresh crisis, because after all she was their own flesh and blood. After a time they came back here to have a look at her. They found that she'd taken the long plaited cord from around her gown, and—"

Tony Scott left the rest unsaid. He took a deep breath.

Croft looked at him. "And that's a matter of stone cold history, I take it?"

"Family history," Scott said. "As in the case of many ancient houses, someone of a literary bent turns up now and again over the years and takes on the job of compiling and publishing a chronicle of the line. We can't doubt the yarn's authenticity."

"And it came true?" Croft demanded. "I mean this curse of Blanche de Castleton?"

Scott was wary. "Depends on how you look at it, my dear Inspector. I'm not a member of the Society for Psychical Research. I try to be a plain, honest-to-goodness sort of a chap like yourself."

"Good for you. You're trying to cling to sweet reasonableness. I seem to have heard, or read, that this—er—chamber—I believe that's the apposite word in these instances—is encumbered by the spirit of the unfortunate Blanche. She occasionally makes an appearance, trailing that same girdle you speak of, and giving vent to mournful cries."

"It's so easy to embroider these things."

"That's what I think," Croft answered. "We've established that there was a curse laid on the male side of the family, but there's no need for us to believe a lot of twaddle, in addition, that the Lady Blanche makes an actual appearance here at intervals. Does Miss Marjorie Castleton believe in the haunting of the Blue Room?"

"No," said Scott in decided fashion. "I'll tell you what, though. This last terrible incident—the murder of an unknown man—has shaken her sophistication and intelligent outlook on life enough to make her believe in the curse itself."

Detective-Inspector Croft was appalled. "You think so?"

"I know so. She's told me that she's quitting. Can you blame her? Remember that she's been fighting alone."

"And the last straw breaks the camel's back. I realise that. Do *you* think the curse has come into operation, Mr. Scott?"

"If you knew the family history as well as I do you might not ask that question, Inspector."

Croft's jaw went out aggressively. "I'm ready to be enlightened."

"You shall be. Mind if we get back to our chairs in the sitting-room? It's more comfortable there."

"Suits me." Croft laid a fatherly hand on the young man's shoulder as they went. "You've got a hell of a problem on your hands, helping Miss Castleton, who has my every sympathy," he said. "But, good lord, think of what I'm faced with! Yet it's pretty certain that I can't make a move until morning. I've done all I can by telephone. So we might just as well spend what's left of the night in yarning, and make an attempt to get to the bottom of this thing."

The man from Scotland Yard refused the offer of a further cigarette from Scott, when they had regained their chairs, but groped in a jacket pocket for pipe and pouch. He rammed tobacco down with a thick forefinger and struck a match. "How about Miss Marjorie Castleton herself? So far we've been dealing with the remote past. Or is there more of it that you'd like to tell me first?"

"You might as well know the rest, in relation to this curse business," Scott said, lighting a cigarette. "It links up, you see. Between then and now—and again I quote recorded family history—there's been quite a few tragic deaths. One man stabbed another in the neck, over a game of dice. I was thinking about the sequence earlier on tonight. Somehow I couldn't get it out of my mind.

"There was a duel, out there in the Great Hall. Somewhere about 1602. Two members of the family fought over a gipsy girl. One was run straight through the chest, and the girl herself was worthless enough to leave the other fellow next day. Then, of course, there was the Civil War, the Great Plague, Monmouth . . . Every time the family copped it properly in the neck. Mostly men, you see, although in and among a female member of the family occasionally came to a sticky end."

Tony Scott spoke rapidly. It was clear to see that he was an enthusiastic student of history. "The curse of Blanche de Castleton seems to have operated consistently all down the

years. In the reign of George the Third, for instance, there
was a squire of Castleton who was shot dead, a few miles
from here, when on his way back from London. A highwayman put a bullet through his brain. During the Indian mutiny,
another fellow was hacked into little pieces and the remains
thrown morning by morning over the wall of a fort into the
midst of his comrades of a British garrison. So it goes on."

He laughed, a little grimly. "That's as may be, Inspector,
but, like you, I don't believe in 'twaddle.' Local superstition
is to the effect that the ghost of Blanche appears every time
immediately prior to these happenings, but there's absolutely
no genuine authority for this. I just can't swallow the haunting business."

"Stout feller," Croft said, as he stretched himself in the
chair and puffed away steadily. "Tell me that you don't believe in this silly curse business, too, and I'm your friend for
life."

Scott laughed again. "Glad to have you so, Inspector. I
don't believe in it. But can you blame Miss Castleton for doing so? It's all very well for us: tough, safe outsiders; yet
think of what she's had to go through!"

"She seems a fighter to me."

"But the fight's been too long and bitter. Everything
seems to be against her. She's left completely alone—the
very last of a long, tragic line; the last Castleton, with her
back against the wall, hemmed in by circumstance—the
culmination of a mounting series of crises. I told you that the
curse was directed to the whole family, Inspector; but the
greater hatred was directed to the male side. Rummy, that.
Whether we believe in it or not, the fact remains that ever
since the males have seemed to be the weaker side. There's
been a preponderance of daughters. That's one reason, I
think, why the finances of the family got weaker down the
years. Dowries went out, instead of coming in. There were
few strong men to recoup the Castleton fortunes."

Smoke swirled around Croft's head as he listened. About
them was the quiet house, steeped in its own peculiar and
tragic history. Dawn was creeping up.

He said quietly: "So much for the past, then, Mr. Scott. Now let's get down to modern times."

Scott extinguished his cigarette in the ash-tray. "Here's where my information is supplemented by facts supplied by Miss Castleton herself. I'll try to present things in order."

He thought for a moment. "I needn't make it too involved, either. Essence of the matter is that Marjorie's mother came from a family in the North of England, called Mead. Her elder sister had married a tough chap of the name of Apperley, some years before. He was something to do with shipping. In this instance there was, again, just one child—Henry."

Croft waved a hand to disperse the smoke. "Need you bring him in?" he demanded a little sleepily, although his mind was still alert.

"I think that he's integral to the present position, Inspector. The Colonel didn't have his only child—Marjorie—until he'd been married for a time, so that his nephew, Henry Apperley, is quite a bit older than she is.

"Well, now, this Henry Apperley is born in the North but detests it. He won't fall into line with its carefulness, its characteristics of hard industry and the lingering on of a Victorian austerity. He craves the good old fleshpots, instead, and there's row after row. Old man Apperley considers that a University education has been wasted; he threatens to chuck Henry out time and again if he doesn't buckle down to an office desk. And every time Henry gets around his soft-hearted aunt, Marjorie's mother—the girl still being fairly young. Finally—climax."

Scott snapped his fingers. "Old John Apperley gets fed up. He does what he'd threatened. The doting aunt intervenes. There's one hell of a family row, and Henry gets kicked out. Okay—Auntie continues to help him from then on. I gather that the Colonel really loved his wife. He'd do anything for her, even to the extent of taking on his nephew, who wasn't worth tuppence.

"Then another tragedy came to Castleton House, while Marjorie was growing up at a public school. Whether the

Lady of the Blue Room walked the same night, I can't say, Inspector. But Marjorie's mother was coming down the huge old staircase to meet guests in the Great Hall. She was wearing the latest in trailing evening gowns and the hem of the skirt caught in a loose board. Something almost imperceptible unless one were looking for it, but understandable in such an ancient house. The poor woman fell from top to bottom of the stairs and broke her neck."

A little hush descended on the room. Croft was busy with his thoughts, pipe going out between his strong teeth. He offered no comment, for the moment.

Scott rubbed one tired eye with a little finger. "The Colonel, who was getting on, devoted all his thought and love to Marjorie. At the same time he strove to keep on with the helping hand to Henry Apperley, whose family had cut themselves off from him completely. The Colonel was finding himself saddled with the effects of the slowing up of his predecessors. Financially, I mean. Things had been sliding at Castleton for such a long time, and he now found himself facing formidable odds. But for the sake of the promise to his wife, he made Henry Apperley his responsibility; and at the same time hung on like grim death to the house. It was the family heritage. He was upholding the old family spirit in lighting to retain the property. Marjorie grew up into the attractive young lady you've now met. She's—oh, about twenty now."

There was a certain fondness in Scott's voice that made Detective-Inspector Croft smile paternally. Good for the boy, he thought.

Scott went on to the closing stages of a story that had been listened to with patience and keen attention. "There's not so much more, Inspector. Henry Apperley turned out to be a bad egg, inasmuch as he was sent down from Cambridge. He turned up here, begging the Colonel for help— wanted to get to America and make a fresh start. The Colonel was already up to his ears in the bouillon and hadn't any money—but again he was loyal to the promise given to his dead wife. I told you, I think," Scott said, "that the Castletons have always considered it little short of sacrilege to attempt to part with any of the furnishings of the house."

Croft stirred again in his chair. "But you did mention that the Colonel wasn't a bookish man."

"That's right. He realised that *something* had to go, and I think he fell in with what might have been Apperley's own suggestion. Apart from his fly-by-night foolishness, Henry Apperley had done well on the scholastic side at the University. He knew what was what when it came to cataloguing the Castleton library that hadn't been touched for generations upon generations. The Colonel set him to work, and Apperley seems to have gone through thousands of old volumes systematically and made a really good job of it. He proved invaluable in disposing of quite a few rarities; raised his fare and expenses to America, and left the Colonel with a decent balance to be going on with."

"Might have been trying to redeem himself a bit," Croft murmured.

"So he might. Hope that I'm not sending you to sleep, Inspector. Time went by; the Colonel struggled on. He now had a hefty great mortgage on the house, but was sticking it out like a man. Then Apperley came back from America."

Scott broke off here, to think deeply. "I dunno, Inspector," he said at last. "He seems to have repaid the Colonel even more by giving him a hand, from which we can argue that he'd struck it lucky in the States. The mortgage was lifted; things went on better. And then—tragedy again. It seems that it just can't be avoided."

Croft nodded. "The Colonel himself? I seem to remember the headlines at the time. Not so long ago, either."

"To round things off, it might do with recapitulation," Scott said, with a little sigh. "Colonel Castleton was out shooting one morning, early. It seems that he was in a little copse. The gun, according to his own story to Marjorie, and as told at the inquest, went off accidentally—a trailing bramble, or something. He staggered out on to a roadside, and a farm labourer happened to pass on his bike. They got the Colonel home, suffering from a terrible internal hæmorrhage, and sent for Marjorie from finishing school. He died shortly afterwards."

"And she believed that this second death in her young life was the result of the curse?" Croft asked quietly.

"I think that she refused to admit it, then. She tried to be intelligent, Inspector."

"Was the Colonel a good shot, do you know?"

"Miss Castleton says that he was. It was one of his favourite pursuits."

"And yet he lets a trailing bramble catch him napping, like a raw amateur," Croft mused. "No wonder that Miss Castleton was tempted to believe in the unavoidable."

"She put away such dark imaginings from her," Scott said. "She found that her father had been unable to leave her very little, beyond the property itself. And she had to find thumping death duties on the top of that. Here, again, the Castleton spirit was almost automatically manifest—cling to the house somehow. But she couldn't cling—not if she sold the place. And it was all she could do. She hadn't a bean. Castleton House must finally go. In her dilemma she hit upon the idea of approaching my people—the National Trust. Her proviso was, if we took over the place as a showpiece, and made her a small annuity for the same, that she should be allowed accommodation with her housekeeper and a couple of servants on the premises, out of the way of everybody. We were glad to agree to this. As it stands, the place is, of course, worth thousands."

"Fair enough," Inspector Croft ruminated. "In that way she ensures the future of the old house that she loves and at the same time she needn't sever her connection with it."

"That's how we looked at it, Inspector. There was a further trifling condition that she made. It seems scarcely worth the mentioning, but you might like to know. The Colonel had expressed a dying wish that his study should be left completely undisturbed."

Croft straightened up. "Why?"

"Tradition," Scott answered. "Pure tradition. That's another Castleton peculiarity. Since Elizabethan times fathers have impressed upon their children that nothing should be moved, taken away, or added to. God knows who originally started it—probably some wise old fellow who wanted the dignity and beauty of the room left as it was for evermore. The strange thing is that this tradition has always been scrupulously respected over the centuries. Even in his death throes, Colonel Castleton was still hidebound by it. We, on our part, felt that we could do no more than comply with his daughter's insistence on the point."

"Quite apart from that," Croft answered, nodding to show that he understood, "I should imagine it's in your own interest. The room must be unique by reason of such an arrangement."

"Decidedly so, Inspector. The Trust had agreed absolutely that during the renovations that we planned to undertake, the study should be completely exempt."

Scott fell silent. He ventured a look at Detective-Inspector Croft, still slumped in his armchair. The weight of words seemed to have told on him. He was busy analysing in his mind, pigeon-holing facts, seeking conclusions. Scott lit another cigarette before the Inspector looked up.

"This Henry Apperley," he queried. "You said that he was integral to the present position?"

"In a way—yes," Scott answered. "You see, he's been pestering Marjorie Castleton to sell out to him. His terms seemed to be generous enough, but she couldn't bring herself to do it. For one thing, it meant her clearing out of Castleton House completely. For another—"

Croft was scraping at his pipe-bowl. "Yes?"

"For another, she doesn't like him. Detests him, in fact. She realises how he helped her father on the return from America, but against that she sets the fact that he drew her idolised mother into all sorts of unpleasantness years ago. She's told me, indirectly, of course, that she resented Apperley's easy familiarity to her as a schoolgirl during the holidays—although that was a long time ago, comparatively speaking. But, in more recent holidays when she's been in residence here, she noted how the mere influence, or even mention, of Apperley seemed to upset her father in some way.

"You see, her dislike of this man, older than herself, is instinctive. Now the wheel comes full circle from where I started, Inspector. I rather think I'd like a word with this Apperley myself."

Scott was trying to keep calm, but there was a dangerous note in his voice. "I blame him a lot for stirring up this idiotic curse business in Miss Castleton's mind," he said, almost in a growl. "Damn him! When I think of him out there . . .!" He jerked his head in the direction of the window, and Croft found himself a little bewildered.

"How d'ye mean—out there?"

Scott tried to grin. "Sorry, I've been meaning to get around to this before now. Apperley loves the old place so much that he's got a houseboat moored fairly close by. Or should I say anchored? I'm no nautical type. It looks to be about a quarter of a mile offshore."

"Does Apperley own it?"

"Not as near as I can make out," Scott said. "It seems that, in America, he picked up a pal named Arthur White. They tell me he's a brilliant artist, interested at the present time in seascapes. Apperley doesn't seem to have the cheek to invite himself to permanent residence here, and I think he has some sort of a flat in London. But he spends all of his week-ends, and as much other time off as he can get, with his crony on the boat and occasionally rows over here as cool as you please, to visit his cousin. There's a strip of private beach below the house, with some sheer cliffs to the left of it and a chain of rocks—some submerged and half-submerged—on the other side. It's like a semi-bay, if you see what I mean."

"I'll take a look by daylight," Croft answered. "So Apperley invites himself here, now and again?"

"He does," Scott said bitterly. "And Miss Castleton can't turn him away altogether, if only out of common courtesy. Those are the times, I think, when he does the mischief. He's poisoning her mind against the place—and purely for his own ends. He wants her to sell to him. Whether it is that such an action would give him some vicarious satisfaction by his being able to turn her out after her obviously shown contempt of him, I can't say. Up to now she's resisted. But now this silly curse twaddle seems to have broken down her resistance utterly. She's come round in actually crediting the baleful influence of the Lady in the Blue Room."

Croft let the other talk. He could sense that he was almost spent by now. Scott said: "In the little time I've had at my disposal, I've tried hard to blow such nonsense sky-high. I was making progress, too. I'd practically succeeded in bringing her around to a sane view of things. She invited me here this week-end to make final arrangements for the transfer of the property. And now—"

Scott stood up. He went over to the diamond-paned window of the little sitting-room and lifted aside a corner of the heavily brocaded curtain. Daylight. The sun coming up in a blaze of crimson and gold that presaged another hot day.

"Now," he said savagely, "the deal's off. She can't face any more. An unknown man brings more blood and mystery to this damned old house. She's given in to the curse of Blanche de Castleton; and she tells herself that, as the last of the family, there's no sense in going on. Let Blanche have her way. Let the house go to a stranger to its high ideals and traditions. She's chucking up the sponge. And in order to do that she's evading me; because she can't face me either, in her present frame of mind."

Scott drove his hands deep into his pockets. And the Detective-Inspector went to him quietly to lay a hand on his shoulder. "Buck up, Mr. Scott. The game isn't lost yet."

He could understand Tony Scott's distress. Not only was he a most loyal and zealous employee of a great organisation that was bent upon preserving such historical loveliness as this, he was also a young man very much in love, even though the object of his affections might not yet realise it.

CHAPTER IV

THE STORM RISES—

"RED SKY AT MORNING," Detective-Inspector Croft said, as he stood with Paynter at the back of the house and looked seaward. "Another hot day for us, but not quite so blazingly bright, I should say. It'll be oppressive and cloudy, if I'm any judge of these matters. So that's the houseboat Scott was talking about?"

The small, neat vessel lay some distance out, riding idly on a long swell. The harsh sounds of swooping gulls came to their ears. Croft brought his gaze back and around to the left of where they stood.

"I'd say that this Arthur White fellow knows enough about the rise and fall of the tide to be quite happy where he is, instead of closer inshore. In spite of the layout, there's only slight protection in case of a blow, situated as he is now, but it's enough, with a good cable, to enable him to ride anything out. Those shelving cliffs coming down to the shingle—pretty sight, eh?"

"Add to the amenities of the place," Paynter answered. "Terraced gardens in the rear, this strip of private beach, a few scattered rocks, then more cliffs to the right and the coast road to Harlingham . . . Yes, I think I can well understand anyone wanting to hold on to Castleton, Inspector."

"Well, we've been all around this choice domain," Croft said a trifle morosely, "and found nothing that'll help us with regard to last night. There's too much gravel, stone flags and what-not to defeat us in the matter of footprints, or other clues. And we've made a brief circular tour as far as the stables—"

He broke off. Inspector Paynter groaned as he turned around at sound of someone approaching them. "The Dragon again. Bright and early—"

Croft patted him on the shoulder. "Looks pretty grim, too. Try to remember that I'm with you."

Miss Elspeth McCracken came up to them slowly but deliberately. Her demeanour was as frigidly starched as the narrow old-fashioned frills at throat and wrists. Croft caught the slight wheeze of her breathing. "Will ye come in to breakfast, gentlemen?"

There was veiled hostility in the broad Scots burr. She waited reply so that she might indulge in further words that were a little sharper. Croft said, "Thanks, but you needn't have troubled to come all the way out here. We'd have found our way inside."

"Miss Castleton sent for me to fetch ye," Elspeth said. "I always have breakfast on the board by eight, an' ye might have known it to be so in a well-run household. I don't thank ye both for givin' me this trapes after ye."

Inspector Paynter looked at his superior with a slight shrug of the shoulders. "Sorry, and all that."

"An' well ye might be," she said. "Miss Castleton, the poor bairn, is rare upset after last night's terrible affair. I'll be glad to see the back of ye, an' no mistake. I'm a plain-speakin' wumman, ye ken."

"I admire you for it." Croft turned with her and began to walk back to the house, suiting his pace to her own, while Inspector Paynter followed a trifle disconsolately in the rear. "I gather, Miss McCracken, that you've not much use for men as a whole?"

"They clutter the place up an' get unner your feet," the housekeeper came back at him, the wheeze more in evidence now that she was on the move again.

"Just so. But you like Mr. Scott?"

"Mr. Scott? He's a braw lad, Inspector, but he's no' a respecter of tradition."

"You mean he doesn't believe in ghosts?" Croft answered bluntly.

"I didna say that, sir."

"How about Miss Castleton's cousin—Mr. Apperley?"

"I try to treat him with respect when he's here," she said in dogged fashion, holding her long skirt aside lest it brush against a drooping flower that bordered the path to the house they were now nearing. "Both him an' that friend of his, Mr. White, the American gentleman. They're Miss Castleton's guests."

"You've known Mr. Apperley for quite a time, I should imagine," Croft persisted. "I'm not asking you to go behind his back."

"Are ye no'?" she said. "Ye're being pretty straightforward, all the same. Ye're wanting an honest opinion on my part, sir. Well, if I'd have had the upbringing of yon Mr. Apperley, he'd have been a better man than he is today."

"I see. Quite apart from you not liking all men in the general, you don't like him in the particular. Is that it?" Croft's tones were insistent.

"I have to like him," she said. "He was a favourite of the mistress's, God rest her! The Colonel—God rest him too!—tried all he could to help Mr. Apperley, for the same reason. And even now Miss Marjorie tries to take him on sufferance because of that."

"He came back from America rather rich, or so I understand . . .?"

"He's canny that way," Miss McCracken replied sharply. "He's hard, strong. But I've no' been afraid of him. I give him the same dish o' tongues that I give to all others who get in my way."

"What's his reaction?"

"He just ignores me. This way, gentlemen." Miss McCracken piloted them inside the house, and Croft entered the breakfast-room realising that his conversation with the dour housekeeper had got him very little farther in his quest for a solution of the mystery of Castleton House.

The days of dining in the Great Hall of Castleton had gone for ever. Here was a fair-sized table with modern appointments, and the Scotland Yard man and his assistant sat down appreciatively to crisp bacon and eggs. While still on his feet, however, Croft faced his pretty hostess. He noted the shrewdness in her eyes, saw, too, the determined set of her small chin.

Tony Scott was already at the table. He greeted Croft somewhat lackadaisically, then looked stubbornly down at his plate. Croft guessed that there had already been words between the pair.

He tried to start a more or less bright conversation. "Inspector Paynter and I," he said, "have been touring around your property, Miss Castleton. As I half-expected, we found nothing to help us."

"I'm sorry . . . " she answered, and crumpled at one corner the starched napkin that lay in her lap. "Perhaps I should have made the effort to have shown you around. But after last night—"

"Please don't apologise." Croft was exerting himself to be gallant. "I quite understand, and there's nothing that you could really have done. But those stables—"

"You found those?" she asked. "Pretty dilapidated, aren't they?"

"Mouldering, Miss Castleton. I saw no cause to poke about them unduly, and I didn't want to keep too far away from the house. As it was, your Miss McCracken had to come out and find us."

She coloured slightly. "You mustn't mind her—gruffness, Inspector. I owe her a lot, from childhood upwards."

"Do you get along with the lady, Mr. Scott?" Croft asked. And Tony Scott almost started as he sat.

"Miss McCracken, the housekeeper? Oh, I don't know." He stirred a cup of coffee, almost violently. "She's a good old stick deep down, I dare say."

"How's the world treating you this morning?" Croft went on, and noted how the movement of the spoon became even more agitated. "Are you one of those unfortunates who can't miss sleep and get away with it?"

Scott laid the spoon in his saucer. It was clear that he was anxious to steer the conversation away from personalities. "I'm all right," he said shortly. "So—the stables didn't interest you, Inspector?"

"Dank, dark, deserted," Croft said. "There hasn't been a horse there for years and years. Of course, we know why."

"Apart from the coming of the motor age," Marjorie Castleton said, in reply to Croft's words, "the family hasn't been able to afford horses for years and years. The place has been nothing but a rotting liability. It still is."

She snapped a piece of toast between fingers that trembled slightly. To himself Croft said: "Oho! a complete *volte-face* on the part of our charming young hostess this morning, apparently." Her attitude as expressed to Scott in the early hours still held—perhaps even more forcefully now.

"Inspector Paynter and I," Croft said, "decided to give the stables a miss, as far as a close inspection went. We merely satisfied ourselves that there could be no possible intruder lurking inside, and then went all the way down to the lodge at the gates, for much the same reason. We found the door boarded up."

He looked across at Marjorie Castleton again. She nodded.

"My father," she said, "was forced to let all the outside staff go. That included the lodge-keeper. He was a widower, anyway, and I believe he went to live with his son, somewhere on the other side of Harlingham. As things stand now, he comes over twice a week with his grandson, who's just left school. It's all Daddy found himself able to afford lately. The pair do what they can, as far as gardening is concerned. But"—she hesitated and sank her voice to a whisper—"no doubt there'll be a different arrangement in the future."

Tony Scott raised his head. "Might I ask your plans, Inspector?"

"You mean my movements, Mr. Scott," Croft chided him gently.

"Sorry—your movements. After all, you *are* a policeman."

"I try not to make that fact too evident. I may have to slip back to Town to make a personal report. On the other hand, I might, after I've seen the Chief Constable of Harlingham, conduct operations from local headquarters under his direction. The immediate problem is to establish the identity of the man who was killed here last night. I don't think I'm giving anything away when I say that my colleagues at the Yard can quite easily handle that angle in my absence, and look after the Press."

"You think that the Press may be able to help you, Inspector?"

"It's often very helpful indeed, Mr. Scott. The local police, I should think, will be able to get some sort of a photograph of the dead man's features at the mortuary in Harlingham. Sorry, Miss Castleton."

"Don't mind me," she said tonelessly.

"Perhaps I shouldn't mention it," Croft said, "but there *is* that point to it. If we can get a picture in the newspapers and a caption—'Do you know this man?'—or something like that, it may help us on a lot. It's been tried before and it's worked."

Once again he brought the conversation back to a focal point. "How about you?" he asked the discomfited Scott.

Detective-Inspector Croft was precipitating a crisis in the table-chatter and doing it deliberately. After all, he told himself, it seemed that Scott wanted it that way. He had given Croft a lead to that effect. Whatever had occurred or been said between the attractive and vigorous young representative of the National Trust and the even more young and attractive Marjorie Castleton, prior to the entrance of Croft and the dutifully silent Inspector Paynter, it looked as though Scott and the girl couldn't sit on it for ever. Whatever had passed between them appeared to be irrevocable to the girl's mind. But it somehow seemed that she lacked the necessary nerve to bring it straight out before Croft. Therefore, Tony Scott, smarting mentally though he might be, was trying to let her down lightly. He was trying to pave the way, so to speak, for that which she knew must be said.

Scott pushed his plate away. "Miss Castleton seems to prefer my room to my company, Inspector. D'ye think that there's room for me at the 'George'?"

It was out at last. Scott looked hard down at the table-cloth. Marjorie Castleton seemed to close her eyes tiredly for a moment. But then she looked directly at Croft, and refused to evade the issue longer.

There was a tiny silence before she spoke. It seemed to Croft that Scott was engaged in mentally biting his tongue. *Too* abrupt.

"That's hardly the way I put it, Mr. Scott," the girl said in her clear young voice. "But it appears to me that that's the way you feel yourself since I refused to take your advice, a short time ago. I don't think, however, that—that even in the heat of our words, I've given you—your marching orders."

She flung down her napkin and got up. At the sideboard she absently arranged tall flowers in a silver vase, and Croft twisted around in his chair to look at her. He saw that her fingers were trembling. So was the rest of her body. Her shoulders were heaving under emotional strain.

Almost instantly, it seemed, Scott was beside her. For a moment it looked as though he would exceed his place, would put out a hand to touch her, to comfort her, then he stood baffled. "Perhaps my phrasing of a delicate point was unfortunate, Miss Castleton. But what else can I do?"

"It will be only curtailing your visit by a few hours if you leave now, I suppose," she said flatly. "That's what you want, isn't it?"

As good as telling him to go, Croft thought. He thought better of attacking the marmalade jar and got up in turn. This meant the finish of breakfast, though Inspector Paynter, with a mere lift of an eyebrow as one who should say that he was but an inferior not called upon to intervene, still sat on quietly munching toast. Croft said awkwardly: "None of my actual business, I suppose. This thing's personal between you, whatever it is. But—"

"But, Inspector," she said, turning around to face him, "it's come to a head now. And it's only right that you should know. I refuse to go on living in this house any longer."

"Your decision, of course," Croft said, trying not to be too gruff about it. "Do I take it that Mr. Scott has been trying to dissuade you from such a course?"

"I have, Inspector," Scott said. "Last night worked the trick for Miss Castleton. I've done my best to advise her honestly. But—oh, hang!—I might as well say it! She thinks I've an axe to grind on behalf of my employers."

"I see." Croft glanced back at the stolid Inspector Poynter, as though motioning him to preserve his tacit silence. "Tell me, Miss Castleton—what do you think of the family 'curse'?"

She shrugged slim shoulders. "I try to be grown up."

"But you're letting it influence you all the same?"

"Not altogether. It's merely that I've had enough. The deaths in this house are unnatural. That may be pure coincidence. I don't know."

Suddenly she turned around, her small hand behind her gripping the edge of the sideboard, with the nails digging into the polished wood under stress of her feelings. "Curse or no curse, Inspector, you must agree that there seems to be no end to these accidents. The sheer bad luck of the Castletons seems to be holding out. I'm left with a pile of debts and a house that is a white elephant. I had ideas of turning it over to better hands than mine; of accepting the settlement that they'd be prepared to give so that I could clear things up, and then settling down here. But, since last night, I'm sick of the place. Sick of it, I tell you! It's oppressive to me—clammy. There's a dead hand over it. I can't and won't stay in it."

She was almost crying. "Don't accuse me of not being a fighter, Inspector. I've tried to fight, but it's no good. Oh, I know there may be a way out if I'll only wait. I know Mr. Scott has told me that, if I must have it so, he'll try to get the deed revised so that I needn't stay here at all if his people take over. But it's not that—it's not that!"

"Then what is it, Miss Castleton?" Croft asked, as gently as he could.

"Don't you see how evil seems to be predominant here?" she said a little wildly. "Don't you see how the past reaches out to these walls? I still insist that I'm grown up. Or try to be, anyway. I'm not fanciful, falsely romantic. I'm trying to be practical twentieth century. I've been educated up to the point of sophistication by—by my father's sacrifices. But I won't and can't go on to try to succeed where he failed."

"If you're set on that," Tony Scott said, almost between his teeth, "why not let the Trust take over completely and pull out from the place altogether? You've just hinted that it can be arranged."

"And pass on the responsibility for what you're pleased to designate 'utter rubbish'?" she flashed back at him. "You'd open Castleton House as a showplace ultimately, I know that. That would bring innocent people here—probably as innocent as the poor man who met a shocking death here a few hours ago."

"He was a marauder, Miss Castleton," Croft said sharply. "An unauthorised person on the premises."

"But it doesn't merit his being killed," she answered. "No, I've made up my mind, Inspector; and this—this friction between Mr. Scott and myself—"

"Has been caused by your quite understandable attitude, Miss Castleton," Tony Scott said. "Before the Inspector came in to breakfast, I tried to argue you out of it, and I think that you took it the wrong way. I apologise if I was too insistent. I don't think that I can presume to dictate to you."

"You're not dictating to me, Mr. Scott," she said with tears in her eyes. "I can understand your side of the affair, but I repeat—I can't, I just can't and won't go on. Thank you for all you've tried to do for me."

Tony Scott almost put out a hand to her again. "Then that means—?"

"That I've changed my mind, Mr. Scott. I told you so a short time after the killing, and I repeated it to you before breakfast. My cousin wants Castleton badly enough. He's been hounding me to sell the place to him. Very well—he can have it."

"If you insist that there is a responsibility in this business," Croft said, "you intend to pass it on to him?"

"I do," she retorted; and her chin went up.

"Well, it's your property, of course." Croft felt himself to be rather helpless.

"I'm not trying to be nastily triumphant on that point," she said. "And I'm not trying to indulge in personalities as far as Mr. Apperley is concerned. I hate to discuss a person disadvantageously when he's not here to defend himself. But I'm bound to say that he's always appealed to me as being a suitable occupant of this house. His general character fits in with it admirably. I should think that he'll enjoy himself despite whatever baneful influence may be at work. I do know that he was a trouble to my father and my mother; that as long as I've known him he's humiliated me by his self-assuredness and arrogance." She took a deep breath.

"All right. Let him try it out as owner of Castleton. I've thought this thing over carefully, and I've had no sleep. I'm determined to open active negotiations with Mr. Apperley as soon as possible. Today, in fact."

Silence fell between them at that. At the table, Inspector Paynter suddenly clicked a knife against a plate and looked up, almost guiltily. Tony Scott turned away from the girl in despair. "So I go to the 'George,' Inspector."

"You're welcome to stay on here until tomorrow, Mr. Scott," she said, half-defiantly.

Scott fumbled for words. "That's good of you, Miss Castleton, but I couldn't presume upon your hospitality. I—I feel that I'd only be in your way. Thanks for—for everything."

Detective-Inspector Croft strode recklessly into the breach. "That your final word, Miss Castleton?"

Her chin went up again. "Is there anything in police procedure to stop me doing what I plan?" she asked. "I mean, I know that this place is under investigation, and all that."

"Nothing at all," Croft assured her curtly. "But I feel bound to say that, metaphorically speaking, you're playing into the hands of the enemy. If there is an unseen influence, as you would seem to recognise there is, then you're simply letting it have its way with you. Here's where I tread on people's corns, yet I just can't help it. I'm made that way. Mr. Scott tells me that your cousin Apperley is a great exponent of this bogy-bogy business that you seem to have here in full measure."

She parried this thrust. "I defy anyone to say that Mr. Apperley, however much I dislike him personally, isn't a man of the world," she said. "He has those very qualities that I despise—avarice, aggressiveness and—as I mentioned— arrogance. He's selfish. And I say that even though he *did* help my father to lift a crippling mortgage on this place."

"You're trying to tell me," Croft said with a sigh, "that if the bogy-bogy business I've just alluded to is good enough for a cynical, worldly wise man like Apperley, then there must surely be something in it. I can't presume to argue the point. I have to get moving."

"Don't think me wilful, spoilt, obstinate," she said, lips still quivering. "I'm so wretched about this beastly affair last night. I'm honestly trying to do what I think is best. So you're going back to Harlingham, Inspector?"

"With Inspector Poynter—yes. I don't think that I need leave any officers behind, Miss Castleton. Unless you feel unsafe, of course."

"Do you anticipate any further danger, Inspector?" Scott asked bluntly.

"No," Croft said. And the girl dropped another bombshell.

"Perhaps it might help influence your decision, Inspector, if I say that I'm determined to get clear of this terrible house. That I intend, after seeing Mr. Apperley today, to close the place up and go to an hotel somewhere. I'll take my housekeeper with me. I won't spend another night in the place."

"Now you *are* chucking me out," Scott said mournfully.

"Here we go again," Croft cut in. "You'll have Miss Castleton saying now that she's just told you that you're welcome to stay here till Monday morning. She might well add to that that you refused by a non-reply. Hence her spur-of-the-moment decision. Well—" He sighed again. "If you're set on that, Miss Castleton, it will simplify my task. I needn't leave a man or two in the house. I would ask, however, that you notify Harlingham Police Headquarters as soon as possible of your whereabouts after you get to this hotel of yours, wherever it may be."

"I'll do that," she said.

Scott looked at Croft again. "I'll keep in touch with you as well, Inspector."

"That brings us round to the 'George' again," Croft answered him. "You'd better put tonight in there, at all events. I gather that you're not expected back in Town until tomorrow. Yes, I think that they'll find you a room on my recommendation. And you'll be close to me. As a matter of fact, Inspector Paynter—who, I see, has now finished his breakfast—is on the point of ringing through to Harlingham for a police car to take us back. Might I invite you to share it, Mr. Scott?"

"I'll have got my few traps together by then," Scott said, somehow avoiding the girl's eyes, as she avoided his. "Will you excuse me, Miss Castleton?"

She turned her head aside, as though she could not trust herself to speak, although Croft guessed that her lips were still trembling. Tony Scott hesitated, as though awaiting reply from her, and then left the room slowly. Behind him, Inspector Paynter took the hint and went out into the hall to telephone.

Croft straightened his tie. The situation was decidedly awkward, but was none of his seeking. "I do hope, Miss Castleton," he ventured at last, "that Mr. Scott hasn't offended you unduly? I mean—"

"I can't blame him," she said, leaving her position by the sideboard and coming back to the breakfast table to pick up and fold the napkin she had dropped. "Would you oblige me by ringing for Elspeth to clear away?"

Croft found an ornate bell-pull. He manipulated it vigorously. "Sometimes," he floundered, "it's hard to—to climb
down . . ."

"I do ask you to believe me when I say it's not that, Inspector," she said earnestly, as she stopped, the napkin still
in her hand, to look at him. "I'm trying hard to view this not
as a quarrel between Mr. Scott and myself, but as a sincere
attempt on my part to resolve a terrible problem. Mr. Scott
opposed that attempt, that's all there is to it. He for his part
was just as sincere as I am, but he took an opposite view. I
hope—"

She hesitated, then suddenly put out a small hand.

"I hope, Inspector, that you'll try to see it in that light, I
hope that you and I will be friends—good friends—but I
can't give way. I won't."

Detective-Inspector Croft took her fingers between his
own. "Of course, Miss Castleton. May I say from my side
that I can dimly sense your motives in this? Somehow you
seem to be trying to prove to us that you *are* grown up. That
the finishing school is left behind for ever. That you're responsible; that you have a mind of your own."

Marjorie Castleton treated him to a wry little smile.

"Something like that. You're actually a very understanding person, Inspector."

"Thank you. One thing more," Croft said. "I'd be a
happy man if you'd do Mr. Scott the same favour, in a few
moments. Shake his hand, I mean. He's feeling pretty sore,
but purely on your account, not his own or his employers'."

"I should feel miserable if he left without doing so," she
whispered. "But can't you *see*, Inspector, that I can't—I just
can't—take his advice? I'm fed up with Castleton. Fed up.
So desperately sick of it all . . ."

"We can only do our best in this life," Croft answered.
"I'm no philosophical humbug when I say that, either. It's
your decision and you've every right to make it. And to stick
to it," he finished. "Buck up, now, Miss Castleton."

She turned and left him, brushing past the suspicious
Miss Elspeth McCracken as she went out. Croft had his pipe

out, had in fact dipped it into his oilskin pouch; and the old housekeeper set down an empty tray with a disapproving bang.

"Rare upset she looks. And I'll thank ye not to smoke in here, sir,"

"I'm on my way out," Croft assured her sweetly. "You'll have the house to yourselves in a short time from now. Look, Miss McCracken—"

The dour old Scotswoman clattered plates into a pile. "Well?"

"You'll be glad to see the back of us, I know. Might I say that your mistress is a trifle headstrong?"

"All the Castletons hae been headstrong," the woman said, scraping a plate in a way that set Croft's teeth on edge.

"Miss Marjorie's a girl of spirit, Miss McCracken. She's determined on a certain course of action. There's nothing anyone can say will stop her." Croft watched the deft old hands move over the white cloth.

"I ken that. I canna stop her, either. I couldna stop her father from plunging into things," the housekeeper said bitterly.

"Just so. But keep a good eye on her," Croft said. "I can't stay here, neither can Mr. Scott."

"Ye're repeating yoursel', Inspector. Does that include the daft loon wi' ye?"

"You mean Inspector Paynter?" Croft asked ruefully. "Of course."

A crumb brush and tray came into operation as he watched. "If," said the enigmatic Miss McCracken, "you're offering that as a suggestion, sir, then I can only say that you're wastin' your breath. I weaned the bairn you're talkin' aboot. If I keep any eye on her, it'll be because of the love I bear the lassie."

Croft ignored the veiled sarcasm. "You've a telephone here," he said, "and it's in good working order. The number of Harlingham Police Headquarters is in the book. So is that of the 'George Hotel,' Marine Parade."

"I ken that fine, Inspector. Now ye'll excuse me."

Croft held the door open, so that she might pass with the loaded tray. "By the way, it's just struck me that you're doing this yourself—"

"Millie and Cook are packing to go," Miss McCracken said simply. "Ye canna expect aught else sin' last night. They've already taken the liberty of phoning up for a taxi frae Harlingham. From noo on, I look after Miss Marjorie myself."

She went her wheezy way, and Croft loaded his pipe and struck a match. Paynter came to his side to engage in a more or less desultory conversation, and a few minutes later Scott brought his bag into the Great Hall, almost coincident with the swish of the tyres of a police car outside. Of the taxi for the two servants there was, as yet, no sign. Croft guessed that there might be Sunday complications.

He tactfully kept out of the leave-taking, terse and restrained, between Marjorie Castleton and the young man who, even at this moment and in spite of all that had been said, was aching to take the girl into his arms. But at least she took his hand, as promised. And Tony Scott held it so long that she was perforce to gently disengage her own fingers. "If," she said, and he could hardly catch the words, "if we never meet again, Mr. Scott, I shall always remember you . . ."

"No hard feelings, Miss Castleton," he said almost roughly, relinquished her hand at last, and got into the police car beside Croft. As they were whirled away he looked back to the lone figure at the top of the worn entrance steps to Castleton House and felt his heart gripped by the strange presentiment. But what, he asked himself dismally, what the hell could he do?

Nothing. There was a storm brewing, both literally and physically. It called to his mind the fact that he had not, in his agitation, paused to ask either himself or the girl just *how* she proposed to get out to the houseboat. But what she had said had been said neither out of sheer bravado nor in a fit of pique. She was in deadly earnest. She must have some sort of resources to do as she planned. She had said that she would see Apperley, lounging on the houseboat in week-end comfort with his friend, and that she would see him today.

From the window of the police car Scott could see momentary glimpses of wayside trees ruffled by a strong breeze. The atmosphere, sensed even in this fast-moving vehicle, had become heavy and oppressive. Almost he could swear to hearing the low rumble of the first distant thunder above the soft hum of the engine. He felt like grabbing at Croft's sleeve and ordering him to stop the car.

Or, better still, to make the driver turn it around and go back. Back to the girl who might need him desperately and that very soon. He felt that, in spite of all that had been said between them, the mere sight of him returning might be welcome to her.

Yet he was borne onward. And to himself he repeated: what *could* he do?

CHAPTER V

—AND BREAKS

THE TIME WORE ON towards midday and lunch, served earlier than usual by Marjorie's orders. But in the giving of those orders she had forgotten the departure of Cook and Millie Smith. Yet as one who would not be brooked in a project by trifles, she went into the kitchen and persisted in helping her old housekeeper.

Miss McCracken slammed shut the door of a refrigerator, strangely out of place even in the modernised kitchen of Castleton House. "An' whit for, Miss Marjorie, are ye needin' lunch so soon? De'il take a lot o' men that's caused all this upset! It's ma kitchen, now. It was bad enough with Elsie in here and a feckless girl to fetch and carry to the dinin'-room—"

"I want lunch, Elspeth," the girl said flatly, "because I'm going out."

Miss McCracken set down a salad bowl. "Might I ask where?"

"I think you know that," she answered. "You were bound to know something of what went on in the breakfast-room this morning." And the old Scotswoman threw a lettuce to the table in despair.

"Ye're daft wrang o' your heid, Miss Marjorie. Ye're never going to *him* in this world!"

"But I am," the girl answered with quiet resolution. "There's nothing going to stop me, Elspeth. This dragging affair of the destiny of Castleton House and all that goes with it is going to be resolved—today."

The housekeeper picked up the lettuce again and began to pull off the outer leaves almost mechanically. "You would say to me, Miss Marjorie, that you've got the feel of the evil of this grim place in your bones. Ye tell yersel' that Mr. Apperley is no' ower guid—that the hoose will match him. That only he can control it. I mind when I boxed his ears once, as I might box the ears of any smart young cockerel who came struttin' into my kitchen here and made his way round Cook to take a couple o' her new tarts between his fingers. An' . . . he turned himsel' around and cursed me in her presence. And I pushed him oot and tellt him to mind his language in front o' females. And now ye'll gang to him . . ."

"I'll try to make a clean deal of it," Marjorie replied, the determined edge still to her voice. "An outright sale at his price so long as it's anything like reasonable. He can get the papers drawn up and signed in Town within the week."

"An' how about me?" Miss McCracken wanted to know, as she broke up the lettuce in the salad bowl. And Marjorie took a long breath.

"I've thought of that. I know that you'll be loyal, bless you! You've been loyal to the Castletons ever since you were a girl. I intend to find a small house or a cottage somewhere. You can still look after me, and I'm sure that there'll be enough for us both to live on." Pain crept momentarily into her words. "I thought that I loved Castleton so much once that I couldn't ever leave it. I told myself that my heart would break if I were ever parted from the place. But not any more. Not after last night. I only know now that my heart will break if I stay here. I can't be lady of the manor to it—not even in one wing. I'd sooner make a clean break here and now."

The wind was rising outside. Gauzy muslin curtains were blowing into the kitchen over the spotless sink. Elspeth went over to shut the window, with a bang.

"And . . . how about young Mr. Scott?"

"He's not my keeper," Marjorie said, almost in a whisper.

"Ye'll gang ye're own gait I suppose. An' ye're rushing me into an early lunch—"

"To catch the tide," the girl answered coolly, and the old housekeeper dropped a knife in dismay.

"The tide, at a quarter past twelve! Good God almighty, Miss Marjorie, it was an ill day when your puir father died! He'd hae taken ye ower his knee for this foolishness, old as you've grown. There's a storm blowin' up like glory—dinna ye hear it growlin'? Yon wee motor-boat of yours—"

"Will take me safely out to the houseboat," Marjorie answered. "I learnt my sailing around these parts when I was a child, and I know winds, storms and water in this locality as I know the back of my hand. I know there's a blow on the way, but I also know the capabilities of the houseboat. And I'm sick to death of delay. You hear me, Elspeth—sick to death of it! I can have lunch, put the boat out on the midday tide and get to the houseboat before the storm breaks. I shall be safe under cover by then, with Mr. Apperley and Mr. White. We'll be talking this thing over in the cabin. Haggling about a price, as like as not," she finished bitterly.

"And ye'll come back when the storm's ower, I suppose?" Miss McCracken said.

"That's how I plan it, Elspeth."

The housekeeper bit back further reply. There seemed to be no use in making one. From the way that Marjorie Castleton was looking at the kitchen clock, it seemed that the girl was busy with some sort of a mental calculation—that she was estimating the distance and approach of the storm. Her coolness in this was inspired by a desperate resolve. She knew what she was doing.

Miss McCracken told herself that she could do nothing else but let her have her head. She knew Marjorie of old, knew her seamanship when it came to the matter of looking after herself in small boats. It was useless to argue further, and she herself was "no' one to boil her cabbages twice." It did, indeed, cross her mind that she might try the expedient, somehow, of telephoning Detective-Inspector Croft in Harlingham. But several reasons militated against that. In the first place, there was Marjorie herself to consider. Constantly at Miss McCracken's elbow, she would not give her ex-nurse and housekeeper the chance to contact Croft or Scott. And, even could that chance be gained, the probability was that neither of the two men could be persuaded to come all the way back here merely to try to stop the headstrong girl from carrying out her project.

They would argue that she knew wind and water—pretty much as she argued herself. And having already had a taste of trying to reason with her, and having been rebuffed, they would be chary of trying it on again.

So that, against Marjorie's rock-like determination, the old Scotswoman could do nothing but grumble to herself and get on with the preparation of lunch. In this Marjorie assisted her to such good effect that it was over and cleared away by just after noon.

"Expect me back for tea, Elspeth," the girl said quietly, as the housekeeper came out from the dining-room, having set it to rights again. "And don't worry. Mr. Apperley can't eat me. Believe me, I'm only doing what I think is best."

Suddenly she came over to the dour old woman and slipped an arm about her shoulders, giving her a little squeeze of affection. "You're an old bear, Elspeth, and a growly one at that. But deep down you know that I'm only trying in my own cussed, perverse way to exhibit a little of the courage that you tried to spank into me as a kid. 'Bye, now."

Hatless, Marjorie Castleton slipped on a short coat and went out by the kitchen door. The wind met her in a sudden snatch; a nearby hollyhock seemed to be bowing to her presence. She looked up at a sky grown heavy and leaden—and went on.

By a tiny rockery, and down brick steps. The terraced gardens had many paths leading to the back of Castleton House. Croft had been to the end of those gardens, with Inspector Paynter that morning, and had looked seaward. Below him he had seen the bare little strip of private shingle with the cliffs that also formed part of the Castleton property to the left and the scattered rocks and greater stretch of cliff, with the coast road to Harlingham, on the right. The shingle had been gleaming in the morning sunlight, the water curling lazily at its edge.

Had Croft gone below the terrace he would have seen how it terminated in a stout retaining wall of ancient stone. Where he and Paynter had stood that morning was a sheer drop beneath them to the shingle.

The tide was in, now. It had risen to its highest and was lapping against the old green-scummed mark on the stone wall. And in spite of the greatest stress that the weather might hold it would never rise higher. The shingle that Croft had admired earlier was now well below water.

The brick steps led down to a stone landing flanked by shrubs that were trying bravely to resist the strengthening gusts. Here Marjorie Castleton turned sharp right, took a Yale key from her pocket and opened a small door inset in the stonework. Lacking windows, the small, cleverly contrived boathouse still possessed enough light for her to see the little motor-boat snug in its narrow dock. The girl walked a narrow plank expertly, bent and lifted up a steel roller door. The wind from seaward caught at her hair, and thunder cracked in the distance.

Wheeling gulls screamed. Her white skirt billowed against her slim legs; the water slapped near her feet. Slapped and clawed and fell back battled. Spray was flung up to wet her ankles, but she lifted her face and laughed. Then a stronger gust came sweeping in to growl at her—to snatch the laugh and fling it out to the misted horizon. She put back a vagrant curl and went soberly about her task of getting the boat started.

The brisk phut-phut of the motor heartened her. With the skill born of long practice she got the tiny vessel out and on to the rolling swell of the tide, the spray flying up over the bows. She went plunging onwards as a jagged flash of lightning split the low clouds to the west; and Henry Apperley, straightening up on the deck of the houseboat after helping his friend White to see that all was disposed snugly before the breaking of the storm that he knew they could now ride easily, looked shoreward and rubbed his eyes.

His lean, dark face with the strong, thin line of jaw, calculating eyes and neat clipped moustache on a wide upper lip showed incredulity. He turned to Arthur White, shorter, stockier, with unruly blond hair and nervous sensitive hands. "Take a look at that, Arthur. By God, she's forcing things!"

White snatched up a pair of binoculars, although the distance between them and the boat was comparatively small. His voice hold a mere trace of an American accent. "And alone!" he said. "After last night—"

"This means that we think fast," Apperley snapped. "Damn' fast. What the hell can she want?"

"Come to ask your advice, like as not," White said. "Or to tell you that she's closing in with that blasted Scott guy. Henry, my son, this fits in with what we were just discussing."

Apperley nodded, as he took the glasses unceremoniously from the other's hands. "Might save us a lot of trouble, at that. How long can we hold off Kreig? That's the point."

"Long enough, with Seldon out of the way," White jerked buck. "That is, if Scott doesn't get his hooks on the place fairly soon and forces us to clear out. By God, Apperley, we've got to keep ahead of time somehow! We're cooked if the Trust takes over. Can you imagine an army of workmen and officials in the place? We couldn't get out from under time. Not with all that stuff to shift."

"We've said all this before," rasped Apperley, watching through the glasses how the distance diminished between themselves and the strong thrust of the motor-boat.

"I know—I know. But your croaking of Seldon has likely put the skids on, as far as Scott and the girl are concerned," White ripped back. "She's come to tell you that she's hurrying up the process of turning the house over to him."

"And with cops in the place?" Apperley said. "Damn, I watched two of them through these same glasses this morning. I can spot them in plain clothes a mile away."

White smiled gently. "And through those same glasses, my dear Henry, *I* watched a squad car go up by the coast road back to Harlingham. And the back was occupied. Well, she's nearly here by now. What were we talking about over breakfast?"

"If she's come to gloat over me with the news that in view of last night's crisis that damned Scott has arranged to speed matters up, then it suits our book down to the ground," Apperley retorted. "She's definitely alone. We've been batting out what few brains we have between us to try to get hold of some sort of a plan—" He lifted the binoculars again.

"Whereby we can snatch the little lady ashore and so prevent her from signing on the dotted line with Scott's fountain-pen," White finished for him. "You thinking as fast as me, Henry?"

"Fast enough," Apperley said grimly. "Damn! How it fits in."

"Telepathy," White said, and laughed. "A poor little motor-boat and a howling storm. We'd have nothing to worry about."

Apperley laughed in turn as White's quick trend of thought struck him. "As usual, we quarrelled," he said. "The impulsive young lady—she's already proved how impulsive she is by coming out in that walnut-shell at all—declared that she couldn't and wouldn't stand my company any longer. *And* the company of my charming friend, Arthur Armstrong White, late of Leavenworth, U.S.A." He bowed towards the other with elaborate sarcasm.

"Correct," White said. "In spite of all we could do, she persisted in going back home. And the storm had broken by then. She threw off our kindly restraint. We struggled with her, but to no avail. We had our own hands full, considering the conditions. She cast off—"

"And hadn't a chance. Terrible! Terrible!" Apperley murmured. "The penalty of being headstrong. Tell you what, Arthur. You're damned right about the back of that squad car being occupied. If the police had stayed on—or even Scott— they'd never have let her come out alone. This proves that there's only old lady McCracken in the house now. And she's no match for my delightful cousin."

"We're wasting time," White answered. "And here she comes. Chuck her a rope, Apperley, while I get down below."

"And have another one waiting for her there," nodded Apperley. "I get it."

"I'll be ready for her at the bottom of the companion-way in the cabin," White said urgently. "Keep behind her as you go down, then grab with me. Okay?"

"Get below," Apperley retorted, as the first heavy patter of rain beat on the deck. He cupped his hands. "Ahoy, motor-boat!"

Twice the wind battered away the girl's reply and made it inaudible to him. Then he caught her shouted reply. "Coming aboard, Mr. Apperley!"

Thunder rumbled. Marjorie closed the throttle and braced her legs against the ominous rocking of the boat as she tried to stand, then crouched. Apperley roared "Stand by!" The boat was almost swirled beneath the counter of the houseboat. The girl missed the line-end, bent like a flash and grabbed it from the milling white froth of spume that surrounded her.

"Tie her close in," Apperley shouted. "You'll have to trust my fenders, such as they are. Up with you now."

He leaned over as far as he could and stretched out a manicured hand to the girl as she clung to a short, swaying rope ladder. "Come aboard," he said as pleasantly as he could and she stepped overside. "I admire your pluck in setting out in weather like this, Miss Castleton."

"Thanks," she answered him shortly. "I wouldn't have come, but I want to get this off my chest. I just can't face further delay . . ."

The rain broke in earnest as she spoke. Apperley took a swift, anxious look around. All snug.

"You'll get soaked if you stay here to tell me," he urged. "Mr. White's down below, making hot coffee. Hold on!" as the houseboat suddenly shuddered violently.

"She'll stand it?" the girl asked, turning her face with its windblown hair towards him, and grabbing at the rail.

"She's been in worse blows than this."

Apperley caught at her arm, guiding her towards the cabin steps as rain and wind beat at them. "We'll get below, Miss Castleton, and you can talk to me there. I've got a sea-anchor on that'll hold a battleship. But don't mind her rolling a bit. She's a flea-bitten old tub, but she doesn't leak and she knows her manners in dirty weather. After you."

Behind her, on the narrow stairs he shut and bolted the twin doors against the driving rain. The roar was muffled now; he could hear the thud of her footsteps, even White's breathing below. Marjorie Castleton said: "Then this gives us a chance to talk—" when White's strong hands closed about her.

Apperley moved in from behind. He clapped a hand over her mouth, put the other arm around her waist, and pushed while White pulled, the American's hands gripping her wrists. The cabin floor tilted, settled back. White braced a knee against a fixture chair secured to it. Apperley half-lifted the fighting girl.

He sat her down violently, and as the houseboat rolled again, pushed her back lest she slide out. Then White scrambled behind her and dropped a prepared loop of the thin cord over her shoulders. He worked swiftly and scientifically in his lashing of Marjorie Castleton to the chair, while she panted out threats and protestations against them. Then he stood back and looked at Henry Apperley in appreciative fashion.

"That fixes her. Let's sit down and take it easy."

"Suit yourself," Apperley rasped, while White disposed himself on a long upholstered corner seat. He himself remained standing, legs straddled wide apart against the pitching of the boat, fingers of one hand curled around a spoke in the back of the screwed-down Windsor chair as he looked at the defiant and now silent girl. "Sorry for the reception, Miss Castleton. It just had to be this way."

"I didn't expect this," she said in a low voice, aware now that louder complaint was useless.

"No more you didn't but I seized an opportunity."

"To drop the mask for good," she said between her teeth.

"You came to me," he answered unsmilingly. "I want Castleton."

"Then you've acted too precipitately," she replied. "But I'm glad that you've done this thing to me—in a way. It confirms my worst suspicions of you. I came here prepared to treat you as—as a gentleman. Didn't you stop to ask yourself why I came alone?"

"I repeat, that I seized the opportunity of your coming," he said, and went to sit beside White who was busy with a cigarette. "I guessed that after last night you'd cooked up a rushed deal with Scott, to turn Castleton House over to the National Trust. You came here to gloat over me; to tell me that, whatever slim chance of acquiring the property I might have had before, now I hadn't a dog's chance in hell of getting it. You were determined to tell me that I needn't call any more at week-ends; that there'd be workmen in the place before another week was out. That's it, isn't it? Thanks," as White gave him a cigarette and snapped a lighter.

He bent his head to the flame and jerked it up again in sudden surprise as the girl laughed.

CHAPTER VI

INSIDE STORY

APPERLEY STARED AT HER. "I'm right, aren't I? You're so damned impetuous that you couldn't wait, even in face of a rising storm, to come out here and taunt me with the news . . ."

She laughed again.

"It's you who've been too impetuous, Mr. Apperley. And you've counted the storm as your friend, but it's your enemy. A few seconds more on deck, if the rain hadn't come pelting down as it did, and I'd have burst out with the news there and then. But you didn't give me a chance."

Apperley exhaled smoke, eyes narrowed. "What news?"

"That I'd made what I fancied was an irrevocable decision. I really came to tell you that I'd decided to let you have Castleton House, lock, stock and barrel, at your price, so that I could clear out for good. That I'd broken with Mr. Scott of the National Trust. That you could do as you wanted with the place. This, Mr. Apperley, is really rich. No matter what you do to me, I think that I shan't ever lose the savour of such a wonderful joke."

Apperley got to his feet and slapped her twice, deliberately across the face. "Savour that, too. And stop lying in sheer bravado."

She fought to get back her breath. Her voice was more sober. "I'm not lying. Scott's gone. I practically threw him out. But I wish to God that I'd listened to his advice, curse or no curse!"

" 'Curse or no curse'!" White cut in sneeringly. "Tell her, Apperley."

Apperley crushed down his resentment that he might speak coherently. "You've opened my eyes, Miss Castleton—let me open yours. In the expressive language of Mr. White's own country, it's 'a lot of baloney.' There's nothing to such an old woman's tale. I used it, I embroidered it skilfully, traded on it in a subtle way, merely to influence you—to get you so fearful and despondent about Castleton that you'd be glad to let the place go to me."

"Then Mr. Scott was right?" she said. "And I fell for the subtle trap of believing that to such a hard-bitten scoundrel as yourself there *must* be something in the legend, otherwise you'd have laughed it to scorn in your worldliness. And just now—just now I nearly fell headlong into full surrender. You fool, Apperley—you hasty fool! But you're too late to do anything about it. Any slight shred of trust and decency that I might have felt about you before, well—I needn't say that it's forfeited completely. I can only tell Mr. Scott that I'm sorry . . ."

"Not forgetting that you might not get out of this alive," White said, settling his back against the bulkhead as the houseboat seemed to dive abruptly and then rise shudderingly again.

Marjorie Castleton looked at him with contempt. "Then why not dump me overboard now? With my hands and legs tied, there wouldn't be a trace left of me in this storm."

Once more it seemed that the queer telepathy existing between White and Apperley was in operation. Apperley looked at the other and grinned. White said: "Didn't we once discuss the possibility of a forced signature?"

Apperley was thinking deeply, the neglected cigarette smouldering away between his fingers. "To answer your question, Miss Castleton: we don't dump you overboard now, propitious as the conditions may seem, because a neat little plan comes to my mind."

"Which is?" she asked, conscious that the thin cord was cutting into her.

"To save myself a lot of money. You came here to sell me the place. Up till now, as the only way out, I was prepared to spend a few thousands—in addition to the money I was forced to give your fool of a father to stave off a blasted mortgage—to acquire the property. That's because I and White must have it, and in a minute I might tell you why, if you're a good girl. White's one of the world's best forgers. Or didn't you know?"

"I'm trying not to be melodramatic in saying that our little heart-to-heart talk promises to plumb the very depths of villainy," the girl answered. "Carry on with the enlightening process."

"I will. It'll help to pass the time until the storm blows itself out. We're partners. We're making thousands. That's how it comes about that I could afford the mortgage redemption and I could have met your price. In genuine cash, I mean," he added.

"In any case," White intervened, "I don't squander my undoubted talent in messing about with note-issues. Bonds, scrip, shares—all the big stuff—that's our pigeon. Get on with it, Apperley."

Apperley laughed. "Certainly. With you out of the way, Miss Castleton, what's to prevent me finding a will among my lamented cousin's effects? As practically her only kinsman, I'd surely be allowed to come to the house and take charge for a while. Oh, I'd arrange it genuinely enough, all right. I'd let Elspeth McCracken—the damned, interfering old fool!—find it in the presence of your Mr. Scott and probably the police as well."

"So that's it. A will, signed by me, and leaving Castleton to you," she said. "Why don't you forge it between you, and save me the trouble of signing it?"

"Because," White answered from his corner seat, "I don't stick my neck out unnecessarily. I know it's a challenge to my artistry and workmanship, and all that sort of stuff, but, solely by reason of circumstances that encompass the dear old house just now, such a document might well be challenged. It'd stand up under scrutiny all right, but I don't like to take the risk unless it's absolutely unavoidable. Get what I mean? Why should I go to all the trouble, anyway, when you've provided us with a safe, easy way like this?"

"Don't trouble your pretty head about the witnessing part of it," Apperley snapped. "We can look after that all right."

"I see," she said, and felt the bonds bite into her even more cruelly as the houseboat pitched forward again and tried to fling her floorwards. "And after you've forced me to sign it? What then?"

"Then the grateful beneficiary, your loving cousin," Apperley mocked, "will have leisure to see what can be done about you."

White put his heel on his cigarette butt. "I ain't scrupulous, Miss Castleton. As Apperley's just told you, I come from Leavenworth. There's always the sea."

Marjorie Castleton's eyes searched for and found those of her scoundrelly cousin. There was no fear in her own; there was no pity in his. She said: "All right. When the time comes for me to go under to suit your ends, well—I'll try to be ready for it. I shan't give you the satisfaction of crawling."

"That's good," Apperley said, unrelenting.

"This whole thing's a puzzle to me," she went on bravely. "You spoke of passing the time away until the storm blows out. Care to keep on talking, Mr. Apperley?"

"Always call your dear cousin 'Henry'," Apperley said, sitting down again.

White laughed until the little cabin rang. "Will you tell her the rest of the story, Apperley, or shall I? We've got to entertain ourselves somehow while we're cooped up here."

"I should imagine that the lady's reactions will be entertainment enough," Apperley said. "Okay, then. How shall I start and try to avoid too much intricacy?" He thought for a moment. "Let me try to get it straight. You know how I was your mother's favourite when I was younger. I've never fancied a life of hard work—least of all at the University. I slacked, got in with the wrong set. My father was too dreary and austere. He couldn't, wouldn't, understand."

"And my mother befriended you time and again," the girl said in a low voice. "And you've repaid her by acting like the scum you are."

"Thank you, Miss Castleton. You sum things up nicely. Perhaps I was only enlisting my dear aunt's support and sympathy with an eye to a coming crash at home. It came, all right. My dear, strait-laced papa showed me the door of our grim Northern home and booted me clear of it."

"And mother made herself responsible for keeping you on at the University," the girl said bitterly.

"She did. My delightful, loving aunt did, Miss Castleton. Then she died. Let me put you *au fait* about this. Her death was purely accidental, purely by coincidence. There was no tom-fool 'curse' operating to force her into catching her long skirt on the stairs that needed overhaul and repair. She was just unlucky."

"And my father?" Marjorie Castleton's words could hardly be distinguished, as the pitching of the boat continued.

"Suicide, Miss Castleton. I'll admit that it might have been murder on my part, but he saved me the trouble. He was pestered by an uneasy conscience, you see. Again it was nothing to do with the 'curse.'

"Oh, I'll admit that there is something about the Lady of the Blue Room in the family," Apperley went on. "I found that out during my historical researches. Blanche de Castleton *did* exist. She went insane in the Blue Room. She hanged herself there. She *did* leave a fanciful curse on the Castletons and all their descendants."

Apperley stood up to take the girl's face between his hands. He looked down into her steady blue eyes and smiled. "The curse of the Castletons, my dear—the curse of the Castletons . . . Utter, complete, old-womanish *rot! I'm* your curse, but I'm my own good friend, and the friend of dear Mr. White, over there."

Apperley's fingers slipped caressingly down the slender column of the girl's white neck. For an instant they seemed to curl and tighten about her throat, then he laughed and went back to his seat. "Let's get this thing in logical proportion," he said. "I'm pulled up short when the University sends me down. What can I do but go whining to your father? I hadn't a bean in the world. And I was dead set on getting to America and trying my luck there. But your dear papa was broke. He was reaping the whirlwind of years of neglect, misfortune, struggle on the part of the Castleton line. He couldn't stake me to a fresh start out of his slender resources."

"He was making hellish sacrifices, sweating blood to keep me at school," Marjorie Castleton said bitterly.

"So he was. But he was between two fires, you see. He also worshipped the memory of your mother. He'd given her a promise to help me, and the poor man began to cast around desperately for ways and means of doing it. I provided him with the idea he needed, I think. Whatever else I'd done or failed to do at the University, I'd put in some promising work in literature. Therefore, at my suggestion, your father set me to catalogue the Castleton library, undisturbed for donkey's years."

Apperley chuckled at the recollection. "I catalogued it, all right. Your father considered it a species of sacrilege to sell anything else in the house, and it was only at my respectful insistence that he grudgingly consented to the sale of anything rare in the book line that I might discover. Well, I discovered enough, by my knowledge of what was what, to raise my stake to America and give your father a small balance in cash to tide him over a few more months. I sold the books for him, in fact.

"And I gave him a square deal in that. But I didn't give him a square deal in the rest. You see, my dear, I found something else, besides valuable books. I found a piece of parchment . . ."

"How romantic!" Marjorie Castleton said witheringly.

"Something from the story-books, Miss Castleton? Of course, but the dividends are handsome ones, all the same. I think I can correctly hazard a little reconstruction of the past here."

White got up. "While you two talk your fool heads off," he said lazily, "I'll get on deck and see about setting the tragic Miss Castleton's boat adrift. We don't want this beautiful storm to die down before that's accomplished."

He picked up Marjorie's short coat from the floor. "Commend me for being far-sighted, Henry. I slipped this off the lady before I went to work with the cord. Evidence."

"See that it's well wedged in under a thwart," Apperley said, admiration in his tones. "What wringing of hands there'll be at Castleton when it's found! By the way, Arthur—try not to pile the motor-boat up on the home rocks. You know what I mean."

"You're referring to those on the right of the house," White said, one foot on the cabin stairs. "Rest easy. The wind and current's not set that way. The lady's cockleshell will go in a completely opposite direction—probably a mile or two before it gets crushed on The Pinnacles."

"If you'd like the information," Marjorie Castleton said in a steady voice, "the minor rocks known locally as The Pinnacles are exactly two and a half miles east of here."

"Thanks," White said. "You'll surely excuse me for a minute or two, Miss Castleton?"

"Where were we?" Apperley smiled, after the commotion of wind and sea had suddenly increased and just as suddenly lessened, consequent upon the opening and closing of the companion-way doors by White. "Oh, yes—the parchment. I said that I'd hazard reconstruction of the past. It's easy in this instance, because it bore signature and date. You remember the eighteenth-century squire of Castleton?"

"I know as much family history as that, at all events," Marjorie retorted. "You mean the man shot dead by highwaymen on his way home from London."

"Correct. The eighteenth century was the heyday of smuggling, Miss Castleton. French smuggling, principally. Does that strike a responsive chord in your imagination?"

"The only cord that I'm worried about is this damned thing around me," she raged. "I'll continue to listen to your hellish story, because there's not much else I can do. But you might try loosening this thing a little. You can still make sure of my hands."

"Right. It would be churlish to repay such a show of spirit by a refusal," Apperley said, and stepped forward to make the necessary adjustment. "There . . . That better? To resume, then. Dear, dear, this business of explanations is a long one, I'm afraid. But it must be finished, now that I've embarked upon it."

He was lolling on the upholstered seat again, one knee tucked up to his chin, the other long leg stretched out negligently to the still-pitching cabin floor. "Back to the interesting Blanche de Castleton. I'll try not to make this too academic for you.

"It's inevitable that a place like Castleton House should have a priests' hole, my dear. You're right in the middle, now, of a real-life adventure story. All good adventure stories that centre around a mysterious old house such as Castleton have a priests' hole. It is inevitable, and who am I to say otherwise? Very well, then.

"So—a priests' hole. But something far more elaborate than usual. The Castletons of the time of Elizabeth discovered a most interesting thing about their property. That was, that the hunk of private cliff they owned, to the left of the house, had a most wonderful cave therein."

Enjoying himself to the full, Apperley lifted a solemn finger.

"A cave, my dear. But with this difference. That, owing to the peculiar configuration of the semi-bay at the back of the house, the fall and rise of the tide by day left the mouth completely submerged. Even when the tide goes out, it's so. But there's a night tide—or didn't you know? That night tide, on the ebb, leaves the entrance to this most interesting little cave free for ingress by a decent-size rowing-boat.

"Now, you see, the advantages were obvious. Priests from and to France, under cover of darkness. A ship standing offshore; a rowing-boat linking it to Castleton House." Apperley's eyes bored into the girl's, held them by sheer malignant intensity. "But the Catholic Castletons weren't satisfied with that—oh, dear, no. They went to work secretly. They bored upwards from the natural cave at water-level when the tide was out at night. They constructed the good old romantic passage under the soft chalk cliff, all the way to the house. Then they broke it, to provide a chapel and living-room for the said priests." Apperley paused. "You're an intelligent girl, my dear. I give you three guesses as to which room it is."

"The study," Marjorie Castleton said witheringly.

"The study. Of course. Under the famous Long Gallery, and on to your dear father's study. Hugh de Castleton had been using it as such. He was Blanche's father. All right, then. He continued to use it as study, but shared it with the priests. And he couldn't trust his servants and chance friends who might pop in."

The scream of the wind came to their ears as White made a reappearance. "I've fixed it, and fixed it for good. Isn't the yarn told yet?"

"Not quite," Apperley said. "Anyhow, I'm enjoying it. Still listening, Miss Castleton? There's quite a bit to come."

"I'm forced to listen," she said. "Go on."

"Our Mr. White will busy himself in preparing that coffee I spoke about at first," Apperley smiled. "In order to ensure the safety of the priests, old Hugh and his sons took three precautionary measures.

"First, they extended the passage clear out to the stables, which have never been rebuilt and which, as you know, are quite a fair distance from the house. They thus had ingress and escape by land and water. Second, they arranged a huge rock, still in place, under the Long Gallery, and merely needing the pull of an iron lever—also still in place—to block the passage up from the study and house completely, Third, Hugh de Castleton started off the idea of the sanctity of the study; that it was sacred—inviolable to the master alone; that no servant must ever enter it, even for cleaning. That idea has persisted to this day. Successive fathers have followed it out, handing it down to their sons. But none of them have quite understood why. Only the eighteenth-century squire.

He found out all right; and he took damned good care to actively revive it.

"Hugh made a sketch plan. Political pressure defeated the family, in spite of all their work. They were forced to embrace the Protestant faith. Blanche de Castleton hanged herself, as already stated, and I think that that may have provided further incentive to the Castletons to keep on being Protestant. The underground passage fell into disuse, was lost to memory. So was the plan. Only the business of the inviolability of the master's study lived on."

Marjorie Castleton had resigned herself to sound of the sneering voice. Outside it seemed the storm was still raging, but now there seemed to be some slackening off.

Apperley resumed. He said: "Years went by. Edward Castleton, the man who was shot by the highwayman, found the plan—or so his notes on the back of the new sketch he made told me. You can easily guess what leapt to his mind, Miss Castleton. Like all later members of the family, he was chronically hard up. Smuggling. What better layout could he have? He made his arrangements and paid his men off in his study—lads of the village who trekked in through the secret stables entrance. The lace and tobacco came in on the low tide via the cave. The most eagle-eyed Revenue man couldn't spot the cave-mouth under water by day. Edward Castleton tucked this new plan away in a little hidey-hole of his own behind some books. He had never had the chance to take it out. But I did."

Apperley got up, went to a scuttle and peered out. "We've had the worst, I think. The worst of the weather, and the worst of my story. I do hope that I haven't bored you."

White came in with the coffee. Apperley said: "Look, I'm untying you sufficiently to let you join us."

He came behind her, and continued speaking as he worked at the knots. "I found the plan easily enough when I dumped armfuls of books from shelves to floor. I realised what it was, but I didn't tell your father. I preferred to see America first and try to get some big money so that I might possibly use this acquisition.

"Well, I made money in America, but I won't pretend that I made it honestly. It landed me in Leavenworth Gaol for a short sentence."

Arthur White looked up from his coffee. "Where he met me."

"That's it," Apperley went on complacently. "We were cell-mates. Shall I go on from there, Arthur? I don't want to embarrass you—"

"By telling the tale myself?" the blond-haired man asked. "Finish it, Apperley, now that you've come all this way."

"I'll try to be as complimentary to you as I can," Apperley said. "My poor friend, White, blames all his troubles on a woman."

White laid a spoon down softly. He was biting his lips.

"He's an artist," Apperley said. "A wonderful creative artist, and a brilliant draughtsman. The woman he married, a girl called Freda, had most expensive tastes. So expensive that—"

"That to hold her I prostituted what talent in draughtsmanship I had," White cut in roughly. "Let's shorten this damned story as much as possible. I turned to forgery of the big stuff to earn more, but even that didn't satisfy her. She met a swine called Ed Munroe—big-time international confidence man. She fell for him, because he could satisfy her craving for luxury."

"The poor boob still loves her," Apperley said clearly. And White spun round in his seat.

"Meaning me? I'll kill you yet, Apperley . . ."

Apperley was cool, unruffled. "I refuse to believe, Arthur, my boy, that you'll spoil a beautiful and most lucrative friendship for the sake of a girl who did you dirt," he said.

"Let me treat Miss Castleton to the rest of the story. Arthur was in the way of Munroe and Freda, so they shopped him. He found himself in Leavenworth, serving a much longer sentence than mine. He told me all his woes. I promised to help him. There was a kingpin States crook, by the name of 'Big Johnny' Kreig. In the past he'd pestered Arthur to work for him, Johnny being a big man on the distributive side of the forgery racket. Arthur had always refused.

"One day, word got around to him by the grapevine of Leavenworth. Danny Callaghan came in to knock the hell out of poor Arthur by whispering him that Munroe and Freda had had him framed. Arthur went crazy. I had to restrain him in my arms all night to save him from the screws. He loved Freda, you see. He'd never dreamed that she could do him the slightest injury. He thought that she was working and waiting for him to get out at the expiration of a long sentence. But not Freda?—oh, no. Danny told the truth when he said that she was going places with Munroe, and helping him work his racket.

"I was going out in less than a week—sentence served. Arthur made me swear to contact Big Johnny and enlist his help. Johnny still needed his services badly; and Arthur proposed a bargain that he honestly meant to keep. Kreig had the means and money and friends to stage a minor gaol-break and spring Arthur. And he agreed. I visited Leavenworth and told Arthur so.

"Arthur *was* sprung. Everything ran sweetly. I holed up with him for a few days in St. Louis. Then another mug I'd done a service to, Legs Donaldson, turned up to tell us as in personal and grateful favour that Munroe and Freda had got wind that Arthur was gunning for them, because he knew of their treachery; and that the pair had lighted out for England. They could operate just as well there.

"Arthur was insatiable. To hell with 'Big Johnny,' he said. He wanted Freda, to talk some sense into her, to take her back, unworthy as she was, and go on loving her. And he wanted the hide of Munroe. It was England or bust. I saw that there was no dissuading him. There came to my mind the parchment I'd found in the library of Castleton House. I saw what I could do with it. I got Arthur to promise that he'd start a forgery racket under the place and that he'd use his skill on our joint behalf. In return, I would try to help him track Munroe and Freda down in England, and do what was necessary to ensure his happiness in that direction."

Apperley took a drink of his coffee. "So we ditched 'Big Johnny.' I recovered a cache of dollars that I'd hidden before I hit Leavenworth. We came to Castleton. I went to the underworld, made contacts, found myself associates who were willing to distribute what we made at a thumping good price, for us. Then I approached your father."

"He never let me go into his study," said the girl, fascinated into submission by the story.

"Up to a certain point," Apperley answered, "he was only adhering to the family tradition about it. He didn't know why—only that *his* father, who didn't know why either, had requested it. But I opened his eyes when I came to him with a proposition that I knew he just couldn't refuse.

"On my return from the States, he was so involved in debt, so hopelessly despairing, so eager to clutch at any straw that should keep him from bankruptcy, should ensure his hanging on to Castleton and provide for his beloved daughter at an expensive finishing-school, that he fell for my suggestion. Especially as I was able, out of my funds, to lift the mortgage."

"In the picturesque jargon of my countrymen," White grinned, "it was a thumping big wad of dough."

"Good job we had it," Apperley said. "It provided us with equipment for our work, too. We shipped it by boat at night-through the cave . . ."

"And you worked down there," the girl asked incredulously, "under the very feet of the servants? Of my father?"

"We did, and were dead safe," Apperley assured her. "All went well until your father got cold feet. He had twinges of conscience. He began to argue with me—me who was providing him with an income to keep you at school, to maintain the property, to keep his mouth shut!"

"So you—murdered him?" she whispered, agony in her eyes.

Apperley was brutal. "I might have been forced to that, if he'd gone on much longer. But it didn't come to that. The worry on his mind was so great that he determined on suicide. But he couldn't face the shame of that. Or so I guess, and I think, correctly. To 'save his honour' it must be an 'accident.' He couldn't, for his own peace of mind, go on with us, and he couldn't, for the sake of himself and you, go to the police."

"And there was no—trailing bramble." Marjorie's face was dead white.

"He may have fixed the trigger in one and stood away with the bramble in his hand and then pulled it," Apperley said. "They went back and found his gun positioned so, didn't they? And it lent credence to his story. So they brought him home to die and sent for you. And I rowed across from this houseboat, fetched by the local police. And while I was being brought—"

"He practically died in my arms," she said, so low that Apperley could scarcely catch the words. "Daddy . . . died in my arms. They'd rushed me to his bedside. He said it was an accident—"

"Because he hadn't the guts, even in death," Apperley rasped, "to tell you the truth. He was too ashamed of what we'd made him do. He told you to keep out of the study, or, if you had children, to leave it inviolable to the master. You thought he was weakly raving about 'tradition.' I tell you that he was shamefacedly covering up for us. Now you know."

The girl's racking sobs filled the tiny cabin. Slowly she lifted her head. "And how about the latest death—the murder of an unknown man?"

"That, I should judge," Apperley said, "is the factor that made you change your mind about selling Castleton to me. Let me explain that. When I read in the Press that you were pursuing the idea of turning Castleton over to the National Trust, that had expressed its determination to engage on instant and extensive renovations, White and myself nearly went into fits and jumped overboard. Not even the ballyhoo about the 'sanctity' of the study could save us. And we had commitments to our distributive associates—still have. There was only one way out, and I took it. I tried to buy the place from you, and to urge my claim I piled it on about the 'curse'."

"Why didn't you get out when you saw this National Trust business coming?" the girl asked steadily.

"Because we have expensive, heavy equipment underneath Castleton," White answered promptly. "That and these associates I mention. We've contracted to supply slush to them—high-grade stuff that takes time. They're not the people to monkey about with; they'd have our skins if we defalcated. But now we've got you, it at least holds Scott up. If we don't get Castleton altogether then we'll at least gain enough time to settle things and get in the clear."

Apperley looked at his watch, then crossed over to open the scuttle again. "All fresh and bright," he reported. "The storm's about over; though I'm sorry for the loss of your boat, Miss Castleton."

"About the unknown man—?" she said, still unafraid.

Apperley twirled home a butterfly screw. "He's not unknown. Not to me and White, at all events. What happened was this: Kreig got a revenge complex, too. He saw that White and I had ditched him. He swore to get us. He found we'd come to England. Obviously he followed. White wanted to kill Monroe; Kreig wanted to kill White. Revenge for duplicity running parallel."

"But with this difference," White rapped, "that I consider myself justified."

"So does Kreig, I expect," Apperley said in his smooth way. "And we can't really blame him. He risked a lot to spring you, then you walk out on him. Naturally he wants to shoot the daylights out of you. And that's where our own associates can't and won't help. They won't take on a private quarrel, not even to enable us to deliver the goods."

Marjorie Castleton eyed the cabin steps longingly. "That still doesn't explain the killing outside the Blue Room."

"I'm trying to tell you about that," Apperley said. "In England, Kreig could only concentrate on London, as being an obvious place. Mind you, all this is guesswork on my part, but I'm forced to think it's correct. He went to the underworld for information, as he always does, but here he laboured under a slight disadvantage. He was a stranger on strange territory. I think that the most he could do was to find out about the distributive organisation I mention. Watch that and he might find either White or myself. So he used a tail, a gorilla that he'd brought with him from the States—a man by the name of William Seldon.

"All right, Seldon saw me leaving certain premises in London. I was on my way back here, last night. It was too late for me to use the houseboat and cave route, and I knew that White was waiting for me underneath the house, ready to start work for a few hours so that we could get back here by dawn. I can only presume that Seldon stood by my elbow at Victoria when I purchased a ticket down here. Then, as like us not, he bought a similar one, phoned up Kreig to tell him 'Harlingham' and got on the train farther down. But he couldn't hide himself from me on the last bus from Harlingham that passes the Castleton House gates. I recognised him as one of 'Big Johnny's' crowd in America. Right. I let him think that he was getting away with it. We turned into the grounds, by the empty lodge. I vanished into the shadows. He was at a loss, went on blundering up to the house. By the time he'd found a window left open in the hot weather, I had nipped through the stables and the study and was waiting for him.

"I caught him as he climbed to the door. I closed with him. He pulled a gun and I grabbed at it. I got it from him, couldn't risk a shot, although I guessed that I'd already awakened you and Scott, and let him have it with the butt. Then I had to work and think fast. I knew this would bring in the police, and there were enough complications as it was. So I risked everything in grabbing at the most obvious identification to stall them for a while." Apperley smiled at the sickened girl. "Time again, you see.

"And now," he said slowly, "I have you on my hands. But it won't be for long, I fancy. Seldon was the spark that touched off a whole train of events. I . . . extinguished that spark . . ."

CHAPTER VII

ON THE ROCKS

HENRY APPERLEY came down the cabin steps and looked thoughtfully at the girl in the chair. "Our Mr. White will give you some tea, although I'm afraid that it'll be a delayed meal. Getting things shipshape above has taken up quite a bit of our time. That's why we brewed the coffee. Nothing like making a guest comfortable, is there? I'm only repaying a little of that damned hospitality that I experienced at Castleton."

Her arms and legs were still bound, although her hands were free. She wriggled ineffectively. "And you're doing it in a most blackguardly way. I suppose you and White have profited by your 'getting things shipshape,' as you call it, to hold a conference about me?"

"Of course. And now that I've told you everything, you'll guess at our next step. I'm going ashore."

"To break the sad news about me?"

"That's about the size of it. Things have quietened down considerably above, although there's still a bit of a swell running. But I think I can manage, all right."

"It'd be too much to hope that you lose an oar, or something easy like that," she said.

Apperley's face was saturnine above the high roll collar of his grey Jersey. "I've always managed to look after myself. There's a lot to do and little time to do it in. But I want to be sure that you're safe and comfortable. I think that I can promise that White won't disturb you. He'll be too busy keeping a good lookout shorewards."

"Glad to learn that," she said doggedly. "And do I sit here all the time like this?"

"Not unless you want it so," Apperley said. "I'll release you if you'll behave yourself. There's a shelf of books over there, and you'll find cigarettes in the locker."

"Thanks, but I don't smoke."

"Sorry. Tobacco's a great thing in forced inactivity. By the way, I'd like to warn you—that scuttle's too small even for your slim figure. This is classed as a houseboat but actually it's a converted cabin cruiser. That leaves the steps."

"You expect me to make a break for it?" she asked.

"I wouldn't put it beyond you, my dear. And that's paying a tribute to your pluck and resourcefulness. But White has a gun, and he won't scruple to use it. Anyhow, give me your promise to stay put and I'll untie you. Well?"

"It's a deal," she said. "But don't think that I shall be altogether quiescent upon your return. Human nature won't stand for it."

"We'll see to that," he assured her.

Apperley's strong fingers released her. She stood up a little shakily, and rubbed her arms. Now that she was free she felt an almost irresistible impulse to strike out at the lean face of this man who called himself her cousin, then she turned her own face away in disgust. She took a few steps around the little cabin. "Aren't you taking a risk?"

"You mean in my pulling over to Castleton? I've already told you—"

"I mean afterwards," she said. "Suppose Scott or the police come hot-foot back from Harlingham? Suppose they insist upon searching this boat? What then?"

"Why should they?" Apperley shrugged. "Up to now they know nothing wrong about White or myself. We've taken extremely good care to steer clear of the law in this country, and we've no reason to suppose that the American police authorities even know that we're in England. Make your mind easy, Miss Castleton."

He kicked the cords into a corner. "And I do beg of you not to underestimate our seemingly placid Mr. White. I've already told you that he'll keep a good lookout on deck. In the very unlikely event of the police, or anyone else, forcing me to row them out here, White will have ample time to gag and truss you and lock you in the forepeak. It's smelly down there, but it can't be helped. And a search-warrant will have to be obtained to get you out of it. But that's a million-to-one eventuality."

"But surely someone," Marjorie said a little desperately, "will report back here to let you know the results of a search. I presume that there'll be one."

"If for verisimilitude alone—yes," he answered. "But I've thought of that one, too. I shall stay ashore until the motor-boat is found. Then I shall come back here sorrowing. All comfy, you see."

"And—after that?" She was trying to hold on to her courage. Ruthlessness, expediency, the future . . . Somehow she would have to face whatever that future might hold. But she would try to face it bravely. And Apperley regarded her with a quizzical lift of an eyebrow.

"Trust us to find a way out. I won't beat about the bush in this, my dear cousin. I've already told you that we've got too much to lose. We can't afford to be squeamish. We can use you to make things run a little easier. All right, so we'll use you. After that—" He shrugged his shoulders and left the sentence unfinished.

"I'm not worried about that. What I *am* more concerned with is that you'll cost us a night's work tonight, because we'll have to look after you here. But don't worry about the proprieties. That's one thing that I can at least assure you of. We'll ensure you a strict privacy in this glorified matchbox we designate a cabin, and White and I will manage with a shake-down on deck."

Marjorie was trying to be as tough and blasé as her captor. "That's something, at all events. Can I count on that?"

"Absolutely," he assured her. "We play for safety first. If this damned Scott or anyone else should get ideas into their heads about paying us a surprise visit under cover of darkness, then we'll be ready to spot them doing it. White and I will take watch turn and turn about. Now I must leave you. Sorry that I can't make you more comfortable."

She turned her back upon him, not trusting herself to speak further. "This damned Scott"—how she would welcome the sight of his broad shoulders now! What a fool—an utter, blind fool—she'd been!

He had tried to warn her, and she had treated him like a child. Like a stuck-up snob. She had tried to be *too* "respectful" to the traditions and legends of Castleton House. She had thought him an iconoclast—one who would ride roughshod over family sentiment; one who, secure in his position in a downrightly prosaic outside world, had been rather inclined to sneer at associations that were centuries old and should therefore be respected.

The closing of the companion-way doors behind Apperley came to her as a little thud. Symbolically it reminded her of how she had cut herself off from Tony Scott and Detective-Inspector Croft, and done it in a headstrong, stupid way. She had only herself to blame for this.

Scott's dislike of Apperley had been intuitive—the dislike of an honest man for someone he felt to be outside his own orbit. That quite apart from her own evident dislike of Apperley, as expressed to Scott in a more or less polite way. She had liked Scott, had admired his forthrightness, but the difficulty between them had had genesis in the fact that merely because she *loved* Castleton she had been too inclined to identify herself as part and parcel of its past.

She had lived too much in the past of the grey, old house. Scott was of the world—as much as Apperley was, but in a different trend. She had been a lonely child at Castleton. There were no relatives, beyond Apperley. Two sisters of the Colonel, her father, might be dead and gone, for all she knew. One had become a medical missionary to Papua; the other lived in single blessedness somewhere at the back of Earl's Court, had a tiny annuity and wrote magazine verses, and was reputed to be "queer." Certainly the Colonel had fallen most decidedly from her favour when he had persisted in marrying "that Mead girl", from the North. Marjorie hadn't even her aunt's address; had, in fact, only seen her twice since babyhood.

No children, of course, in that direction. The Colonel had had no other brothers or sisters. There seemed to be an odd lack of distant relations, either on the Mead side, or anywhere else. The Apperley crowd had cut themselves off completely when Marjorie's mother had mistakenly tried to take the worthless Henry under her wing.

Marjorie had had a lonely early childhood. Lonely holidays at Castleton. Only school friends in her life at all. Perhaps it was this very factor that had largely robbed her of contact with the outside world, although her education had made her sophisticated enough. It was just that if she had had the friends or relatives to have "gone around with," the grip exercised by the Castleton past might have been broken, or at least weakened.

She had not even been able to share holidays with school friends. By reason of his position, her father had been so lonely, so worried. It would have been cruel not to come back to him at Castleton and cheer his life for a period.

Therefore, life—and through nobody's real fault, but just by the blindness of circumstance—had been one-sided. From Castleton House to school; from school to Castleton House. Castleton, Castleton, Castleton ... there had been nothing else for her in the world. It had been the hub of her universe, in fact.

That and her father. She had known no one else who really mattered. Perhaps that was why, when Tony Scott had come into her life, she had been so attracted to him. She had not known men, beyond the loving, yet reticent figure of her own father and the slightly-domineering, "clever" Henry Apperley. Scott was startlingly, dynamically, opposed to the two.

Because he *was* different, she had perhaps mentally opposed him. She had, perhaps, been a little afraid. Add to that the fact that he had struck, however sympathetically, at cherished beliefs of the Castleton universe, she told herself, and the misunderstanding between them might be explained.

Not that she was trying to excuse herself now. Even though the Castleton mental aspects were ingrained in her more deeply than might be the fact with one who had experienced a freer, more cosmopolitan, life; even though, as a matter of plain psychology alone, she might be excused her more than half-belief in the iron fate of the Castletons that might not be denied; she knew that she had been stupid and obstinate. She had riled Scott, and he had tried to be patient in his greater knowledge of a world she had not yet experienced.

And Scott had been courteous in taking his *congé*. Manifestly she had made the situation impossible for him. And Croft. But Croft was tough; and had other work to do.

Marjorie's thoughts went around in circles. Bitter circles. Her father . . . Even though she now blamed herself, could she blame him?

She could only find a deep, aching sympathy.

And Apperley? Apperley and White. Thought of the precious pair sent her hot and cold by turns. Whatever they did to her, in the ultimate, she would not give them the satisfaction of cringing to them.

For his part, Apperley admired that spirit. But he had already come too far to possibly relent in any way. It was now all or nothing, sink or swim, for himself and White.

Murder, now. He and White had raised an elaborate structure of falsity. The stakes were high and the rewards great. The penalty for failure was abysmal. If the luckless Seldon had not blundered haphazardly into things, something might have been done about "Big Johnny" Kreig. Apperley and White might somehow have temporised. But not now. Seldon's murder had been an enforced one, but it was still murder.

And it would bring Kreig down upon them. But there was this to it—he had to find them. Apperley knew his man. He knew that Seldon would have obviously tipped off Kreig as to his destination of the preceding night. But in that he would be general, rather than specific. There was, too, the fact that Kreig would be sure to know sooner or later, if only by medium of the Press, that the police were now interested in things. That same information would enable Kreig to couple Apperley and White and Castleton House together, but then—Kreig was a crook himself. And if Castleton House now had a police focus . . .

Apperley pondered all this as he lay to his oars and pulled for the private strip of beach that Croft had admired. With all these factors to consider, it meant that he might yet gain the little time he so desperately sought. That and the playing of his cards right. With police in the offing, Kreig would be prudent. He must lay off, even temporarily. He couldn't just come charging in to try to take them both apart. Not yet, anyway.

Apperley's strong muscles worked rhythmically. As he lifted his head now and then he could see the diminishing figure of Arthur White, alert on the deck of the houseboat. There was not yet complete calm. The sun was obscured by low, heavy clouds shot through with an angry red. There was a chill, stiff breeze; the gulls were wheeling and crying against a dark sky. On the whole, it suited his mood.

A fairly long pull. Apperley felt the boat grounding beneath him slightly, shipped his oars and flung a seabooted leg over the side. Pebbles crunched beneath him as he bent to drag the boat up higher, Then he straightened up and looked around.

Elspeth McCracken by the kitchen door, looking stonily out to sea, gnarled old hands folded inside her apron. Apperley went padding in her direction, wet footprints following. The boat-house inset in the terrace wall was now high and clear. There were pools of rainwater on the flagged path where he strode. Leaves and flowers were beaten down. Their crushed perfumes came to him mingling with the scents of wet shrubs.

Apperley felt ungainly on the brick and stone steps of the main path to the back of the house. Nearing the old Scotswoman, he saw her lined face, lips still unmoving. For a moment he felt like calling out a greeting, then lowered his eyes stubbornly. He went on to stand before her, and it was then that he noted that her old eyes were like flints.

She left it to him to speak first, and the tactic somehow baffled him. Canny, canny, devilish canny. The old, grey, crippled eagle. The strong, calculating beast of prey that approached. Apperley said, "Well, good afternoon, Miss McCracken—or, rather, good evening."

Somehow he was smiling. Then he realised that such a move was wrong, and he puckered his hatless brow in mock anxiety. "Naturally, I've come about Miss Marjorie," he said slowly. "Did—did—? She got home all right?"

Elspeth McCracken breathed in sharply. "Come away in," she said. "We'll no' be talking oot here."

Apperley put his back against the inside of the door of the spacious kitchen. "An' ye'll stop leaning against those curtains," she said sharply. "What's your news?"

"News?" Apperley feigned to be puzzled. "I came *here* for news. I've been anxious—terribly so. I tried to stop her—"

"So did I," the old woman said, and was unyielding. "Ye say that ye've come to find out if the girl got hame safe. Is that it?"

"*Isn't* she home?" Apperley asked. "Good God, Elspeth—"

"Miss McCracken to you," she said. Her breathing was deeper, her face more grey. Slow death to the old eagle of the crags. A useless, feeble flapping of aged wings. Pain and sinking down so that there might be a weak striking out in defence. The sere lips of Miss McCracken parted as her breathing grew ever more laboured. The years and the world were against her. She put out a hand to the white-topped kitchen table.

Apperley was curt. "Sit down before you fall down," he said. "Stop treating me like dirt."

"That's twice she wouldna listen—"

"Hell!" Apperley said, and knew that he hated the sight of her, that her reluctant but not to be denied weakness of spirit and body jagged at his nerves. Get it over with. She saw through him and he saw through her. He was brutal; she was pawkily barbaric. He dragged out a chair. "Then she didn't get home?"

"Did she *leave* you?" the old woman whispered. "Did ye no' keep her on the houseboat?"

"I tell you," Apperley answered roughly, "that I've come here to find out if she made it all right. Stop beating about the bush now. You should never have let her come in the first place."

The eagle struck feebly. "Could you yersel' restrain her, Mr. Apperley? You've always been clever, strong, big. But I'm only an auld wummun. If you couldna restrain the lassie from puttin' back in a peltin' storm, then what chance had I when it was still calm? So she left ye?"

"We quarrelled," Apperley said, trying to keep his patience.

"I'm no' surprised, ye big black de'il. She was climbing down, an' there's only me and hersel' can know what it cost her to do it." Her voice rose in anger. "Did ye want the cursed auld place for naething at all? Did ye batter the poor girl down so that she spit in your worthless face and turned away in her high spirit?"

"We didn't fall out about the price," he retorted. "I was willing to meet her in that. She flung an insult at me immediately after and, when I replied to it, insisted that I'd mortally offended her. She said our deal was off, that she'd go back, in spite of the storm."

"You should have held her back, by main force if necessary," Elspeth flung back at him. "Ye were two so-called men."

"With our hands full with the management of the boat?" Apperley snarled. "How *could* we do that? I tell you that Miss Castleton simply evaded us. She'd left her boat accessible at the side and she was down to it and away in spite of all I could do. I shouted to her to come back, but it was no use."

The old housekeeper struggled to her feet. Her footsteps were dragging as she made her way out of the kitchen. For a moment or two Apperley stood undecided, then finally elected to follow her. He caught up with her in the Great Hall.

"Ye'll stand there an' see me struggle wi' this de'ilish contraption," she said in a shrill, weak voice; and Apperley wrenched the telephone from her hands. She fumbled at her sparse breast, then, for ancient spring pince-nez, and Apperley snatched up the slim local telephone directory and thumbed through it rapidly. "Get through to the police." she said, through greying lips. "There's a Detective-Inspector Croft, frae London. He'll be there. He tellt me—"

"Sit down!" Apperley said, and dialled. Croft was not available. Apperley explained things and was rapidly put through to the energetic Inspector Paynter.

"Hold on," Paynter said, after Apperley had explained the state of the case. "I don't quite know just where Detective-Inspector Croft is at the moment. And I won't go into the rights or wrongs of things, Mr. Apperley. I'll get a coast-guard search organised at once. And I'll send over to the 'George' and inform Mr. Scott. He'll probably come over to you right away, but you can expect that. You know him, of course?"

"We've met," Apperley said, a little coldly. "Yes, I should think the poor chap will be cut up, and no mistake. I know that I am. And he can look after Miss McCracken, anyway. I can't stay a great while after I know the worst, or otherwise, of this tragic affair. And I should say that the lady's in no state to be left alone. Will you keep in touch with me by telephone?"

There was a pause, while Paynter answered. "Good," Apperley said, and replaced the telephone. Miss Elspeth McCracken got up with difficulty from her hall chair and left him without a word. Here was silent hate.

Apperley put his hands in the pockets of his soiled grey flannels and stood looking around him, seabooted legs strad-dled wide. In the sleepy silence of the old house, his keen ear picked up the slow, grumbling tick of the grandfather clock on the turn of the stairs. He went to the foot of those same stairs, with never a glance in the direction of the study, and still with his hands in his pockets, stood regarding them. A mere lifted corner of a loose board; a thing so slight that a maid in her polishing of the spot would not think it worth reporting. But enough to catch the trailing hem of an elaborate evening gown. To catch it, to jerk the wearer back as she descended a step or two below. Then the sudden slip of high-heeled silver court shoes on the edge of a stair that had been religiously polished for decades . . .

Apperley grunted to himself. That was one thing he was *not* responsible for.

He clumped his way over to the great front door, opened it, leaned his bulk against the jamb. He could only wait.

And then Scott came, in a taxi. An agitated, fighting, but for all that somehow dangerously restrained Tony Scott. As Apperley had indicated to Paynter over the telephone, these two had met a week or two before at tea. For Scott, it had been a flying afternoon's visit to the girl, who had thought in her innocence that he might like to meet Apperley consequent upon Elspeth's gossip that the latter was coming down from London for a break of a few hours in mid-week. So that here was no meeting of complete strangers.

Scott said; "How are you?" and automatically put out his hand. Apperley brushed it with the fingers of his own. "Sorry to bring you out like this."

"Paynter's told me everything," Scott said. "He rang me up. Good man, Paynter. Well, Mr. Apperley, I don't want to argue with you, but I can't admire what you've done."

Apperley had half expected such hostility. "I've done nothing," he said smoothly. "I can't be responsible for Miss Castleton's foolishness."

"Foolishness?" Scott said, as he heard the swish of the departing taxi at his back. "Come, Mr. Apperley. She's just a headstrong, impetuous girl. We both know that. But we also know that she's unprotected and with no one to help her."

"She won't *be* helped." Henry Apperley was blunt. "I know. I tried it myself. But there's a difference, I think, between leaving this house as I did, because I couldn't stay on unwanted, and letting her deliberately cast off into the teeth of a thundering storm like the one we've just had."

Apperley showed a brief flash of his white teeth. "There's a hell of a lot to do in the teeth of a thundering storm, Mr. Scott. Try it sometime. Try being with just one other man on a houseboat the size of ours, with everything being battered to glory, a cant of nearly forty-five degrees, rain and wind blinding you, and a determined girl lashing out and kicking at you in her efforts to bolster up her damn-fool pride and get away. Could *you* have held her?"

Scott walked past him into the near chill of the Great Hall. He turned around. "Before I'd have let it happen," he said clearly, "I'd have risked everything in one good swing to her jaw. That'd have stopped her."

He walked slowly back to Apperley and looked deep into his shifting eyes. "It might even stop you," he said.

"Meaning?"

"Meaning I don't know quite what, Mr. Apperley. But I suspect your motives in this. Always have done."

Apperley hunched his fists at his side. "Try clarifying that, Mr. Scott." Crisis. How much did Scott know? But how *could* he know? Was he going to tell him—?

"I don't mince words," Scott retorted. "I merely say that, from the amount of love lost between you and Miss Castleton, I wouldn't put it beyond you to have let her go without much effort."

Apperley breathed again. So that was what the fool meant. "Harsh words, Mr. Scott. Then you think that I've been wilfully negligent?"

"I do." Scott was clearly spoiling for a fight.

"And you're convinced that a poke to the chin might help me to remedy such a failing." Apperley looked the neat lounge-suited figure of the other man up and down and laughed. "I invite you to try it."

"Suits me." Scott lunged forward and grabbed a handful of the grey jersey. He pulled Apperley towards him, then paused at sound of the housekeeper's voice behind them. It was weary, dispirited, but still held the chill of authority. "An' will *this* mend matters, gentlemen?"

Scott dropped his hands with a groan. "No, it won't. And it's not my house to fight in."

"You wish it were," Apperley snarled. "Don't waste our breath by retorting 'So do you.' That's not the point. What *is* the point is that if you care to step outside it I'll be delighted to give you the hiding of your life."

"Ye'll bide still, both of ye," Elspeth McCracken snapped. "There's greater things afoot than bein' senseless and fighting like beasts o' the field. Think of that poor bairn away on the watters. I'll get you both a wee sup of tea and some sandwiches."

Greater things afoot . . .! Apperley smiled cynically to himself. Let Scott go, for the moment.

Tony Scott himself tried to still his throbbing pulses. "We'll defer this," he said to the scowling Henry. "But don't forget, my fine friend, that I'll catch up with you yet, and when I do—well, look out, that's all."

He turned away disconsolately, and suddenly a mental vision of Marjorie Castleton came before him. So young, so lovely, so proud. To have that sweet loveliness broken, clawed down by the pounding sea . . .

Both tried to change the conversation, as though by mutual consent. Both went into the kitchen by tacit agreement and insisted on taking the meal there. And while they ate both let the old housekeeper indulge in her sorrowful memories of Marjorie Castleton—the girl she had come to regard as her own.

Somehow they kept the pretence going. Somehow they got through until a quarter past eight, when the telephone rang.

Both were eager to answer it. But Henry Apperley stood aside, hands again in his trouser pockets, his eyes directed moodily, he hoped, towards the floor. Scott's conversation with Inspector Paynter of the Harlingham Police was brief and to the point. He put the instrument down gently, and his voice was utterly broken.

"She—" He rallied strength to his words. "Bad news, Mr. Apperley. They've found the boat."

"And the bairn?" Elspeth McCracken was wringing her hands.

"No hope, I'm afraid," Scott said.

Apperley squared his shoulders. "What does Paynter say exactly?"

"That the motor-boat's been found smashed on the rocks they call The Pinnacles. It held her coat, jammed beneath a seat. Apparently there's her name on a tab inside the pocket. They're out now—looking for the body . . ."

Tony Scott put out an arm to support the old housekeeper, but somehow she took a grip on herself and turned slowly away. Clearly, she could not trust herself to speak, but preferred to go back to the kitchen. They let her go. Scott locked his fingers behind his back and faced up to Apperley.

"You know these parts better than I do, especially with relation to the sea. What chance do *you* give her?"

Apperley breathed in, deeply and noisily. "The poor kid hasn't—didn't get—the slenderest of chances," he said. "It's my frank opinion, since you've asked me for it as one who has a little more knowledge of this locality than you, that however strong a swimmer she might have been she couldn't possibly have lived through the hellish packet that's just been thrown at us."

He paused, then: "If she clung to the boat when it went on to The Pinnacles she'd be knocked unconscious. And, of course, she'd drown. The sea would sweep her off the rocks and drag her under."

He cleared his throat, somewhat self-consciously. "Don't think that I'm a prophet of gloom, Mr. Scott; or that I'm getting any satisfaction in seeing you squirm because I just don't like you. It's just how things are—nothing else. I know The Pinnacles. I'm—sorry I couldn't stop her . . ."

"I suppose the wind did it," Scott said miserably.

"It was beating strongly in that direction," Apperley answered him. "She just managed to contend with it, with an engine to help her, coming across to me. But when the rain started and the storm broke in real earnest, the wind got up like all hell let loose. *We'd* have known it if we'd been anchored broadside on."

"So that, when she tried to get back," Scott said, "it would just beat her in the direction of The Pinnacles, engine or no engine."

"It's my guess that the boat would be so flooded that the engine would soon stop functioning altogether," Apperley said.

"And—" Scott seemed to be swallowing something. "How—how about finding her body?"

"That I can't say. We're dealing with the sea, you know—not a stretch of inland water or a river. They might never find her."

Scott nodded, face pale and strained. "Excuse me." He left Apperley, and a moment later that worthy heard him from the kitchen. Apperley nodded his head, as Scott came back.

"She won't leave the house, eh, Mr. Scott? I shouldn't try to persuade her further. Let her stay here. I'm sure that she'll be quite safe, and unhappy anywhere else. Sorry I can't give you a lift anywhere, but I didn't come awheel. I'm going back to the houseboat."

Scott nodded. "Perhaps," he said, "we *shall* meet again, Apperley. You'll excuse me if I don't shake hands."

"Suit yourself," Apperley said, with a shrug. "Next time there may not be an interfering old woman to come between us. Going back to Harlingham?"

"Elspeth tells me that there's a bus due shortly," Scott answered him. "One last word before we break up, Apperley."

Apperley turned. "Well?"

"If," said Tony Scott in low tones, "if there's anything in this damned awful business that isn't on the up-and-up as far as you're concerned, I'll hunt you down and break your filthy neck."

Apperley laughed. "That eases your mind, doesn't it? Well—I'll be seeing you."

"I hope not," Scott answered, and there was a world of meaning in the words.

CHAPTER VIII

UNFINISHED PICTURE

ANOTHER MORNING. The sun was strong again, the breeze a mere whisper. Marjorie Castleton had been glad of the blankets in one of the cramped berths of the cabin. She had merely removed her shoes and frock; and, strangely perhaps, had managed to get off to sleep. Not that sleep had been altogether undisturbed.

Three times she had awakened, to consult her watch and to hear the heavy footsteps of White and Apperley on the deck above. And then, for a short time, she had lain miserably staring up at the deck beams, dimly seen above her head. She had tried to think, to plan. But she was young and healthy, and the long rolling swell of the sea was a powerful and natural narcotic. Off she'd gone again, in spite of thoughts of the dour Elspeth, the disgruntled Scott, Croft, her father, the mysterious Kreig.

Eight o'clock, now; and she was kneeling on the long upholstered cabin seat, looking through the scuttle out to sea. It was almost dazzling under the sun, slightly choppy and dancing in the bright light. Craning upwards, she could just glimpse a heavenly blue sky with a few fleecy clouds. Then Arthur White came lumbering down the cabin steps with a tray containing her breakfast.

It was well served, and it was good. Whatever other failings or accomplishments the American might have, he could certainly cook. The tea was nicely brewed, eggs done to a turn, bacon satisfyingly crisp, with toast and marmalade on the side. He set down the tray and looked around.

"Glad that you managed to find the wash-basin and towels," he said, with a half-smile. "I pride myself on that concealed fitting and the miniature pump and faucet, though I'm sorry I've never been able to arrange hot water. Apperley and I have had to do with a bucket over the side."

She was still unafraid. "It's not my fault that I've upset your domestic arrangements," she said.

He sat her down in the same Windsor chair, screwed to the floor, to which she had been lashed last night. The seat was a revolving one, enabling her to swing around to the small folding table that White now arranged for her. He emptied the tray on to it carefully. "There. I'm probably booked for hell, my girl, but you can put at least one good deed to my account—I served you a darned good breakfast that I cooked with my own fair hands. English style, too."

She looked at those same hands as he poured her tea. Strong, but slim. Tapering fingers, almost like a woman's, but with squarish ends. Intensely capable hands, the hands of an artist and craftsman gone wrong.

Somehow she could almost find pity for this man, though none for Henry Apperley. Last night, in the brief intervals between sleep, she had pondered about Arthur Armstrong White. A woman at the bottom of all his troubles, or so Apperley had said. A woman . . . Freda White, because she seemed to be undivorced. Strange how this man let her play havoc with his existence. Strange how it appeared that he still loved her. But here she sensed, in her unschooled way, that his artistic temperament might well be responsible.

In many ways, White was not as ordinary men. True, he was crooked like Apperley, but not deliberately so in the first place. Henry Apperley had gone wrong from the start simply because he wanted to go wrong. He demanded a life of ease without hard work. Women to him held no serious implications. He felt himself to be immeasurably superior to them— even the tough, sophisticated ones—let alone ex-high schoolgirls. To Apperley, women were just a necessary adjunct in the world—nothing else. He met and defeated the clever tough ones; he treated the naïve, not so experienced others with contempt. For a Beatrice or a Joan of Arc, a Grace Darling or a Florence Nightingale, he would not have lifted a finger.

But White had not the same heart of stone. He was, in a way, romantic merely because he was an artist. Women to him were necessary, vital, a subtle part of the artistic tempo that dominated his life without being altogether self-evident. And, on the same life lines, one woman, and one woman alone, gripped him to the exclusion of all else. He was not as other men, although his romanticism was not unduly sentimental. But where other men would have been "sensible" he was blinded, and completely so.

It would not have needed an Apperley, in the first place, to refuse to turn to all the risks of crime, to pervert artistic talent, merely to satisfy the craving for luxury of one woman. She was so obviously "no good," and nine hundred and ninety-nine out of every thousand practically-minded men would have kicked her out without further demur. The thousandth saw her in a totally different light. She didn't have to be a Beatrice or a Florence Nightingale; White was content to sweat after her cruelty and hold her as a sort of Manon Lescaut.

One woman—one woman alone, or none. He had put her on a glowing pedestal, and when she kicked it down in his face he only became more determined to set it up again. And determination bred determination. Apperley had spent hours in arguing until his astuteness had told him that further argument was useless. So, because he was clever, he accepted the inevitable.

Hours of talk in the steel cell of Leavenworth Gaol. White had simply said that Freda was worth it. She was beautiful, the world owed her tribute. In a way he could understand how such beauty and intelligence needed luxury for its setting. He wondered how she had fallen in with him at all in the beginning—simply because he *wasn't* like other men. He supposed that it was the price he must pay for her interest in him at all.

But with all this, White was not one to be despised. The flaw in his character, if flaw it was, was amply compensated for in other directions. He had an agile intelligence. He was a match for Apperley and a dozen like him. The iron will he exhibited, even towards the worthless Freda whom he still deemed worthy, had the vengeful Kreig and the cunning Apperley together completely beaten.

He would find the woman, hold her yet, in spite of everything. He would bend her to his loving will. His love was big enough, or so he told himself, to break down every barrier. When he had finished she would see that further resistance was useless and the glory of his achievement in winning her back would bring about the required mental change in Freda. She would at last love him in return, change her life for his sake, because his determination had mastered her. And at that she would be worth the having. And he would have her, or die.

A squat, monkey-jawed little man had drawn White into the shadow of a buttress beneath an almost unscalable wall menaced constantly by machine-guns and searchlights. He had pressed White for "the makings," had skilfully rolled tobacco in rice paper while he spoke hurriedly from the corner of his mouth. His interest in telling White what he did was not a purely personal, friendly one. It was dictated solely by the fact that the underworld hates and detests a raw deal. The blunder can often be forgiven; the deliberate double-cross, never.

It was why the rat-like Danny Callaghan broke the news to White on the hot exercise ground. Nothing to do with him personally, but the canons of the underworld demanded that he be told. White's face went grey as he heard the hurried words. He choked. He caught at the rough prison denim of Danny's collar, and Apperley, lounging nearby, sprang forward. He thought quickly and acted quicker. The heel of his right palm came down on White's biceps in a paralysing blow and he dragged him away as a guard hoisted his carbine to the ready and came towards them. Apperley said: "That damned Danny wouldn't give him 'the makings' back. I try to keep my pal from trouble," and smiled. Then the whistle went for fall-in, and they were saved.

Back to the cell. Here White threw himself into a corner and sobbed. Apperley blocked the steel-barred door with his back and hurled fierce, whispered imprecations at him. He was trying to save them both from solitary confinement,

Somehow he quietened him down. Somehow he got him through supper, taken in company of hundreds in a vast, echoing dining-hall, the guards with their clubs strolling up and down the aisles between tables. Here Apperley had been filled with presentiment. Fate had it that Callaghan, only arrived that morning, should be allotted the seat just left vacant by a paroled man and which faced White directly. Apperley had long since "worked it" with a "trusty" that he should be seated on White's left hand. He curled his right leg around White's as the latter suddenly dropped a spoon and advanced a hand across the table. Danny Callaghan looked apprehensively around at the nearest "screw."

Then Apperley breathed again. White was whispering a plea for forgiveness. He had thought it out, had realised that Danny had only tried to help him, that obviously there was no earthly inducement why he should make up a lie. Danny understood as much in a flash. He gripped White's right hand in his own left one, and the monkey-jaws smiled delightedly to show three missing teeth. The same "screw" of the prison-yard saw the action and nodded approvingly. The tobacco row had been settled.

All this was going through Arthur White's mind now, as he watched the girl start her breakfast. The reason was simple: Marjorie Castleton was a woman, and a woman recalled Freda to his mind. The events of the past hammered at his brain.

It had not been as easy to dismiss Freda and Munroe as it had been to dismiss Danny from culpability. White was ominously quiet until some time after lights-out, when he suddenly squirmed out of the lower bunk and went near-berserk. The torture of his mind was too great for further restraint. He crashed tinplate utensils to the stone floor, shouted once—

and Apperley jumped down and hit him cleanly behind the ear. He caught him in his arms as White sagged downwards, hugged him in a fierce embrace on White's bunk, as a guard on the brilliantly-lit landing said: "What the hell!" and came running to peer into the shadows. Once more Apperley was plausible, speedy, quick-thinking. White had been half-asleep in his getting up for a drink of water, had cannoned against the steel table in his clumsiness, had shouted in pain from the blow . . .

The guard had said: "Then get your buddy back to bed," and had turned away. White moaned and struggled; Apperley held him and whispered in his ear as fiercely as any lover. "Don't do it!" he said. "Keep quiet. Quiet, or you'll rob yourself of the chance to get even."

Information laid anonymously by Munroe and Freda to get White out of the way so that they might pull out together. Danny had phrased such news pithily. Another four years, as balance of the forgery sentence that White had thereby re-ceived, still remaining to him on the slate. Three days left to Apperley, unless White involved him in a fracas that would rob Apperley of good-conduct time, however innocent he himself might be. In his arms, White went quiet. He thought of "Big Johnny" Kreig and returned whisper for whisper. Passionate, pain-racked whispers of hate and revenge, of subtle planning and fierce desire. "I'll work my fingers to the bone for the damned man, only make him get me out! Out, I tell you! Johnny'll know; Johnny'll understand. He knows I can put a fortune in his fingers any time, only I've kept away from him because I didn't want to become involved for the sake of the future . . . with Freda. Johnny'll risk it for me; it'll be worth his while. For God's sake, Apperley, go to him. Get me out—get me out!"

"Quiet!" Apperley snarled, "or I'll be able to do nothing. How—?"

"Main 71400," White had gabbled. "Ask for Legs Donaldson. Tell him who you are. He'll arrange for you to see Kreig. Tell him how I'm fixed, but don't mention Freda or Danny."

Right enough, there. Danny didn't like Kreig the over-lord. Freda's cool flight with Ed Munroe from New York to Cleveland was also beneath Kreig's notice. It had not been brought to his notice, either, being the mere trivia of the un-derworld.

Apperley reluctantly made his promise to White. Here his own motive came to view. White was a gilt-edged asset to any crook with brains. Fate had made him Apperley's cellmate, and Apperley had been quick to foster a friendship, although he never mentioned why, but merely told White that he was from England, and was lucky to escape extradi-tion. A longer sentence, instead of the short one he had re-ceived for the simple theft of a car, might have ensured that.

He yet hoped to be able to do something with White. And at the back of his mind there simmered the birth of a staggering idea. In the long nights when he couldn't sleep in the heat and White tossed fitfully below, when the steps of the guards rang hollowly on steelplate landings and there sometimes arose the demoniacal screams and smashings of "stir madness," Apperley thought it out. Thought of the per-fect set-up that might be organised beneath Castleton House, at peace thousands of miles away.

Apperley's lip curled. He had stolen a car in a hurry to enable him to cache nearly thirty thousand dollars of spend-able currency, results of a one-man robbery of a department store in a fair-sized town. He had done it alone and thereby reaped the advantages of loneliness, negotiating watchman and alarms where a gang would infallibly have come un-stuck. He had left nothing by which he could possibly be traced. Not for him explosives and confusion—there was a better way. A partner-cashier of the store had a small hunt-ing-lodge in the mountains, where he often spent a few days completely *solus*. His murder by Apperley was worth it.

An old man on the verge of retiral. At the lodge, a score of miles from anywhere, Apperley threatened him with a gun, got the combination of the safe and particulars of his watchman's movements and the location of a secret alarm off-switch and the fact that takings were only banked on Mondays from him, and then shot him dead.

To a daring man the rest was hazardous, but fairly easy. The watchman was too hoary to be much of a nuisance. Apperley side-stepped him easily and kept out of his way, to pull the switch, open the safe and clear it of a week's cash, and then get out by a goods' door at the back. Luck was wonderfully with him all the way. As wonderfully as it was later, when his careful planting of effects at the hunting-lodge led to a supposition of suicide by the old man. Whether that suicide had anything to do with the missing money, no one knew. Certain it was that he alone knew the combination whereby it had obviously been opened, and that on Friday night, when the store closed for the week-end, he had set out for the lodge.

Perhaps he had taken the cash with him, intending the lodge to be a jumping-off point for his escape from his partner, might have lost the money or been robbed of it on the way. Probably, then, committed suicide in utter despair. Key to it all—something that persisted in sweeping aside improbability—was that only the old man had had the combination.

Such a fuddle, in fact, that Apperley got away with it. Then luck let him down on a point so tiny as to be laughable. He had selected his cache beforehand and was determined to use it—beneath an old-fashioned rural bridge over a stream a few miles from New York. Half-way there his own car broke down. Apperley saw another parked by the roadside, the occupants of which—a courting couple—had strolled among the trees to observe the beauties of romantic nature. His need was desperate. By means of the stolen car he cached the money, and on the way back to town was picked up by a motor-cycle patrol who had the number of the missing car radioed. Seeing how the land lay, Apperley had the very good sense to keep his mouth shut. Only six months—five if he behaved himself—and there was no possible suspicion about any missing money.

No suspicion. Because of that he was able to retrieve the cache in perfect safety when he "came out."

But that was after he went to Kreig.

"Big Johnny"—silk shirts and champagne in a well-screened atmosphere of luxury—weighed the proposition up and pulled various wires. White was "sprung" from Leavenworth by the exercise of mass co-operation, money, superhuman ingenuity and risk worthy of a better cause. For his part, he had fully intended to keep the bargain—to work for Kreig and attend to Munroe and Freda on the side. But such a major operation as White's escape could not fail to have repercussions among the criminal fraternity, especially as a kingpin was involved. Munroe and Freda fled in fear. Munroe might have handled White; "Big Johnny" being on his side was another matter. And England was as good a place for an international confidence-man and his moll as any.

And if White's "love" for Freda and his terrible passion for revenge on Munroe whom he counted as her "seducer" had been sufficient to make him break gaol by Kreig's help, then it was strong enough, in spite of Apperley's entreaties, to make White determine to ditch Kreig and cross the Atlantic in pursuit. Apperley saw that his friend was inflexible. He was still taunted by avaricious dreams of the Castleton setup. He had no wish to stay behind alone to face Kreig, who would, of course, blame him. Therefore he threw in his lot with White, saw how well things fitted together, and told him about a slip of parchment.

Yet he made one tiny and quite understandable mistake. He had told himself that only the cracked "love" of the enigmatic White would impel a man to cross all the way over to another continent in search of revenge. A man like Kreig who had everything to live for and attend to in the States and who must, withal, walk warily by reason of police and federal authorities, would be more prudent. He would swallow a bitter pill of resentment, but forcedly so. He would take a vow to cut his losses and tear White and Apperley into little pieces if they ever came to the States again. But that was all. There was nothing else he *could* do. But Apperley was wrong.

Dead wrong. The double-cross was too blatant, *too* much of an affront to the big man's pride. Added to this was the fact that the heat was on just now, from the law, and Kreig had a pile to spend. He needed a break, and he determined to combine business with pleasure. But it took him some little time to clear things up against his return and fly to England.

He took his "mug" with him—Seldon. And in England he found himself somewhat handicapped by the fact that native crookdom was loath to help him, an interloper.

Arthur White sighed. That was as far as it went at present. By reason of Seldon, he and Apperley knew that Kreig was in England. He would never have sent Seldon alone.

White looked appreciatively at the little pile of bedding folded neatly by the girl. "I'm glad that you're trying to make the best of things."

"Am I?" she asked. "I wonder if I'll be able to keep facing up to things in the same way?"

"Don't get sentimental," he warned her. "It's my own failing, and I can't avoid it."

"What's to be done with me?" she asked point-blank.

"We've already hinted at that," White answered. "Just because we're treating you as decently as possible at the moment doesn't mean that we're relaxing anything. Far from it. And don't try to get around me personally, Miss Castleton. I assure you that it won't work—indeed it won't."

"You're a strange man," she said slowly. "Apperley I can get in perspective, all right. There's scores of people in this world like him, I suppose—plain, unadulterated rotters with precious little to redeem them. But you're—different, and I don't quite know why."

"Change the subject," White urged. "I don't like to be embarrassed, and I still think that you're trying to get gradually around to an appeal to my sympathies."

"I'll change it slightly," she said. "I gather from what's been said that the forged will business can't be put into operation immediately. Do I stay down here all day?"

Arthur White smiled. "I was coming to that. Having a lady aboard has put us in a bit of a quandary.

"Apperley has to go to Harlingham. He has a stone-cold nerve, I'll say that for him. He wants to forestall the police coming here, and he wants to find out how the land lies. We have this man Kreig to consider, too."

Marjorie Castleton poured herself a second cup of tea and tried to be calm about it. "How does that actually affect me?"

"I want to give you an airing," White said. "You see, I'm still trying to make things as easy for you as I can. But I can only do so by your co-operation."

"An airing? Ashore?"

White shook his head. "That *would* be a dumb move, wouldn't it? No, Apperley and I have been discussing this thing.

"Look," he said. "First of all, my valued partner needs a shave and a change of clothes to go to town. That means you've got to clear out of here for a few minutes. Then back you come for a short while to enable me to row Apperley to a point nearer to Harlingham than your little strip of private beach. We always use the same spot. It means a bit of a scramble and crossing some sandhills, but it brings us out quite near to a bus stop on the coast road. Apperley will catch the bus and get into Harlingham and will come the same way back. I'll have the boat ready for him at a certain time this afternoon."

"Then the 'airing' you speak of is only a few minutes for me on deck?" she asked coldly.

"You can extend it a bit, if you play ball with me," White answered. "You have to stay locked in here while I row Apperley across, and I could keep you below under the same conditions until he's safely back here. But I tell you, I'm soft with women. Don't take that as meaning that I'll let you put anything over on me," he warned.

"When I come back with the boat, you can go up on deck again with me. But you'll keep down—understand? That matchbox we call the wheelhouse—I've put some cushions behind it. You can make yourself easy there—but facing out to sea. Get it? Try to stand shorewards with the wheelhouse behind you and I'll slap your ears down and tote you straight back in here. And I'll tie you down. Understand?"

"Perfectly," she said.

"Good, then finish your breakfast. And get this through your pretty little head, Miss Castleton—there's only one woman in the world that I'm interested in and that's my wife."

She looked into his eyes as he faced her then. They were the eyes of a fanatic.

White left her for a short time, then came back and took away the tray. Returning again, he ushered her up the cabin steps and out into clean, sunlit air. The three-sided wheelhouse was immediately adjacent to the companion-way, and she stepped straight behind the structure without so much as a glimpse of her lithe young form being visible shorewards. Apperley stood by a pile of cushions.

"Good morning, Miss Castleton," he said ironically, then walked straight past her and down the cabin steps. She looked around hesitantly and found White's hand on her shoulder. Gently he pushed her down on to the cushions. And she was silent, her outraged young heart too full to bandy words further.

She found herself thinking again of Tony Scott. Where was he now? What was he doing? And Detective-Inspector Croft, of New Scotland Yard? He seemed, for all his official position, to be almost a non-active participant in this dreadful business.

Here the sun was warm, but tempered by a slight breeze from the Channel. She could only relax and try to take things as easily as possible. Apperley was not long. He came up from the cabin with a jaunty step, clothed in smart gabardine flannels and a checked sports coat. A light grey, snap-brim hat set off the dark handsomeness of his tanned face. He was shaved and spruce and carried a little pile of magazines. "Get on with these," he said abruptly, "and be a good girl while I'm away."

"You must experience an inward glow from treating me like a child," she said.

Apperley laughed. "Perhaps. Surprised at the appearance of the reading-matter, Miss Castleton? It's amazing the stuff we have down below, in all sorts of cunningly-contrived drawers. I wonder that you didn't get around to opening them. Mr. White has quite a lot of painting junk."

"Both for diversion and appearance," White said. "Long-range stuff in oils. Most afternoons after I've slept I sit out here on deck and paint. There's a most interesting shoreline you know. And sometimes I row in to it and do closer work. *The* perfect camouflage to our—er—nefarious activities."

Henry Apperley bent and put a none-too-gentle hand beneath her right armpit and jerked her to her feet. "All right, Miss Castleton. Down below again until I've been put ashore and White comes back."

"Take your hands off me!" she bit out, twisted herself free and brought up her right hand in a resounding slap on Apperley's freshly-shaven cheek. Apperley caught her by the wrist.

"Tit for tat after the smack I gave you last night. But I haven't time for such pleasantries; there's too much to be done. Get going."

He thrust her roughly on to the cabin stairs and locked the double doors of the companion-way upon her. Almost sprawled there, she suddenly gave way to tears, and for a few moments sobbed her heart out.

Then she recovered. The Castleton spirit—the proud Castleton spirit—came to her rescue. She got up, dried her eyes, squared her shoulders, and went to work on the lock of the doors. But they consistently defeated her.

Apperley had a hard jaw and stony eyes as he deftly scrambled ashore without wetting his smart tan brogues. He said to White: "When we finally have to put paid to this damned girl, Arthur—"

White was just as cool. "After she's signed what we want her to sign. Well?"

Apperley laughed unpleasantly. "I told that cockerel of a Scott when we tangled last night that the Channel doesn't give up its dead so very easily. But perhaps I was wrong in my opinion. Think she'd float in with the tide?"

"Very probably," White said. "But it wouldn't be too soon. She'd be in such a state that there'd be no saying with any certainty just how long the body had been in the water."

"Which ties up with the motor-boat," Apperley said, and laughed again. "Don't give her a chance to cut up rough, Arthur. I still think that you're a fool to let her out on deck until I get back. But then, she'd probably drive herself mad by pounding and yelling down in the cabin. Six o'clock, then. Pick me up on the turn of low tide."

"Right." White clapped him on the shoulder. "And, Apperley, don't forget my copy of the *Daily Mail*. Buy it first of all—when you get off the bus." And Apperley stared.

"Oh, yes. I'm not going all through a damned minor argument again, but I still don't see why you must have it. An evening paper would be more in line by the time I get back. However"—he shook his head—"I suppose that you must be humoured in your madness. Get aboard now, and look after her."

He turned away, body bent against steeply rising ground. White pushed off.

He felt a little tired after last night, as he pulled back to the houseboat. But he promised himself a lazy afternoon. The girl couldn't but behave herself on the pile of cushions behind the wheelhouse.

Back at the houseboat, he unlocked the companion-way doors and went down for a further word or two with her. But she was curled up on the wall seat, below the tiny scuttle. Her mood had become one of sullenness—of obstinate, silent defiance. White shrugged his shoulders and left her. When he brought her lunch she again refused to speak.

After the meal it seemed that he was determined to have her up on deck with him. She threw off his hand that would direct her to the cabin stairs and sulkily began to mount them. Perhaps she could not trust herself to speak. Perhaps it was that her mind was too busy with desperate plans to somehow get away. Like an obedient child she dropped to her knees on the gay cushions and opened a magazine, not seeing its contents. White grunted appreciatively and busied himself with an easel and blank canvas that he had laid ready to hand.

The breeze caught his blond hair as he stood at the opposite side of the wheelhouse to the cabin, facing shorewards. He had a folding stool and an expensive mahogany case of oil-colours, with a cedar-wood palette in the lid and brushes and bottles neatly packed in their appointed places. "Come around this side," he flung back over his shoulder, "and down you go below under lock and key again, Miss Castleton."

"You're wasting words," she said icily, more to tell him that she had heard and understood, than for anything else.

"But not time," he retorted.

White settled himself on the stool, arranged his primed and stretched canvas and took a piece of charcoal between his fingers. Marjorie Castleton tried to read, but the sense of the story eluded her. Almost fearfully she leaned on her elbow, to the left, then greatly daring, craned her head around the side of the Wheelhouse. White had twisted around on his stool and was regarding her.

"Cat and mouse," he said pleasantly. "Only don't try my patience too far. I can assure you that I'm alert. And I'm only doing this in case someone at the back of Castleton House, after your tragic and untimely demise of yesterday, may be watching this damned old hulk through glasses."

"Then they'll have seen you take Apperley ashore," she said.

"So they might. That is, if there is anyone at Castleton aside from your tottering old woman of a housekeeper," he answered. "But I'm not worried about that. Apperley's going ashore was perfectly reasonable and quite to be expected. No harm in that."

He drew a skilful slight curve. "Or in his coming back. The light's quite good this afternoon."

Marjorie went back to her magazine. Let him alone. Let him become absorbed and paint his way to hell, for all she cared. There seemed to be nothing she could do.

An article on country gardens. She dropped the magazine again. It reminded her all too vividly of the grounds of Castleton House. The latest in soufflés . . . No.

Her throat was constricted with the ache she felt there. She found that her fingers were tearing desperately at a corner of the paper. Tearing tiny fragments that were whirled away from her in the breeze. White seemed to be enjoying that same breeze. It was not strong enough to disturb his enjoyment of what he was doing.

So the afternoon wore on.

The girl had forced herself to concentrate and read through a twelve-thousand-word "long complete" before she dared try the manœuvre of head-turning again. This time White did not have his body slewed around to catch her at it. He was laying on colour with a firm hand. And he was absorbed in what he was doing. White the crook and a companion of a crook was fast becoming absorbed in White the pure artist. Marjorie drew her head back and sat thinking. Then she rolled over to the left, on to her stomach.

She drew her knees up beneath her and so inched her way forward and up to a standing position. The hollow of the empty Wheelhouse was now on her right hand, a brilliant bar of sunshine lying over the idle wheel and binnacle. She flattened herself back against the narrowness of the partition edge. Then she risked a quick look round over her shoulder.

Marjorie jerked her head back just in time as White finally wrenched his mind away from study of a drifting line of cloud and looked back in her direction. He did it as an automatic duty, sighed contentedly because he could see nothing of her, and became absorbed again. Now her crisis was upon her. She must tiptoe lest the planking ring hollow beneath her feet, despite fairly soft-soled shoes with low heels.

God knew what she proposed to do exactly. Only—he was sitting down and she was standing up. She had her mind focused; his was concentrated in a different direction. If she failed . . . well—her life was forfeit already, anyway.

Oh, for Tony Scott beside her now!

She loved Scott. Even in this fleeting moment of utter peril when she must concentrate with every scrap of vision, guile and intelligence that she knew, she could not help the shock of the sudden realisation. The mere longing for him in this crisis snapped the last mental barrier of reserve. She might never see him again, but she loved him.

On tiptoe, then. On tiptoe with a prayer to the high gods that she would find some way out. Arthur White was placidly whistling now, beneath his breath. His sensitive fingers and yet more sensitive faculties were revelling in the joy of creation. Marjorie Castleton held her breath as she came up behind.

For a second she stared down at the tousled blond head, shining dully in the sunlight, snatched at her breath and plunged her hands downwards. At the same time her right foot kicked the stool from under him, and White went down with the easel toppling drunkenly across his chest.

His left hand flailed upwards wildly. She caught a brief reek of turpentine on the knuckles that grazed against her forehead and made her feel momentarily sick. Her knee, hampered by a skirt, found his ribs. She felt a suspender snap, and plunged her weight downwards on the rising arch of White's own tough body. His heels thudded against the deck, the backs of his crepe-soled white shoes crumpling.

He was on his elbows now, heaving the easel away from his body so that he might somehow roll over. In that frantic moment his strong shoulders found the leverage he sought. He was on his knees, panting, so that a fierce backward sweep of his left arm sent her spinning. But before he could rise fully she was on him again.

Back to his knees. A swift, chopping blow upwards that caught her shoulder, sent her away again. White's face was bleeding where her nails had raked him. She ran into a more powerful blow as he finally gained full balance. Even as she crashed back into the front of the wheelhouse, the lightning thought came to her that if there were anyone engaged in observation of the boat from the rear of Castleton House, then here was something to get excited about.

But she could not know, as heaven and earth and sea seemed to be reeling and crashing about her, that the only one at Castleton was dour old Elspeth McCracken. That in her own housekeeper's sitting-room upstairs, she sat in a grey silence, eyes grown tired and misted with unshed tears. That an album of cherished photographs of those she had served so long and faithfully had slipped from unresistant fingers . . . that the slow mental death-throes of the exhausted old eagle were being accomplished.

Coatless, and with his thin blue silk shirt ripped away at one shoulder, Arthur White was clawing at his hip-pocket for a gun. As he jerked it clear, Marjorie Castleton came at him yet again, her breath sobbing in distress. Before he could take aim she ducked, grabbed at his ankles, felt the barrel of the revolver graze her shoulder, went past the staggering White on her hands and knees and scrambled upright again. Then she was over the rail and hurtling downwards towards the water before he could fire.

No time for a dive. She almost smacked into the slight chill, spreadeagled. White hurled himself against the rail, craned over, finger curling around the trigger as she forced herself into a quick over-arm stroke in the direction of the shore. He squeezed, and cursed as he remembered the safety-catch. But, as the fingers of his other hand flicked across to it, he thought twice. A floating corpse and a bullet-hole . . . a forced will . . . He scrambled over the rail in turn, edged along to the tied skiff, lowered himself by his hands and worked feverishly at the painter.

Damned bad luck, although White was not to know, in his agony of apprehension, that there *was* no unseen watcher at Castleton House. Quick as he was to get going on the otherwise deserted water with not another craft in sight, the girl had already made considerable headway. White pulled away like a man possessed, came alongside her, cursed at her to tread water and let him pull her in. But she fought on. White

leaned over, tried to grab at her with one hand while he retained his grip on an oar with another. She pumped in air.
The dinghy rocked. White felt the oar nearest her, that he had
left swinging in the rowlock, slip its pin, and made a plunge
for it. Marjorie Castleton felt its heavy bulk strike her on the
head.

Under she went, as White fought to get control of the oar
and both hands free. Somehow he managed it. Somehow he
dragged her aboard by an exhibition of brute strength surprising in one of his build. She lay stunned, hair lying wetly
across her eyes, the soaked dress sharply outlining breasts
that rose and fell labouredly with her agonised breathing.
White dashed sweat from his forehead and swore in fervent
manner.

His muscles were aching as he hauled her back to the
deck of the houseboat. He kicked aside the ruined painting
and the broken easel, felt a tube of colour squish beneath his
heel, and bent to lift the unconscious girl. If she had wanted
Scott, he now wanted Apperley. He felt exhausted as he laid
her out on the berth she had occupied the night before.

Then, because he was interested in no woman beyond the
one known as Freda White, he went automatically about the
process of taking off the girl's wet upper clothes. She came
to with the slight sting of sal volatile on her lips and temples,
and the realisation that, in her wet underwear, she was cosily
wrapped up in the warmth of blankets. And, barring the wet-
ness, that was how she had started the day—in her underwear.

CHAPTER IX

STRATEGY

TRUNDLING ALONG THE COAST ROAD towards Harlingham, the local bus caught the sun dazzlingly on glass and paint-work, and by the stop, with his back to the sea, Henry Apper-ley was glad to shield his eyes with a hand. The conductor-driver nodded to him as a casual acquaintance—one of hun-dreds—and slid open the bus door from his seat. Apperley climbed aboard, thrust his fare at the man, received his ticket and went to the back of the vehicle as it started off again.

For most of the journey to Harlingham he was in deep thought. Uppermost in his mind was the question of "Big Johnny" Kreig—something had to be done about him. And there seemed to Apperley one very good method of finding out about Kreig, which was to go and see someone in charge of the Seldon murder case.

If Selden had by now been identified, even unofficially—even, that is, if the police had found out who he was and were keeping the information from the general public for some reason—he meant to somehow find out about that fact. Skilful, ingenuous "fishing" at Harlingham Police Headquar-ters might accomplish a lot in his favour. He might gain some inkling, no more, of where Seldon might have come from; might, from that, more or less pinpoint a spot where "Big Johnny" might be expected to be.

The chances were that even if the police succeeded in backtracking Seldon's movements they could not be ex-pected to get a line on Kreig, simply because they did not link the two together. But Apperley did. And if he knew very roughly where Kreig was likely to be or even had been, then he and White might strike cleverly and fast. "Big Johnny" might yet he beaten to the punch and their future saved.

Not only that. To avert suspicion from him Apperley must needs put in an appearance to the police, following the "tragedy" of Marjorie Castleton's death. Apperley guessed why officialdom had not yet paid a visit to the houseboat—it was preoccupied with Seldon. It knew that Apperley was in receipt of the news about the smashed motor-boat, therefore there was no sense in squandering precious time to go out and inform him.

And by reason of the adroit way in which he had handled affairs with Tony Scott and the old housekeeper, there was no suspicion of foul play. Until that suspicion arose it was a job for the local coroner rather than the police. Apperley had known that last night, which was why he and White had slept securely—though somewhat uncomfortably on deck—on the houseboat.

But this morning was a different matter. In respectability —Apperley smiled to himself as the word came to his mind—in respectability he couldn't be expected to defer a visit to police headquarters any longer. As loving cousin to Marjorie Castleton he would be expected to be eager for any news of the possible finding of her body, might want to see the motorboat that the coastguards would now have towed in. He would want to know: what was all this business, that had surely come to his ears by now, about a man being killed up at Castleton House?

So much was surely expected of him. And additional to that, he had to make his own side of the story good. The story of how he had tried to restrain his pretty but headstrong cousin and, in face of her proud spirit, had failed.

Apperley didn't think that he could possibly be blamed. Wasn't there Scott and the old housekeeper to testify to the girl's obstinacy?

On the whole, then, Henry Apperley thought it an astute move to walk boldly into the camp of the enemy on this bright July morning. And, if nothing else—if they *weren't* possibly expecting him—then the surprise they would experience would surely send up his stock several points. Why come to them if he had anything at all to hide?

He got off at the terminus in Market Square, and looked approvingly about him. Three blocks away (Apperley could not forget his American associations) was busy Marine Drive and police headquarters, housed in smart red brick of modern design. Apperley knew where the place lay all right. When he had embarked on this bizarre, but strikingly original business at Castleton House he had been prudent, and had made it his business to know, in case of possible future eventualities.

And on the way he passed a tobacconist's and newsagent's shop, remembered, turned around and retraced a few steps. White, he supposed, must be humoured. He thrust the *Mail* into a side-pocket of his smart sports coat, lit a cigarette and went on. At police headquarters he went up a few broad steps, through swing doors, into a wide cool hall. There was a big glassed-in inquiry-box presided over by a uniformed sergeant almost facing him and he strode over to it briskly.

The sergeant had greying hair and a bored manner, but he was courteous. He pushed a "lost and found" pad away, put his pen behind his ear and cocked an eyebrow towards Apperley who stood with an elbow on the ledge outside. Apperley removed the cigarette from a corner of his mouth. "Good morning."

"Can I help you, sir?"

"I'd like to see someone about the—the Castleton affair," Apperley said glibly, and gave his name. He was beginning to settle in with the atmosphere of this brisk place by now, was finding added confidence and sang-froid. "I'm the poor girl's cousin."

"Inspector Paynter is in charge of that unfortunate business, sir," the sergeant said. "A sad affair indeed, Perhaps you'd like a word with him?"

"Is he—?" Apperley hazarded.

"He'll be able to do anything necessary for you, sir. He's head of our local C.I.D." The sergeant picked up a housephone to make inquiries, and Apperley waited. Not for long.

A uniformed constable came to escort him along a wide passage to somewhere at the back of the building. They went through opaque-glazed double doors into a big room with a high two-sided desk, with long chromium rails dividing the slopes, running the length of the place. Black-lettered doors marked various offices leading off it. Apperley continued to finish his cigarette in perfect coolness.

Inspector Paynter came to him and put out a hand. Not for him to deny Henry Apperley such courtesy, even though Croft had discussed the man, *vide* Tony Scott, as being a probable "bad egg." " 'Morning, Mr. Apperley," he said. "What can I do for you?"

"Isn't it obvious?" Apperley asked, forcing himself to assume a grave face. "I came to see if there's any news of Miss Marjorie Castleton . . ."

"I wish there were," Paynter answered. "I know how you must feel about her, but up to now there's nothing to report."

"The coastguards?" Apperley murmured, looking around as though in quest of an ash-tray.

"Dump it on the floor, Mr. Apperley. We all do. No,"— Paynter shook his head—"they're still out searching, as a favour to us, but there's no sign of the body yet."

Apperley said sorrowfully: "I wish there were something I could do. It makes me feel so terrible . . . You've seen Mr. Scott by now, of course? And the housekeeper? They'll have told you what happened on the houseboat."

"Mr. Scott is here now," Paynter said. "He's in with Detective-Inspector Croft of Scotland Yard, the one assigned to that other unfortunate affair. You know, Mr. Apperley—the death of an unknown man in Castleton House." The detective shook his head. "The family certainly seem to cop it, sir. You have all my sympathy."

"Thanks. I understand Mr. Scott is staying in the town now?"

"That's right," Paynter answered. "He's come pretty much upon the same errand as yourself, I fancy, Mr. Apperley, only he knows the Inspector better than you do. Well, I'm sorry that you've had your journey for nothing. There's just no news I can give you, but if you care to keep in touch—"

It was a polite way of saying that Inspector Paynter had other duties to attend to. Apperley said: "If you don't mind, I'd rather like to see this Detective-Inspector Croft of yours. I'm just as interested as Mr. Scott in that mysterious shindy of a couple of nights ago, at Castleton. Mind if I wait?"

"Not a bit, sir." Paynter arranged a chair for him at the end of the high desk where a sprinkling of the law's minions were engaged in pounding typewriters, despite the polished slope, making up sundry ledgers, checking in small items of other people's property. The two-way double doors swung open again and again, as blue-uniformed figures came in and went out on various errands. A lost child was brought in and sobbed, was questioned and led gently away. Apperley sat on serenely. But Scott and Croft seemed to be a hellishly long time. For want of better distraction he pulled out the copy of the newspaper he had purchased.

"Do you know this man?" asked the front page, and Apperley stared at the skilfully retouched photograph of the face of the yet-unidentified William Seldon. Retouched because he had died in agony from a fractured skull, and the susceptibilities of the public must be protected. Apperley read the few facts contained in the story beneath the picture. Nothing much there, but the "picturesque" side had not been neglected. Had the curse come true again? was the implication—an obvious "snip" for any enterprising newspaper man to write up.

And in an adjacent column, the story of the terrible believed "death by drowning" of Marjorie Castleton, last of the line. Obviously in the next column—the tie-up was too good to miss. From somewhere or other, the paper had managed to get a photo of The Pinnacles. Apperley wondered how long it might be before reporters, national or local, might get around to circumventing the boredom and trouble of a trip by dinghy to the houseboat. Well, if they came today, White would be ready for them. As with any probable visitation by the police or Scott, he had the estimable advantage of being able to spot them putting out and quickly bestowing the silenced girl in the forepeak.

The Pinnacles, Apperley thought to himself. The local name had arisen solely by tact that the rocks were sharpish but they were certainly not tall and altogether impossible. They were only worth a couple of buoys by way of warning to general shipping; even the houseboat could have avoided them easily enough had it been in the immediate vicinity of them in the storm. But a small motor-boat had been an entirely different matter.

Apperley was considering lighting another cigarette when he saw a door at the farther end of the long room suddenly open and the broad-shouldered figure of young Tony Scott come striding out. Scott looked worried, haggard. Apperley refolded the newspaper, put it in his pocket and got up.

"Well, Mr. Scott, we *do* meet again."

Apperley had remained by his chair until the other had come up to him in his walk to the exit from the general office. But there was no extended hand, only a mocking half-smile. Scott pulled up.

"I might have known it'd be you. Sorry I haven't the time."

From the corner of his eye, Apperley saw Inspector Paynter going across to the office Scott had just left. "Of course not," he said smoothly. "And I can understand your feeling a trifle unsociable. My poor cousin . . . I feel damned miserable myself."

"No news from your direction, I suppose?" Scott asked brusquely.

"I wish there were, Mr. Scott. I came here to see if I could pick anything up."

"So did I, yet I'm sorry to say that there's nothing doing," Scott answered him. "But I'm glad of the opportunity of seeing you this morning, Apperley."

"Indeed?" Apperley's smile was still soft and inviting.

"Yes. It gives me an opportunity to repeat what I had to say yesterday evening."

Scott was uncompromising, cold, but inwardly worried and aching. Apperley looked across to see Paynter coming out and towards them. "Don't like me, do you, Mr. Scott?"

"I'm sure that the feeling must be reciprocated," Scott said. "Tell Croft I said so, if you like. I think that he'll see you now. By the way, if you *should* want me for anything, I'm putting up at the 'George' for a few days."

"You mean," Apperley said, and his voice had grown deadly, "that I might like to call and accommodate you in that little matter of trying to knock my head off. I can see that you're still set on such foolishness. Good-bye."

Scott crushed down further words, nodded to Paynter and left the office. Paynter said: "Detective-Inspector Croft will see you now, Mr. Apperley," and led the way back. He tapped on the door, opened it, and Croft looked up from the desk placed at his disposal.

For the first time he and Henry Apperley stood face to face. Croft was trying to be pleasant; Apperley was quickly getting the measure of an arch-enemy. Perfunctorily he engaged in the usual handshake, and complied with Croft's invitation to take a chair.

"Smoke if you wish, Mr. Apperley," Croft said. "Sorry I can't offer you a cigarette, but I only carry a pipe myself."

"You might like to try one of mine," Apperley answered, bringing out a packet.

"Thanks, but this'll do me." Croft picked up his pouch. "Well, sir?"

"I think," Apperley said, "that your Inspector Paynter will tell you why I've come. You can't imagine how terrible I feel about this—this tragedy. And the killing at Castleton." He tapped the newspaper in his coat pocket. "I've just been reading about it."

Croft rammed down tobacco and regarded him over the flame of a match. "I think—" he said between puffs, "that I—understand—how you feel. You saw Mr. Scott on his way out, I take it?"

"We passed the time of day," Apperley said, with a faint grin.

"He told me all about it from your angle," Croft said, blowing out the match and dropping it in the waste-paper basket. "And Inspector Paynter went out last night and interviewed Miss McCracken, the housekeeper. Incidentally, she won't leave the place, and until there's some sort of a legal settlement as to whom it shall go, I don't think that we can get her out. She's quite all right in her mind, and she's not scared."

"I've been a little worried about her. Do you know, Inspector," Apperley said, "it's never crossed my mind about who the old place shall go to, now that poor Marjorie Castleton's gone. I suppose that there's no doubt about it?"

"Her drowning?" Croft asked. " 'Fraid not. And as to who'll be her heir—that's for the lawyers to decide, if there isn't a will."

"Of course," Apperley said slowly. "If there isn't a will. She may have made one, Inspector. No doubt there'll have to be a search. But—" He pulled himself up sharply. "Don't think badly of me for saying that, will you?"

"She has to be presumed dead, first—if her body isn't found," Croft answered. "And that, I suppose, will be a matter for the local coroner. All sorts of complications, aren't there, Mr. Apperley?" He paused. "I can't help saying that you might get the house after all. You're her cousin, and from what Miss McCracken told Inspector Paynter last night, there doesn't appear to be anyone else much. Forgive me for saying that you've certainly tried hard enough to get the place otherwise."

Apperley sensed slight hostility in Croft's words. He said a little stiffly: "I don't think that there's much wrong with that, Inspector."

Croft twisted the mouthpiece of his pipe into alignment with the bowl. "I'm only trying to say that it appears to me that you rather put the poor girl's mind into a turmoil. Let me ask you something. As a man who obviously knows what's what in the world, do *you* believe in what is so glibly called 'the curse of the Castletons'?"

"Depends on how you look at it," Apperley answered.

He had not altogether expected this, and was indulging in some quick thinking, while Croft watched him steadily. The Scotland Yard man said: "I can't altogether believe, myself, Mr. Apperley, that that kind of thing appeals to you. *You* aren't a child."

"People in this world," Apperley said, "have a right to believe as they choose."

"Granted. But we've got to think of what they choose. They choose in conformity with their characters and mental outlook. I just won't have it that you're of a mental age to believe in this rubbish that you handed out to Miss Castleton. I know, Mr. Apperley, that you came here seeking sympathy, and I extend it to you in the matter of her unfortunate death. But I'm a plain-speaking man, and I'm saying that I don't like the way you tried to influence her to let you have the house."

"Good enough," Apperley replied, forcedly respecting Croft's position of authority. "Only, my dear Inspector, I put it to you that there's a lot of men, of the mental age you flatter me as belonging to, who wouldn't like your words. There seems to be something a little ugly underneath them."

"Such as?"

"Such as that you might be leaping to utterly wrong, absurd conclusions. I think I know how the official mind argues to itself. You're a policeman and naturally a policeman is always ready with suspicions. Things seem to add up with you, although you may be wildly wrong."

Apperley restrained his thoughts at that point. He was subtle. Croft made the expected answer to him.

"You're trying to tell me, Mr. Apperley, that I'm seeking to link up things where I haven't a right to be linking them up. That you were, in a way, unscrupulous by the use of suggestion in your efforts to get Miss Castleton to sell you the house; and that therefore it might possibly be thought that, following those efforts, there might be something fishy about her death as far as you're concerned. I'll tell you what you've come for. You've come here to find out whether or no I think you may have been mixed up in some foul play in the matter of the girl's death. That's so, isn't it?"

"You can afford, in your position, to be devastatingly blunt," Apperley said. "Let's sift this thing down to bedrock, Inspector. I'll admit, fully and frankly, that I don't believe in such old-womanish rot as 'the curse of the Castletons.' I know from historical fact that such a curse exists, but I don't believe in its potency. Neither do you. Of course you don't. But there's absolutely no law—possibly beyond a moral one and I don't care a fig for that—to preclude me from saying I believe in it and from using such ostensible belief to further my own ends."

He got up to stand behind his chair, fingers gripping the top rail. "There's nothing to prevent me wanting Castleton House, Inspector. If I've always admired the place since my youth and I thought that I'd like to help my poor cousin out financially by giving her a better price than the National Trust could, well—I repeat that there's no law against that. If wanting the place becomes so strong with me that I seize a weapon laid ready to my hand, and use it on one I thought not sophisticated enough and less resistant, then that course of action can't be held against me."

"I follow your argument, Mr. Apperley," Croft said in his serene way. "I'd like to hear the conclusion of it"—as Apperley paused for breath.

"I'm not fighting with you, Inspector."

Croft was imperturbable. "Of course not. You're just indulging in plain speaking. No doubt you'd like to tell me that you've a right to it. But so have I. All of this, I feel, leads up to the death of Marjorie Castleton. What lies behind it is that you're trying to tell me that I've no right to be suspicious of you."

"Something like that," Apperley said. "I feel that it's best for both of us to be frank. Scott—"

"Now we get to the meat of the matter, Mr. Apperley. I was rather expecting this. Has Scott been accusing you of some sort of funny business in connection with the girl's death?"

There was challenge in Croft's words, and Apperley met it. "He's gone farther than you, Inspector. In fact, he's made himself damned unpleasant. I've just admitted to you that I tried to scare the girl into selling Castleton House to me because I thought it was a legitimate way of doing it. There's as much bluff and hooey used in business every day of the week. But there's a limit to what I'm prepared to admit otherwise. Scott seems to have some damned silly idea that I took things a step farther—"

Henry Apperley was pleased with his own guile in this. Even Croft had to go his way, though it was no easy matter. It meant a show of bluster, but it was worth it. Worth it and necessary—vitally necessary. At all costs Apperley must know Detective-Inspector Croft's hand, so that he might successfully play the game out to his own satisfaction in the future. Was he suspect by Croft himself? Could he afford to go on with the plans he had made with White; or must they now devise quick emergency measures?

Scott could, for the moment, be discounted. The two great dangers facing the pair were "Big Johnny" Kreig and the police. Find out how they stood, and White and Apperley might know which way to jump for the best.

And Detective-Inspector Croft, of New Scotland Yard, played up to Apperley's subtle strategy in the way that he hoped he would.

"All right; let's get things straight," he said. "Mr. Scott came here merely to tell me that he'd been in telephonic communication with his employers in Queen Anne's Gate. London. He was supposed to have returned to Town last night, Sunday, and report progress at his office this morning. But in view of what's happened, he's naturally interested in staying on for a few days more. His people have agreed to that. After all"—Croft shrugged thick shoulders—"whoever'll turn out as the probable heir to Castleton might have to be approached. I take it that the Trust is still interested in the property."

"Fair enough," Apperley admitted, and waited for Croft to speak on. Information was coming his way.

"Mr. Scott merely came to tell me that," Croft said. "Nothing more. We discussed the fatality, of course, and inevitably your name cropped up, but nothing derogatory was said about you beyond the fact that he disliked you for trying to influence Miss Castleton's mind with a lot of superstition. But, there again—he's a right to think so. You've been talking about rights; and we've already discussed that angle. I myself have a right to dislike you, on the same principle—and, frankly, I do."

The candid eyes of Detective-Inspector Croft were turned full on Apperley's face as he stood running his fingers along the rail of the chair. "So it all boils down to this, Mr. Apperley. I'll admit that the circumstances of the case appear to be sticky. You want the house and she wouldn't let you have it. You might well be her heir. You let her cast off from that houseboat of yours into what was practically suicide." Croft held up a hand. "All right. I know your side of the story. You've already done your best to clear yourself, and that, again, is your perfectly natural right. But what I'm trying to get around to is this. That neither Scott, the housekeeper, myself, nor anyone else is accusing you of anything. We don't even hold you under suspicion."

Croft struck another match as he sat comfortably. "That satisfies you, I hope. But because I dislike you, Mr. Apperley, I feel that I must qualify the statement. To this effect: that I'm in the hands of the local coroner, as I hinted before, and there's simply nothing to justify Mr. Emerson advising him on a criminal verdict. If there were, I'd have had you picked up before this and you wouldn't leave this office in freedom now."

Inspector Croft paused, thinking. "That tells you what you want to know, doesn't it? As regards the inquest. The facts have been reported to the coroner in the usual formal way, but he likes a body to inspect. They all do. Sometimes the body can't be found, in which case the inquest is deferred as long as possible until there's no hope left. It also," Croft said, again looking Apperley straight in the face, "gives the police time to make a final check if we want one. I'm warning you, you see.

"You're not under suspicion yet, but you may be. And I don't think you can quarrel with that. We may have to let the verdict go as 'Presumed accidentally drowned.' But," Croft said, "if it should be something else—'Murder by drowning by some person or persons unknown'—then"—he stopped significantly.

"You seem determined to insult me," Apperley said without a smile.

"Haven't I told you that I dislike you?" Croft asked. "Well, what else can I do for you?"

"I've already said let's not fight, Inspector," Apperley came back at him. "How about the affair of the death of the unknown man at Castleton House on Saturday night? I presume that he *is* still unknown?"

"You read the newspapers," Croft answered, looking at Apperley's pocket.

"That's another inquest on the way, I suppose?" Apperley said, ignoring the minor thrust. "Murder this time, of course."

"Naturally," Croft said, bringing his gaze from Apperley back to the wall opposite the desk and the previous year's calendar, only retained because of the coloured view of Lake Coniston thereon. "I'm quite satisfied, so is the Chief Constable, on that point. Once again I refer you to the newspapers. I know very little more than they do."

Croft laughed. "While we're in the mood for confidences, I'll tell you everything, and that'll prove how much I trust you."

"And those same newspapers get it tomorrow, eh, Inspector?"

"It'll hurt nobody," Croft said. "I went back to Town yesterday, in spite of it being Sunday. I had a conference with a superior officer at the Yard. I went through so many photos in Records that I turned the job up in disgust. That's why I wasn't available when you telephoned Inspector

Paynter about poor Miss Castleton. I only got back by a late train, last night.

"All I can tell you is this. We don't know the name of the man who was killed at Castleton House on Saturday. We're appealing, as you know, for information from the public, and the Press is co-operating there. That's my strongest—in fact my only—hope. I do know that he's probably an American."

Apperley restrained a slight start. "Interesting, Inspector."

"But simple," Croft assured him. "He has the appearance to me of a low-grade crook, although I hope that I'm not maligning a dead man. I'm only going by his face and my experience. And say 'probably an American.' He might have pinched the suit he was wearing, might even have bought it or had it given. But it struck me upon closer examination of his clothes, that they didn't look English. Right enough, there was a tab in the inside breast pocket. Weiss and Harmer of Boston. I've checked up on that with the Yard.

"It's a firm of multiple tailors. It turns out wholesale, off-the-peg stuff. All bespoke orders that are individually tailored have the customer's name indelibly inked on the same tub. This one merely had a blank space." Croft smiled thinly. "It's amazing what information is stored away and what specialists we have at the Yard."

If that were another thrust to make him feel uncomfortable, thought Apperley, it was feeble enough. "What then, Inspector?"

Croft looked critically at Lake Coniston again. "If the suit was mass-produced," he said, "it was of very good material. That's why I say good enough to pinch. On the other hand, if it was the rightful property of the man who had his head bashed in at Castleton, then, although he might have been a cheap crook, he was obviously a cut above cheap digs and lodging houses."

Croft stood up to stretch his legs. "So—a medium-class hotel in London, since we know that he came from there by rail. He might have stayed at one with a pal."

With a pal! For an instant Apperley mentally panicked, as he thought of Kreig. Then he breathed again. Wasn't it an inviolable rule of the kingpin, when it came to hotels, to stay at a superior one himself and make his underlings lodge snugly in lower-grade ones? His far-sighted caution might now stand Kreig in good stead.

Apperley's near-panic was caused by a swift circle of thinking. It Kreig *were* picked up, he might spill all he knew about White and Apperley merely because he hated them and was determined to get even. If he himself were held by the law, then he couldn't take his own revenge as planned, because he would lack the liberty to do it. What more natural, then, to ensure that Apperley and friend got it in the neck by means of a murder charge?

Merely mention Apperley's name to the police and the fat would be in the fire with a vengeance. The connection would be too sound not to be unprofitable to Croft. Apperley, Castleton, the by-then-identified William Seldon. Intensive work by Croft and the whole secret of White and Apperley's activities and Seldon's murder at the hands of Apperley would come tumbling out.

There was a double twist to this thing, as Apperley realised. In one way he wanted to know if there was any hint of Kreig's movements known to the unsuspecting police. In another way he was desperate that there shouldn't be, because the pulling in of Kreig by Croft might well mean his own and White's downfall.

And yet . . . He hoped to temporise. Hoped to find a middle course. He would have liked Croft—too much to hope for!—to have told him that they suspected Kreig, had some vague idea as to his whereabouts, so that White and Apperley might get in before them and settle Kreig before he settled them.

Croft said: "We have men making inquiries around the hotels, Mr. Apperley, but that takes time. And hotel police aren't usually co-operative with the regular police, unless they have to be. They're too afraid of being drawn into possible trouble, you see. They don't like what they term 'undesirable publicity' and although we always try to do our best for them, we aren't always able to provide a screen. Someone may volunteer information, or skilled questioning on the rounds may reveal it. On the other hand, the man may not have stayed at an hotel at all. I just don't know; and something tells me that we're going to have a hard time finding out."

Henry Apperley sensed that the interview was almost at an end. One last question, then. It was his turn to look Croft full in the eyes.

"And how about his killer, Inspector?"

Croft was silent for a moment or two, then he spoke, and it appeared to be after much deliberation.

"Not a trace, Mr. Apperley. And I think that I'll have an oven harder time in cracking that problem. But"—he held out his big hand to Apperley in dismissal—"I *shall* crack it, never fear."

Apperley smiled to himself and went away. "A damned hard time," he said beneath his breath as he went down the steps and into the street again.

CHAPTER X

PREPARATION

FOR ONE IN Henry Apperley's position, that gentleman had a singularly pleasant and relaxed afternoon. He had a good lunch, then went to the pictures.

This was not particularly because he had a yearning to go that must be satisfied. Neither was it altogether dictated by a complacency of mind consequent upon his recent interview with Detective-Inspector Croft and the knowledge that up to now he and White were fairly in the clear. Rather was it because of the tide, in getting back to the houseboat.

Therefore, Apperley first indulged himself in roast duck and a half-bottle of somewhat indifferent wine, and later in a superb Technicolor film that strangely enough dealt with pirates and a wronged heroine. The ironical coincidence struck him forcefully, and he lay back in the seat and laughed softly to himself. He had taken pot-luck with the feature attraction when entering this convenient cinema, and had not expected this. He could enjoy the implication simply because he had no conscience.

Being an exceedingly super-cinema, it also provided him with tea and cakes, brought to his seat by a ghostly attendant. So that Apperley was quite at ease when he came out into the early evening sunshine. For all his relaxation he had kept a careful eye on the time; caught his bus and got off at the point where he had waited for it that morning. From his seat next a side-window he looked out over the sea, waiting for the turn in the road that would bring the fairly distant houseboat into view.

All seemed to be quiet aboard. Doubtless the girl would now be locked in the cabin again, and White would be pulling inshore to meet him. Pretty good, Apperley told himself.

The bus stopped at his request. He got out, strolled away negligently until it had gone, then made for the sandhills that he must briefly negotiate. And, slap on six o'clock, there was White.

He seemed to be a trifle ruffled. Apperley was shrewd to notice his actions, the way that he greeted him. "All in order?" he asked him, and White grunted a little surlily.

"I've *made* everything go according to plan," he said. "But that damned girl!"

"A hell-cat," Apperley said. "Has she been giving trouble?"

"Don't blame me for it," White said, as he turned the boat back to where she was imprisoned. "This is what comes of trying to treat women like her gently."

"I became weary long ago of pointing that fact out to you," Apperley replied. "Especially in relation to one woman. All right, Arthur—don't get sore. What happened?"

"She tried to make a break for it."

"And—?"

"I went after her. She got a ducking and a crack on the head."

Apperley clicked his tongue in annoyance. "Bad. Bad. I told you to look out. Did she take a header overboard?"

"She did," White snapped. "After a bit of a shemozzle between us on deck. I pulled after her; that's how she got a clout with an oar. I put her to bed in your berth and locked her in."

"You're a fool with women," Apperley said, and there was a double meaning to his contemptuous words. "What are you sweating about now? You've told me, haven't you? And I'm your pal? I haven't grown blazing mad about your little confession—in fact, I'm quite tolerant at your clumsiness."

"Can it," White answered. "You know damned well that I've never been afraid of you. I'm only worried about a possible watcher at Castleton. If there was, or is, one, then—"

"Your violent upset with the girl will have been duly noted," Apperley sneered. "That it? Let me make your mind easy, Arthur. There's no one there but that sour old fool of a housekeeper, and I gathered that she's sticking to her own room indoors."

Perspiration shone on White's broad forehead beneath the dunk blond hair. "Second sight, Apperley?"

"I told you," Apperley retorted, "that I gathered as much. And I could only do so from an informant."

White forced a grin as he worked. "So you managed to get into police headquarters?"

"I did," Apperley said, and went on to detail all that had occurred there as they neared the houseboat. White grunted his satisfaction.

"Good—damned good," he said, as he secured the skiff and came aboard following Apperley. "This gives us time to breathe again. I see that you brought the *Daily Mail* of this morning, that I asked for."

Apperley had forgotten that he carried the paper. He clapped a hand to the side-pocket of his coat. "Of course. I might have lost it, for all the care I've taken."

White paled a little and put out a hand. "But you haven't."

"Eh?" Apperley looked at him queerly. "Enjoy yourself with it while I slip below and take a look at our fair captive. You might prepare a tray in the meantime. She'll want another meal."

He unlocked the companion-way doors and Marjorie Castleton heard him coming and breathed a sigh of relief. She was dressed again, but only just in time. Apperley halted in surprise.

"Back again, you see, Miss Castleton. But I don't understand."

"Don't understand what?" she asked coldly.

She was feeling better—stronger. Her fighting spirit was back and the enforced brief rest had done her good. Apperley said: "Weren't you supposed to be shivering in blankets in the berth I've been glad to let you deprive me of? And here you are, hopping around in full rig—"

Marjorie Castleton had grown more subtle—less of the innocent ex-high schoolgirl, more of the hard, tough woman who was gaining experience in a hard school. She was less gauche in her standing up to Apperley. "I see what you mean," she said. "Compliment me on being a clever girl—or at least resourceful."

Apperley was instantly alert for a possible dangerous move. "How?"

"The scuttle," she said, and jerked a head over her shoulder. "You were quite right when you said that, however slim, I couldn't squeeze through."

"Then you've tried?" Apperley smiled. "Naturally. And I can't blame you. I'd have done the same thing myself."

"Not altogether," she answered. "I didn't make such an attempt, especially as I was soaking wet. Good job I was out cold, or your delightful friend White wouldn't have taken my things off as he did."

"He was doing a good turn," Apperley said. "Such a thing means nothing to him. As far as you go, he's completely detached. But this is interesting, Miss Castleton. Do go on. About the scuttle—?"

"I found that I could get an arm right out," she said coolly. "It didn't take me long to wake up after White had tucked me into the blankets. I just couldn't lie there in wet underwear, so I risked him coming back. But I judged that he'd more or less had enough of my company and I wouldn't be disturbed. I found that there was a stretched rope, or a stay or something, just underneath the scuttle."

"Part of the equipment of this magnificent tub," said Apperley. "I *do* compliment you, Miss Castleton. The sun and the breeze were in your favour of course, and in such conditions it wouldn't take very long to dry out the complete outfit that you're wearing. That's one of the advantages of being a modern woman, isn't it? Now, in Victorian days—"

She was saved what might have been embarrassing remarks by the appearance of Arthur White, again bearing a full tray. It seemed to her, even in face of the danger in which she stood, that there was something a trifle ludicrous in this. But she was glad to see the well-prepared meals. No sense in jibbing at them in mere pique. She was trying to be sensible, trying to tell herself that she must keep up her strength. She might yet he presented with a further opportunity of escape, in spite of her failure, and when and if that came she must be ready.

Apperley said: "The lady has managed to dry herself out. Good job you didn't come down, White. What have you found for her? My, my! Eggs and chips, Miss Castleton!"

White put the tray down. "I hope that it'll be your turn to do this soon, Apperley. I'm not complaining, but—"

"We have to have hewers of wood and drawers of water," Apperley retorted lightly, "although the metaphor is not exactly applicable to this noble vessel." He noticed how White's hand was a little unsteady as he rattled a cup in a saucer, and looked at him sharply. The eyes of the other man were gleaming as though with suppressed excitement.

Apperley became subdued. His sixth sense of impending trouble told him that here was something that was beyond joking. White put the empty tray beneath his arm without a word and turned to go on deck. Apperley took a quick look around to see that the girl was all right, noted that she was pouring her tea, and followed.

He went to the rail and lit a cigarette while he heard White banging about in the tiny galley. Surely the fellow wasn't piqued about having to get meals ready? Normally Apperley shared the chores with him, but today he had had to leave him on an errand necessary to both their well being. Or was it that the girl's attempt at escape had ruffled him unduly? Yet White had met tougher spots in a hectic career.

Apperley went to him. White was cutting a peeled potato upon a scrubbed board. The long knife he held deftly crossed the white slices. Near at hand boiling fat sent up a faint blue smoke. White tossed the chips into a wire basket. He did not turn around, but reached for another potato. Apperley said: "Same dish, eh?"

"Good enough for all of us," White said, "though I don't know if you've had some tea."

"I'll join you in this," his companion answered. "You couldn't call mine a meal—"

There was a folding table on deck. Apperley got in White's way to lay it roughly with plates and cutlery, and brought up two slatted folding chairs. The breeze was freshening as they sat down. The face of Arthur White was set and pale, and Apperley watched him as he dug viciously into the sugar basin.

"What's gone wrong, Arthur? That damned girl upset you? Forget it."

"It's not that," White muttered. "By God! you've got to listen to me, Apperley . . . "

"I've told you that everything's hunky-dory," said Apperley, taking a slice of bread on his plate. "Don't get cold feet now when it seems that we've got a damned good chance of seeing things through to our mutual satisfaction."

But White shook his head. "I'm not scared, if that's what you mean. Only—"

"Only what?" Apperley prompted. "Out with it, man."

"There's something else cropped up. I see that I'm forced to tell you. But I'm not backing out. Get that, Apperley? I'm not backing out."

White brought the copy of the *Daily Mail* into view from his hip. Apperley was cold, wary, but with a puzzled look in his eyes. "You seem to set a hell of a store by that paper," he said softly. "Enlighten me, Arthur. You've just hinted that you've reached a stage when I must know."

White folded the paper and laid it before him, indicating by a slim forefinger an advertisement in the personal column. His voice was harsh. "That mayn't mean anything to you, but it does to me. Look at it, Apperley. 'Agree. Meet you Metropole H. tonight. F.' "

Apperley looked up. "The aitch is on the wrong side, Arthur. As an abbreviation, shouldn't it read 'Hotel Metropole'?" And White set his teeth.

"It means," he said with a deadly calmness, 'Harling-ham.' That's what the aitch stands for, Apperley. The Metropole, Harlingham."

"And the 'F'," Apperley said, with as much danger in his voice, "stands for 'Freda.' I get it."

White caught the deadly inflexion in his tones. His hand went to his chest as though buttoning the torn blue shirt. "You won't stop me, Henry."

"That remains to be seen when I've heard your story," Apperley said. "Good God in heaven, White! Can't you lay off the woman? I've told you that she's smart—smart and utterly worthless. She dropped you and lighted out with Munroe and there's a pair of 'em. Precious beauties I wouldn't risk my neck for. And I've argued with you; damn' well pleaded with you, in fact—"

"And I've told you scores of times that you're wasting your breath," White snapped. "When I came into this deal in England with you, you promised that you'd do your best to help me locate Munroe and Freda and in return I said that I'd lend you my skilled assistance. Right?"

"We can do nothing without each other." Apperley had his elbows on the table.

"No more we can, Apperley. You've got commitments—we both have—that can't be carried out unless I work over at Castleton House of nights. We know the penalty for failure. Those we turn the stuff over to for good, genuine cash are strong enough to root us out and destroy us and we wouldn't have a chance to evade them, if we defalcated on our ar-rangements. They won't take on a fight with Kreig on our behalf, but they'll take thundering good care to keep us in line."

"Well?" Apperley asked, and watched the hand of the other man still plucking idly at the shirt button.

"I'm willing to go through with that," White said and his voice sounded strained. "I know that I've got to go through with it—with you. But there's something inside me . . . Oh, hell, Apperley! How can I explain it to you? I'm not a snivel-ling pseudo-romantic; I've had to watch my step as a tough, practical guy. I'd tear the guts out of anyone who told me otherwise."

"And you want to tear out the guts of Munroe," Apperley said. "And, damn you, you're content to let Freda tear yours out in fretting for her."

"I've *got* to have her!" White said. "Y'hear me, Apperley—I've got to have her! I don't care what she's done, or how she's done it. Munroe's the one to blame. He turned her mind and took her away from me. He poisoned her affections, and I'll get him for it. But she's not to blame. I can straighten her out. I can love her—make her love me. You've got to listen to me!"

"I *am* listening. So you've got in touch with her? And you didn't tell me—"

Apperley was trying to keep calm. Things were critical. Now, of all times, he could least afford the sudden cracking up of his partner. "Look," he said, "we're likely to be in a jam. There's Kreig and the girl on our hands."

"I put this deal through before Seldon or the girl came on the scene," White answered him. "You can't blame me for not anticipating that."

"But you didn't tell me," Apperley insisted.

"I didn't, by God I didn't. Because I knew that you'd oppose me—that you'd try to talk me out of it. I argued that if I got the thing moving then it would be too late to back out. That when I told you, you'd be forced to let me go through with it, because you couldn't afford to have it otherwise. If I'd known about that damned Seldon and all the trouble he was to bring us, I swear I wouldn't have taken this business on."

"But you embarked upon it when the sky was still clear, before Seldon came barging in?" Apperley asked. "That it, Arthur?"

White's food was untouched, although his companion had been making some pretence of eating. "I've got to go through with it now, Apperley. I shall die without her. This damned woman . . . "

"What did you do exactly?" Apperley demanded and knocked the folded newspaper to the deck. "Let's have it straight now."

"When you sent me to see Griffiths in Paddington . . ." White said. "You remember Griffiths?"

Apperley did, and nodded his head in agreement. The mysterious, outstanding distributor, internationally, of the impeccably forged material that White and White alone could turn out. A back room in a frowsty street off Paddington Square, used as a blind to meet and investigate his contacts. Apperley had been forced to stand before him, to be carefully weighed up and passed. Then White, coming alone on orders, to "inquire for a room," and to give his name in a casual way. The smell of the house had sickened him.

Apperley bisected a chip. "So you spoke to Griffiths about attaining your heart's desire. And you did it confidentially, unknown to me?"

"I made a little bargain with him," White said. "And I *didn't* tell you, Apperley, for the reason I've already explained. But I figured that with the men and the big organisation at his disposal he could help me. He knew the underneath of things; and I realised how much he needed my services."

"Almost as much as 'Big Johnny'," said Apperley, with a taint sneer.

"So—I bargained with him," White went on. "And he agreed. After all, it was a mere nothing to him. His boys soon did the trick. He sent me a letter poste restante to Harlingham, and when I was getting in provisions one day I picked it up."

"But," Apperley cut in, the sneer becoming more pronounced, "I nearly rumbled you then, Arthur my boy. You lied, lied skilfully and fluently, and you got out of it for the time—I'll say that for you. But I think you realised that you couldn't pull that same trick again. Hence the advertisement in the *Mail*, eh? Smart. Damned smart."

"I swear to you," White said, "that this business was well in swing before all this happened with Seldon and the girl.

Griffiths located Munroe and Freda for me. Of all the damned places in the world, they were staying at the Berkeley Court Hotel in London and doing it in luxury. The old con. business. And they get away with it."

Apperley could not resist a cruel dig at his companion. "There *are* other artists in the world besides yourself, my dear White. Munroe's smart, and he knows his lay all right. He doesn't go in for chicken-feed, hence the swell address. Well?"

"I wrote them from Harlingham post office," White said, and his voice was husky with the strain. "Munroe is using an alias, of course. Major John Hanlon, late United States Army. I wrote that letter convincingly, Apperley—damned convincingly. I told them that I was prepared to lose everything if they turned me down or tried anything funny. I mentioned Griffiths as being on my side. I said it was two against many. I think that they saw the point."

Apperley was sarcastic. "And they determined to come running to you to be wiped out?" he queried.

"Not quite that. I took a middle course. I told them that I honestly wanted to talk things out," White replied. "I said that I was willing to let Freda choose between us. That if I could only get an opportunity to talk to them, I hoped to influence Freda. Then if she wanted to come back to me—"

"You'd take Munroe apart if he tried to stop her," Apperley finished for him, and said it brutally. "But how about if she *wasn't* willing to break with him and come back to you?"

White's fingers were still playing with the shirt button. He seemed to have forgotten his meal utterly. The wind lifted at his blond hair as he stared unseeingly into the distance. "I—refused to face that," he said. "I still do. I can't think of life without Freda. She's got to do it. She's got to come back."

"And you're willing to forgo your satisfaction of tearing his damned head off, if only she'll leave him?" Apperley asked in incredulous fashion. "The cussedness of human nature! The unpredictability of it!"

"If I can only come face to face with the two then I can settle it one way or another," White answered him stubbornly. "I've got to get this business out of my . . . I—I shall go mad . . . They knew that, with Griffiths on my side, let alone an anonymous tip-off, as a poetic revenge, to the police, they just couldn't refuse. Munroe knows my mettle, by now. No doubt he thinks, like you, that I'm plain crazy."

"But that craziness is too dangerous for him to overlook," Apperley said. "So it all resolves itself into this—that Munroe and Freda have been forced to agree to meeting you. They realise that you're quite capable, apart from myself and Griffiths and what we might do to them if they side-step you, of going completely off the rails. That you can drag them down, even if it means destroying yourself and me in the process. That you and Griffiths can make life such an utter hell for them that it's best for them to get this issue settled, come what may. Do I interpret things correctly?"

"You do," White answered, fingers twisting at the button. "Now I've told you."

"And when's this meeting to take place?" Apperley wanted to know.

"Tonight. Ten o'clock in the lounge of the Metropole Hotel, at Harlingham. The advertisement that I told Munroe to insert in today's *Mail* agrees to that," White said. And Henry Apperley started in dismay.

"Tonight! And you expect me to help you? Of all the confounded, blasted silly messes you get yourself into! That's the complete idiocy of working with someone who's artistic—"

"But necessarily so," White said with a bitter twist of the lips. "The artistic have their foolishnesses and failings. They're not like other men, but you can't do without 'em. You flatter yourself that you have the practicability, that you wouldn't be such a mutt, but you'd be lost without the artist and his blundering in what you call 'life,' just the same. Hell, I'm not trying to give you a sermon, Apperley."

"There's damn-all time for sermons," Apperley flashed at him. "Can you come out of the clouds sufficiently to think of what's involved? That everything's hanging by a thread just now? That Kreig's on our tail; that Scott is aching to pull my ears off; that a flatfoot by the name of Croft is waiting to pounce on us ashore or here, just as soon as he gets a bit more sure of himself? And you expect me to go through with this craziness—and tonight! I know that you won't and can't set off without me, and I think even you won't argue about that. But—" Apperley paused.

White brought his gaze back from the distant point that had seemed to hold him as he talked. "But—?" he asked. "Come on, Apperley. Give me an answer? What's it to be?"

Apperley sensed rage swelling up within him. "Suppose I say 'no'?"

The nervous fingers of Arthur White left the button and reached swiftly inside the sagging breast of the blue shirt. His wrist felt the smoothness of the edge of his plate as he menaced Apperley with the gun he had placed in readiness. "Not even you are going to stop me. Say 'no,' and as God's my judge I'll put a bullet between your eyes and dump you overboard. Then I'll leave the girl to sink or swim and I'll go on alone. And to hell with Scott, and to hell with this fellow you call Croft. To hell with Griffiths. I'll settle with Munroe and Freda once and for all, come death, come life—I don't care which. If I'm spared, then I'll fight it out alone. But I shan't need to do that, Apperley. You're coming with me."

"Put it away," Apperley said. "I always try to think quickly. You don't need *that* to influence my decision." He put out a hand and gently shoved the nose of the weapon aside. "I suppose that I've got to go with you for the safety of us both. This business is too far advanced to back out of now. Munroe and Freda will be at the Metropole at ten. And we can't leave them hanging fire there. I value my neck, Arthur, just as much as I value not having a bullet in my hide right now. I'm forced to go with you."

He put his hand over the clenched fingers of White and the revolver, so that the gun was lowered to the table. And presently the fingers relaxed. The gleam of subdued excitement was back in White's eyes. He was about to attain his desire.

"But, if you kill me on the spot or I hang later for it," Apperley said more strongly, "I make one condition. We can't leave the girl here."

"I'll . . . meet you in that . . ." White answered him in almost a whisper.

Apperley was again thinking, thinking cleverly and fast. "You've convinced me that we're forced to go through with meeting Freda and Munroe. If, tonight, someone—Croft or Scott—decides to come snooping, they'll have full opportunity for a protracted search, if we aren't here to bluff it out. Then they're bound to find the girl. But it's no crime to leave the boat. So that if they come and find no girl, nor any trace of her, then there's nothing they can do."

White was getting back a little of his natural buoyancy, now that things were going his way. "We're having a quiet evening ashore, eh, Henry? The shock of the poor girl's death drives us to a spot of what they call 'pub-crawling' over here. And there's the hut—"

Once again the almost telepathic planning between them came into play when they were both in frank co-operative mood. Apperley was swift.

"Old Tom Clyde, so they tell me, hadn't chick nor child, Arthur. He kept a leaky boat and worn-out nets in that rotting old hut on the other side of the sandhills. He broke his leg, sold the gear when he decided to make do with his old age pension. And he died a month ago. No one's been interested in the place since, any more than they were interested in it while he was alive. He was cranky and quarrelsome, wanted to be left alone. The place is deserted."

"Trust you to find out about it and mark it down as holding future possibilities," White said.

"Thank God that these parts are deserted," Apperley went on quickly as his thoughts raced. "We'll get the girl in the boat beneath a tarpaulin, gagged. When we beach she'll have to have her legs untied. It's too early for the tide for us to get into Castleton with her, by the cave."

"Suits me," White said. "We leave her there, and risk it."

"There'll be little *to* risk. I tell you that not even courting couples ever go there. And there's a padlock and a hasp on the door."

White looked at him. "How about a key? Damn! are trifles going to upset things now we've started?"

Apperley laughed. "This padlock I speak of. It's rusted inside. It holds, but you can spring it with a tug of the fingers. When you snap it to again it looks right.

"And put that rod back in your pocket," he said evenly. "And Arthur—don't ever try it again. You hear me? I may not always be in . . . a cleft stick."

There was hidden menace in the words. Arthur White looked at him and seemed about to speak, but thought better of it. He poked distastefully at the congealing food on his plate.

"Not hungry?" Apperley said. "We'll have to move—the time's getting on. For God's sake get washed and into something decent. I'll clear away."

"Bring my stuff up here," White said. "The girl—"

"Right." Apperley got up, started to clear the table. White moved away.

The breeze was dropping now, the sun getting low. There were banked clouds in the west. Apperley scraped a plate over the side and thought savagely of the future.

A minor irritation, but it was there, amid the turmoil of greater business. The girl's tray could wait now. When they got back from this damned expedition White would no doubt clear it away.

Apperley went down into the cabin, where the girl sat patiently, hopelessly. But her eyes were bright with defiance. She ignored a forced pleasantry by her cousin and turned her back on him as he went about the task of opening drawers and collecting what White needed. "Time for you in a minute or two," Apperley thought, and left her with his arms full.

He washed up and put crockery and utensils away, while White stripped off the torn shirt and went to work with a bucket and soap. Apperley hung the dishcloth across two nails in a corner of the galley and dried his hands before re-suming the checked sports coat. White had prepared himself quickly.

He looked much better now. The blond hair was brushed down smoothly. The tapering fingers were clean. He sported a neat blue suit with a maroon tie. Apperley pitched a ciga-rette-end into the sea and straightened up from his lounging position by the rail.

"Ready? Let's go."

There was a new length of thin cord that he had secured while waiting for his partner, together with a big blue silk handkerchief, now stowed in his pocket. Not only that, but an automatic. Getting it out from a drawer, while the girl had still had her back turned coldly towards him, Apperley had fought down an impulse to go up on deck with it in his hand and try conclusions with White there and then. But the same careful, lightning thought that had been his over the table on deck came to influence his judgment again. Even if he put White out of the way, there was still Griffiths and Kreig. Still Freda and Ed Munroe waiting at the Metropole Hotel, in Harlingham. If they were *not* met—

Therefore the gun had been slipped into his hip pocket. Well he knew that White would also pocket his own weapon when he changed into the smart blue suit. Well, let him. Be-fore this fateful night was out they might both need the help of not one but two loaded messengers of destruction.

And Apperley had already proved, in that strained con-versation between himself and his crooked partner, that both could be trusted with a gun against each other. Fear, instead of bullets, brought about respect and trust. And it would be so to the end.

The cracked tarpaulin lay ready in the bottom of the boat, alongside. Apperley led the way down into the cabin, and the girl, who had been standing with her back to the steps, sunk in deep and bitter thought, spun round to meet them. There was, she felt, something different afoot. This was no meal-time routine, although the tray had not yet been removed.

Apperley's actions in collecting clothing and other miscellanea from the cabin drawers had convinced her of that.

And they had no time to be subtle now. Apperley said directly: "Listen, Miss Castleton, you're coming with us and you're coming quietly."

She clenched her small fists. "You're optimists. I shall yell my head off."

"Not with this around your mouth you won't," Apperley answered, producing the silk handkerchief.

She looked at him contemptuously. "And the usual cords, too, I see. What then?"

"We're taking you for a trip," Apperley said, now as always spokesman for the pair of them. "Sorry, but this is urgent business and we can't delay it. I'd advise you not to resist."

She clung at a desperate straw. "Suppose I give you my word to be quiet?" But Apperley shook his head.

"I wouldn't take it, Miss Castleton. You proved to our friend White, this afternoon, what you can do in the way of trying to stage a getaway. Oblige me by turning around and putting your hands behind you."

For a moment it seemed that she might yet put up a fight, but then she saw how useless resistance was. She was trembling with a stark, seething, inward rage; but she was too contemptuous of these men to break down and show weakness. The look she gave them spoke volumes of hatred. Yet it held power. Power in passive resistance.

Marjorie Castleton felt the cord whip over her wrists, felt it pulled tight. She felt again the cruel biting in of it over her shoulders, through her thin frock and on the skin of her arms. Yet her teeth were digging into her lower lip as they worked. She would not cry out.

But they left her legs free. Apperley folded the gag and tied it expertly in position. Then he put an arm around her and guided her up the cabin steps with White behind so that he might assist her.

If she had thought that there might be great difficulty in getting her over the side and into the boat, she was mistaken.

James Corbett

Two men skilled in such lifting and a weak, helpless girl . . . . She was forced down into the bottom of the dinghy and the tarpaulin drawn over her.

And then, a little later, she was lifted cleanly ashore in the waning evening light. The place seemed to be utterly deserted. Between them the two men hurried her some distance over tufts of coarse grass, stones, sand. She felt that the rough ground was rising a little beneath her dragging feet. The darkness of the decaying little hut came up to greet her as she was thrust inside and on to a pile of old sacking in a corner. It enveloped her in terror.

Then Apperley dragged to the creaking door, thumped in the rusty padlock; and she was alone.

CHAPTER XI

THE MAN WITH THE SCAR

AT MUCH THE SAME TIME that Detective-Inspector Croft was conducting interviews with Tony Scott and the suave Henry Apperley at the red-brick Harlingham Police Headquarters, Scotland Yard itself was at work in Croft's absence.

It was necessary for such an arrangement to be carried out. Focal point of the case of the murdered unknown at Castleton House was Harlingham and district. Therefore Croft, as having been called upon to assist the Chief Constable of Harlingham, must needs make it the place from which he could direct operations. And his colleagues in London, collaborating with him, were just as able to undertake routine inquiry work as he was. In fact, he couldn't be in two places at once.

In a very handsome service-flat in Kensington, "Big Johnny" Kreig read his morning newspaper over his breakfast and started to think rapidly. The British Press, unless he got a move on, might prove to be his undoing.

All the dailies carried what the Sunday newspapers had been too early to secure—the story of the murder at Castleton House and the "fatality" that had occurred to Marjorie Castleton. Here was a Monday-morning shock for Kreig.

The last he had personally heard of or from Seldon was when the latter had telephoned him hurriedly on Saturday night to the effect that he had located Apperley coming out from the house he had been deputed to watch in Paddington. Seldon had telephoned from Victoria Station, whither he had followed Apperley. And, as Apperley himself had guessed, Seldon had taken advantage of the crowds and bustle in that congested place to attach himself to Apperley like an unseen limpet.

Seldon had slipped right behind him, in fact, when Apperley had taken his ticket to Harlingham. He had let the quarry move away and then had purchased a similar ticket himself, at the same time inquiring about the next train. With ten minutes to spare, he had been prompt in ringing up his boss, Kreig—alias Christopher Medway, wealthy London visitor from Maine, U.S.A. Kreig had rasped: "Keep on to him," into the telephone, and had hung up, jubilant that at last he seemed to be within striking distance of his two enemies—Apperley and White.

The powerful Griffiths, even if he would not risk trouble in carrying the war to Kreig, would not stand for any on his own doorstep, as it were. It would not only have been dangerous, but downright foolish for Kreig and his lone assistant, Seldon, to attempt to start anything in Paddington or anywhere near it. Two men against a mob. Kreig was too wary for that.

But he also sensed that Griffiths would "keep in his own backyard." Kreig was aware that, in England, he filled very much the same role as he himself did in the States—he was a big and careful distributor of high-class "slush", *i.e.* the products of brilliant forgery. As such, he kept to the distributive side. So long as his associates gave him a square deal, kept their mouths shut and themselves out of danger and brought him the goods regularly, Griffiths stayed out of their private affairs. He safeguarded himself from interference— and surely any sort of an attack on Apperley and White *through* Griffiths would mean interference—and he paid promptly and liberally in genuine hard cash that was not "hot."

Therefore, if Kreig wished to strike at Apperley and White, especially as he only had one henchman in England to assist him in the doing of it, he must try to do the striking well away from Griffiths altogether.

Seldon was all right for what Kreig had hired him for, quite a long time ago. He was a good slugger, a personal bodyguard, someone to do the dirty work and the errands. But he left the thinking to his boss, because he was a bonehead himself. Proof of that had been his question to Kreig over the telephone. "Just whereabouts in this damned country will this place Harlingham be?" And Kreig had withered him with brief invective. "Work it out for yourself, blast you," he had said. "You're dealing with the southern region of the railways. Surrey, Sussex, Kent . . . An' how much have you paid for that ticket? You've been long enough in this country to be hep to its currency by now. You pay a two-bit fare an' then wonder where you're going . . . "

And so on. And now Seldon was dead.

When he had not put in an expected appearance on Sunday, "Mr. Christopher Medway" had made it his business to find out just where Harlingham was. An A.B.C. railway guide told him that, easily enough. But he had resisted an impulse to go chasing after Seldon. Yet why didn't the damn' fool get in touch with him somehow?

Kreig decided to wait, and spent anxious hours in doing so. The drama at Castleton—the murder of Seldon, the appearance and departure of Detective-Inspector Croft, and the ingenious "snatch" of Marjorie Castleton—was played out while he dallied time throughout that Sunday that seemed to him to be an eternity. In one thing he was hopelessly handicapped. He had chosen to come to England and pursue his implacable pursuit of revenge on the two men he classified as rats, and he had come with only one trusted helper, Seldon. There were good reasons why it was so. Not only expense, but safety. He could rely on no one like the man who had now been bumped off on his behalf. Where two of them might get by, when it came to evading the law and the British underworld, more than that might make things decidedly uncomfortable.

With men at his command, Kreig might have got busy before now. He could have had Seldon reinforced, might have sent other helpers to find out what had happened. But he was alone and a stranger in a strange land. So he waited, and with the advent of Monday morning and the newspapers realised that he had waited too long.

News of the killing came to him as a shock that confirmed his worst fears. Unless the laws of probability were wrenched around unbelievably it meant that either Apperley or White, or both, were responsible for Seldon's death; might, indeed, be the actual killers. How else could he think?

And that connected them up with Castleton House, which meant that he, Kreig, knew where the precious pair might be found. At Castleton House or somewhere very near by.

The death of the trusting though not sparklingly intelligent Seldon was the last straw for Kreig. It fed the fire of a bitter hatred until it roared up within him. The cool, unashamed, blatant, walking-out on him by White and Apperley had been sufficient to make him come all the way from America to get even with them, and his vengeance had not cooled with the delay he had experienced in settling things up there and leaving. That delay had enabled Apperley and White to dig in with the late Colonel Castleton at the old house. Weeks had gone by; they had breathed in relief at thoughts that Kreig had stayed put. But, unlike them, he had been unable to "light out" straight away. In the interim he had nursed his feelings for them. And now, with Seldon's death, those feelings were increased tenfold. He was determined, more than ever, to get them.

Kreig crumpled the newspaper and flung it from him as savagely as though he were crumpling up his joint enemies. Then he started to think, and think deeply. Seldon's murder meant that there was a lot more to it than just going down to Harlingham in Sussex, finding White and Apperley by what he judged might now be a fairly easy effort, and waiting his chance to eliminate them both in safety. There were ways and means of doing that—alone. It was not like London, with all its hazards. He might catch them afoot, for instance, and be in a car himself; might mow them down from behind with an automatic and be away. Kreig was skilled enough in such matters.

The difficulty lay in preserving himself now that Seldon had "got his"; and not only preserving himself from Apperley and White who might have ideas of striking first, or even from Griffiths, but from the law.

This was where things became involved. "Big Johnny" Kreig cursed the fact that he had been too clever.

Three master-blocks for five-hundred dollar bill reproductions had come Kreig's way just before he left America. Their acquisition at great trouble and expense had caused part of the delay he had experienced in following on to England. Normally Kreig did not deal in the actual work of forgery—he took it from others and paid for it. But the master-blocks, such marvels of cunning workmanship, were well worth having. He could bargain, gain power and money, from employing them in the hands of others while still retaining their ownership. It was clever of him to snap them up.

It was also clever of him to trust neither associates nor apparent places of safe-keeping in the States, but to bring them along with him, carefully packed in the false bottom of a cabin trunk. And cleverer still to make Seldon the custodian of them. In all things "Big Johnny" thought of himself first and others afterwards. He played for safety, when he engaged his luxurious Kensington service flat, by having Seldon keep them in his own place. In the event of any possible trouble by the police or anyone else, a break-in and a search, the blocks would be safe.

If Kreig were ever found out, then they would come to Kreig. And Kreig would save his own hide. It by some mischance the law connected him with Seldon and investigated him first, then Seldon might well take the rap. And he was not intelligent enough to be anything but loyal to Johnny. That was how Kreig had arranged it.

But now Seldon was murdered, and the newspapers were enjoying themselves. They had Seldon's picture on their front pages, by police request. The gist of it was: "To hotels, boarding-houses, doss-houses, bed-and-breakfast dives: if you know this unidentified man, have accommodated him, ring Whitehall 1212." Like as not, the police were combing out such places in London without sitting back to wait for response. Sooner or later, someone would come forward to identify Seldon. In this case it would be an old woman.

Then would follow a routine search of Seldon's effects. The master-blocks would come to light and, in addition, enough evidence to infallibly ensure the picking up of "Big Johnny" Kreig inside of twenty-four hours. With the police in on things, he would be finished.

One factor alone would damn Kreig, if nothing else. He had a scarred face, impossible to hide. Years ago, in Chicago, in his more humble days, he had been embroiled in a gang fight and had been "carved." No hair would grow on the ugly white serpent that writhed its way from forehead and eyebrow down to his chin on the left-hand side of his fleshy face. He had even thought of the theatricality of disguise but had put it aside as being cumbersome and impracticable. Yet it marked him down as infallibly as though he had had "Johnny Kreig" stamped all over him. Up till now, both at home and abroad, he had managed to keep out of the hands of the police and so clear of all records.

Yet the old woman would know him as a visitor to Seldon at her place. She did not run a hotel, but furnished rooms in Shannon Street, Elephant and Castle—a prudent hide-out for Seldon, or so his boss had deemed. Inquiries for the unidentified would switch from Seldon to Kreig himself. Look out for Scarface. Arrest or detention. Inquiries. The master-blocks. Scotland Yard and the F.B.I. were astute.

How neatly the pieces of the puzzle would fall into place!

But not if Kreig could get in first to kick a few of those pieces to hell. Not only had he to consider his own safety now; he might also be robbed of his insatiable craving to bring down Apperley and White if he didn't move quickly. And bumping them off in a place like Harlingham, and bumping the old woman off in a congested area, were two very different matters. Now, while it was still early and before she got around to talking, he might somehow slip past her and lift the master-blocks to safety.

By nine o'clock Kreig was in a taxi, heading for the Elephant and Castle.

He got out at the corner of Shannon Street and approached the house on foot. Mrs. Bolton answered his knock and stood peering at him on the doorstep: an old, wrinkled woman in a soiled floral-patterned overall, with greasy white hair falling into her bleared eyes. Kreig eyed her in disgust. He'd sometimes wondered if, even in the interests of their safety, it had been such a bright idea, after all, to have Seldon hang out in such a lousy spot.

She had never been given Kreig's name, as an alias or otherwise. She merely knew him as a friend of the lodger who had his own key and whom she had not heard moving around. She had regarded Kreig's scarred face with abhorrence. It was so noticeable to her. She put a pair of steel-rimmed spectacles, by the help of which she had been perusing the morning paper, into her pocket, and didn't give Kreig a chance to talk.

Damnation! he thought and pushed her back into the hallway. "Hell, mother," he said roughly, "I've read it. You'll keep your mouth shut, if you know what's good for you. Have you told anyone?"

"I've not had the chance," she trembled. "But it's terrible an' bad. I never liked him—"

"I'm going up to his room," Kreig said, in a deadly voice. "And you're coming up with me. Behave yourself and I shan't hurt you."

"Look, mister," she said. "I'm seventy-two. Leave me alone and go away. Take 'is key. Here." She dived into the overall-pocket that her spectacles had bulged and brought out an old-fashioned key that Kreig guessed was a duplicate. "I 'ave to clean after 'em," she said. "Go on up yourself."

Dead scared of this big man. Kreig stood six feet three in his socks, and had the massive frame of a bull. Not for nothing had his nickname clung. He wavered, then decided not to argue further. But damn this reception! He had meant to approach her quietly, reasonably. She might have let him in and upstairs more easily then, and he would have had little or nothing to worry about. But it had been plain bad luck that she had already got around to reading the morning paper, early as it was. The mere fact that she had recognised the photograph as being that of William Seldon, her lodger, and that William Seldon was dead, made things awkward for Kreig.

She was now suspicious of his movements, of his motives in coming here at all. Still, he hadn't time to argue. He would scare her into keeping quiet. "See here, now," he said. "I'll only be a minute or two. Make a move outa here or try to raise a shindy that'll bring anyone else—"

"There's no one here but meself," she said in a whisper. "I keeps respectable lodgers an' they're all out at work."

"And there ain't a phone in the house," Kreig said. "Okay, now. Stay there."

He mounted the narrow stairs whereon he knew his way. On the first landing he slipped the key into a worn lock and went inside Seldon's room with agile movements of his great bulk. It was not much to rave about. Rickety furniture; a window that looked out on to a sooty oblong of starved garden, bounded by a low wall. Kreig went over to a tallboy, and a used razor blade rattled in a cheap glass ash-tray on the top as he bent down to pull out the bottom drawer.

Underneath folded garments he came to that which he sought, and even as he hauled out a locked attaché-case heard the front door click.

"Gone for a cop . . . " Kreig told himself malevolently. The situation had become desperate by reason of his misjudging the old woman. But against his desire to have her with him as precaution had been the fact that he had not wanted her to see what he was up to in this room. And he had not really credited her with the courage to slip out like that.

Yet she had found that courage. Kreig thought fast. He had time yet, he told himself. If she *had* gone for a policeman, then surely he would gain a few precious minutes while she found one.

He slammed the attaché-case on the none too clean bed, then realised he could not open it. It was locked, and Seldon had the key . . .

Had had the key, although he was not to know it. The desperate Henry Apperley had grabbed at Seldon's keys after he had struck him down with a revolver butt—grabbed them in a desperate effort to stall for time with the police. Kreig was now faced with an attaché-case that he had selected himself as being a tough proposition to open for anyone opposed to himself and his dead henchman.

And inside it was evidence that could not fail but to ensure to Kreig a long, long sentence.

In his desperation he looked around, saw a poker in the old-fashioned fender before the dead firegrate, and snatched it up. He tried to force the slender point beneath a hasp of one lock and wrench, was defeated and rained down useless blows upon the leather-covered steel of the case in his anger. He looked around for a further makeshift, but there was none. And in that instant his keen ears caught from below the sound of the old woman's panting shuffle, followed by hurrying footsteps. The front door opened, and Kreig stiffened where he stood.

Easy to see what had occurred. He was unlucky. A millionth chance had come off for the old lady inasmuch as she had had only a few yards to go and had found a patrolling constable on his beat, instead of having to range street after street in her distress, looking for one.

Kreig could hear the rumble of his voice; sensed that he was putting a heavy foot on the bottom stair. He determined to run for it somehow. The case must be abandoned. Were he crazy enough to burden himself with it, he could never hope to succeed in a wild dash for safety. If only he had not been such a cunning fool, had looked after this vital evidence himself, or at least have retained a key!

"Big Johnny" was over at the window with its dirty half-curtain in a flash. He pulled back the dusty catch and tugged upwards at the sash in an agony of impatience. But for his strength he might have been lost. The window did not move easily, by reason of disuse. But he got it open and swung his legs over the sill as the footsteps on the stairs became rapid. The constable had not yet gained the frowsty little room before Kreig hung by his hands and dropped to the scrubby garden beneath.

For one hellish moment he thought that he had twisted an ankle in his fall, then scrambled to hands and knees and so to an upright position. Then he was away, nearly crashing one shoulder into a wooden clothes post as he reeled. He was by the wall and turned as the constable leaned out of the window and shouted. Kreig looked the young officer full in the face over the intervening distance. Then he swore violently and reached his hands up with a little spring.

A combination of factors saved him. One was that the wall was low. He could grip the top of it. Another was that, although the constable had sufficient training and mental ability to register a snap description of the face, dress and figure of the escaping man, he did not have the experience and initiative to pursue a direct course in pursuit. That was, to clamber in turn through the window, streak through the garden and get over the wall.

His split-second decision was, however, a natural one. He would have more chance of catching the fugitive, he told himself, if he hurried out of the house and got around to the back of it. He argued that he would be speedier than the other, getting over the obstacle he had chosen to negotiate. He could run where the other was doing, as it were, a crawling struggle, up and over. And no doubt, in the ordinary course of events, the officer would have been dead right.

But in this instance he was dead wrong, through no fault of his own. He was downstairs and scrabbling to open the front door before the old woman could make him listen to her frantic words. And then he realised that this was a street of close-set houses; that there was no easy way round to the back of them. That it meant going right to the end of the street and doubling around into another to get to the rear of the premises. He damned these decaying terrace houses and set off at a run. Perhaps he might yet pick up the man who was negotiating the wall, might at the least—if he had managed to get over—see him somewhere ahead.

He might even be lucky enough to barge into him, if the other were fool enough to run in the direction of the end of the street that the constable must enter.

But the man had not bargained for the length of the squalid blocks of property. He had at least three hundred yards to go in each direction—up one street and down the next. And before he had accomplished one of those parallel distances at top speed, with the old woman gasping far to the rear, "Big Johnny" Kreig had got over the wall.

Then, again, luck came to him in full measure—the luck that ebbed and flowed during his remarkable and risky career. He turned to the right, whereas if he had turned left and gone in the wrong direction he must inevitably have made contact with the constable running towards him. The only other immediate occupants of the street seemed to be a child on a tricycle pedalling solemnly along the opposite pavement and a milkman who stood near by, leaning against a house-front and making an entry in his round book. And a couple of yards from where the man stood, Kreig saw an intersecting street—a short thoroughfare that was like the upright of a rough T. The house nearly opposite the street, from the wall of which he had just dropped, was, as it were, on the crossbar of that T.

Kreig saw the surprised eyes of the man, as he looked up at sound of the fugitive. Before he could open his mouth to speak, however, Kreig was across the road and openly running up the short street that lay before him. Here he found another long thoroughfare of terraced houses, similar to the one around the corner of which the constable was now frantically turning. To the right again, and Kreig got back his breath in utter thankfulness at sight of a main road.

Although he had been to Shannon Street more than once, he was not familiar with the locality. It was sheer damned good luck, he told himself, that he should be where he was now. And there was a bus. A bus heading for a stop a couple of yards away. "Big Johnny" broke again into a shambling trot, swung himself aboard as the vehicle slowed down to receive the only passenger waiting for it. As it picked up speed again Kreig lurched upstairs, found a rear seat and flattened himself back against it. He was safe, but for how long?

The policeman would question the milkman, who had been too surprised, too slow, to either speak or try to stop the man who had appeared so suddenly before him as he looked up from his book. At the other end of the intersecting street, or at the main road if the constable had sense to turn in that direction, the trail would be temporarily lost. The constable would summon assistance, go back to the house in Shannon Street. The attaché-case would be seized, opened at the nearest police-station, and the contents of the case would no doubt be soon recognised for what they were. They would be forwarded, like as not, to Scotland Yard, together with a report and a description of the man who had tried to steal them. That description would be a very good one.

Not only would it be furnished by the old lady—who knew him by no name or address at all—and by the astounded milkman. That description would also emanate from the trained, retentive mind of a police officer. That in itself might be enough, without the scar that singled him out so damningly from other men.

Yet Kreig was thankful for one thing. All that would give him time. He was one of London's millions, but he knew where he was going. And he could think as fast as those who would now be on his trail.

Back to his service flat, where the rent was paid until the month end and he might come and go as he pleased. Kreig got off the bus after taking a threepenny ride, because he knew that he must—otherwise he would be taken well out of his way. He travelled back to Kensington by Underground.

What price the newspapers again? There was not one solitary thing that might lead the police of London to believe that Kensington was, or had been, his habitat. Scotland Yard would have to begin the painful process of looking for the needle in the haystack. And the metropolis was a hell of a big haystack. It occurred to Kreig that if he could keep cool and level-headed he might find ample time to get out of this jam. But he couldn't stay in London, that much was certain.

London was where the search would be intensive. However unpromising the start of that search, and however handicapped Scotland Yard might be in making it, still—Scotland Yard was clever, there was no mistaking that. For Kreig to stay in the capital might be asking to be picked up.

And—he almost ground his teeth as he thought of that which came so searingly to his mind—he had a score to settle. By God he had!

Now he knew that it must be settled in Harlingham. Two ideas went together in his mind with an obvious ease. Get out of London, get into Harlingham. If he must go somewhere then he'd go where he had a chance of somehow getting on to those two rats, Apperley and White.

And then . . . "Big Johnny" Kreig set his teeth again. Then . . . it would be *his* turn; and this time there should be no slip-up. He would see the job through himself.

Damn that old lady in the opposite seat who was staring at his scarred face with such sweet compassion! Kreig could sit no longer. He went from his seat to stand by several straphangers near the doors of the Underground train compartment, although there were still several stations to go. He changed trains and stood again, although he might have found a seat. And, throughout, his mind was seething. Thank God that Scotland Yard had nothing on him in the past!

Plans raced through his brain. He had plenty of ready money—enough to see him through any eventuality. His settlement with Apperley and White must be quick—damned quick—lest he find ways and means of getting out of the country and back to America closed against by the police who were merely looking for a man of his description, now known to be implicated in forgery. Kreig got to his flat, locked the door, and sank down thankfully on a settee.

For a minute or so he sat there, then went over to a handsome cocktail wagon, opened it and mixed himself a stiff drink. He lit a long Panatella to soothe his nerves, gulped off the highball and mixed himself another. He was tired, desperately tired by his recent adventure.

But he couldn't afford to let up, although he must eat. He had time—he knew, he had worked that much out. But not too much time. He picked up the telephone and got through to the hall porter. Sandwiches and bottled beer.

Kreig went into his ornate bedroom and commenced to pack. The young porter brought him his order from a nearby restaurant and "Big Johnny" tipped him lavishly—as always. He wolfed down the food, eyes ever and again flicking to the handsome gold watch on his wrist.

Then he brushed crumbs from his lap and went back to the big suitcase in which he was trying to pack as much as might see him through the job in hand. He had arrived with three such big pigskin affairs, plus a cabin trunk, but manifestly he must now make do with one. He had thought, for a start, of leaving all luggage behind, but prudence went against such a course. He might not be able to get back to the flat. And such was his vanity, as well as his careful planning, that he told himself he must have some sort of a kit with which to make a getaway.

And once he had accomplished that getaway—after he had settled with White and Apperley—he swore by all his crooked gods that he would get back to the States and stay there. "Big Johnny" yearned for his home territory, for plenty of men at his bidding, for facilities that seemed to be totally lacking in this strange, battling country that they called England.

He kept telling himself that there was still that one very good point in his favour: the police didn't know where to begin looking for him in the vast warren of London. They didn't know his name or who he might be, where he came from, where he might be bound. They only knew that he was an American, obvious from his accent that even the old woman of Shannon Street must have placed correctly; that he was dressed in such and such a way; that he was roughly of such and such a height and build; that he had a scar on the left side of his face. The description might have fitted hundreds of men in the metropolis's huge floating population. And the beauty of it was that the police could not possibly know where any one of those men could be found.

Kreig would get out of London. That area of bafflement that Scotland Yard would encounter—although with its brilliant organisation and resources it would not be baffled for long—would then be extended to the whole country. True, the Metropolitan Police might get around, sooner or later, to the fact that their man might have left the capital; that he was important and astute enough, from the nature of the evidence he had forcedly left behind, to probably indulge in flight from the city. But even so, Kreig told himself, there was absolutely nothing to warrant the Yard drawing a possible inference: that the unknown man with a scar was in any way linked up with the Castleton affair. There was nothing to start them thinking in the direction of Harlingham, Sussex.

Therefore "Big Johnny" slammed down the lid of the pigskin suitcase and locked it. There was no sense in avoiding the porter. If the Yard by some miracle got on to his track as being the tenant of this luxurious service flat that Kreig was unregretfully leaving, then they would pick up his trail soon enough, without that obliging servant. Kreig got through to the man again and asked him to get a taxi. Then he went to a neat wall safe and took out a thick wad of notes. Genuine stuff that should see him through, together with a perfectly good passport.

But he refrained from telling the driver his destination—Victoria Station—in the presence of the porter. To the latter, as he pressed upon him a final crackling tip, he said that he was going away for a day or two, but would be back. Probably by Wednesday night. At the back of Kreig's mind was a rough idea that such a statement might help a little. If the cops *did* get around to this block of flats, then they might waste time waiting for him to come back in a mere couple of days, after the porter had obligingly spilled his information.

Information as to his return, but not where he was going by taxi. Kreig told the driver where to go, once they were clear of the pavement. In spite of the summer weather, he had donned an expensive cream mackintosh, lightweight and belted. It gave him some sort of excuse for hiding as much of his scarred face as possible. "Damn everybody!" he thought. "I can wear this damned thing in the sunshine if I want to. an' I can turn the blasted collar up if I want to. Don't they say it's a free country over here?"

Better, he thought, as he bought his ticket for Harlingham, to be deemed eccentric in the wearing of a mackintosh when all others were carrying them over their arms or had come without altogether, than to let everyone in the hurrying throng of the station see the scar. Before this, he had not troubled to hide it much, refusing to be over-embarrassed. But that was before the police had been forced to take an interest in him.

Victoria Station might be a danger-point, he thought nervously. Police might concentrate on exits from London, perhaps on the assumption that if the man with the scarred face knew he was wanted he might be tempted to fly the capital as soon as possible. So "Big Johnny" kept the collar of the cream-coloured mackintosh well up.

And it didn't look *too* out of place on the station. After all, he was a traveller; and travellers very often wore raincoats in sunny weather, to save themselves the labour of carrying such garments. Kreig went about finding his train in his own way, going from direction hoard to direction board rather than making inquiry. Then he spotted what he was looking for—time and platform number, and made his way to the barrier.

He told himself that all he had to do now, as there had seemed to be no notice given him of having to change anywhere on the journey, was to sit back and watch the stations. When he caught sight of a platform sign that said "Harlingham" he would get out. In fact, as he realised, there was no need even for that. His destination, the well-known but not yet over-run seaside resort, was terminus for the train.

It carried him mile by mile nearer his revenge. So much had happened to him now—Seldon's death and his own narrow escape from the law—that, if in the past there had been any possible question of him giving up and forgoing that revenge, now he was more implacable than ever. In the corner of a first-class carriage that he had managed to secure to himself, "Big Johnny" Kreig smoked another Panatella and brooded.

Handicapped as he was by lack of exact knowledge of the movements of the hated White and Apperley, he was yet trying to plan the way ahead. One question that arose was that of accommodation when he reached Harlingham.

Several factors influenced his judgment in this. Once more there came to his mind repetition of the fact that the police couldn't connect him with Harlingham merely in his capacity of the unknown man who had scaled the wall of the house in Shannon Street, London. And if, by some miracle, they did get around to thinking in the direction of Harlingham, then he would surely be safer in the last place they might think of looking for him—the biggest hotel in the town. Kreig might yet find advantages in lurking behind a façade of really high-class respectability.

There was, too, of course, the natural inclination that he had always fallen for—luxury. All right.

He liked the clean look of Harlingham Station, took appreciative lungsful of its bracing air as he came out into the station yard. "Taxi!" he said; and, as he put his case aboard and climbed in, "Say, what's the best hotel in this place?"

The "Metropole," the cabby assured him. And Kreig settled back and said: "Okay. Take me there."

The imposing hotel appealed to him as he paid off the driver and had his suitcase carried in by an alert page. At the reception desk, "Big Johnny" Kreig was ready with yet another alias—a new one this time. He must have had Connecticut in his subconscious mind, as a good American, for he signed the hotel register as "James Hartford, New York."

The page marched before him with the case. The pair stood by the lift gates, waiting. Kreig idly glanced about the big vestibule.

And he saw, coming arm in arm through the revolving entrance doors, a couple whom he instantly recognised—but almost the very last persons in the world he expected to see—as Freda White and Ed Munroe.

Impossible *not* to recognise them. He had been too familiar with them on the American scene in the past. Kreig turned his head quickly, thankful again for the thrust of the upturned mackintosh collar. Then the lift arrived and he stepped into it quickly.

He was confident that they had not spotted him. As he was swept upwards he began to think more furiously than ever. Here was a new card that had been dealt unexpectedly. Perhaps an ace, since it seemed to point to White and Apperley. Where Freda and Munroe were—in Harlingham, of all places—there White and his crony might be expected to forgather. And . . . "Big Johnny" Kreig would be there also.

Unexpectedly so. If, as he could only surmise, there were some sort of a meeting afoot—otherwise why should Freda and Munroe be in Harlingham at all?—between White and Apperley and the man and woman who were engaged in running one of the safest and sweetest confidence rackets in the country, then "Big Johnny" would make it his business to be in at that meeting.

Yet another Panatella, unlit, was between his fingers as he stood in his room at the "Metropole"—alone. Under stress of his murderous thoughts the long brown cylinder snapped, was crumbled to pieces. Kreig threw it away from him.

What he must do was obvious. He must keep Freda White and Ed Munroe under observation; must follow them without being seen. Kreig fancied he could do that. He had the advantage of their not knowing of his presence in Harlingham, and that went a long way. Sooner or later they must lead him to the two men he sought.

And then—he would strike, and strike to kill . . .

CHAPTER XII

RECOGNITION

IT WAS NOT EASY for Tony Scott to try to relax throughout the dragging Monday afternoon, once he had got through lunch at the "George."

Croft had been kindness itself, knowing as he did the state of Scott's feelings towards the girl he had parted from so formally. It had become evident to the hard-bitten Inspector that there was more than just ordinary friendship between them, but pride and mistaken motive had decidedly come between them. Now, it seemed it was too late.

If Scott had only dimly guessed the fate that had befallen Marjorie Castleton, what might he not have done to retain his place by her side at the old house! But she, by reason of excess of mistaken feeling, had as good as sent him away. And *his* feelings had prompted him to go.

Any other girl he might have forgotten in time, even though she too might have met the "tragic death," news of which had caused Scott to mentally reel. But not Marjorie. Their new-found love had been an implicit one, not even mentioned between them.

Detective-Inspector Croft had been quick to realise as much, even as early on as in the small hours of Sunday morning, just after the murder, when the girl had retired to her room and he had had his long conversation with Scott. How remote and far away *that* seemed to be!

Now that it seemed that the girl had met a terrible fate, the groping, unexpressed, shy love of Tony Scott for her had blossomed fiercely, although he had still kept it to himself.

And he was suffering thereby. Even the sympathetic Croft was not to know the depth of such mental anguish.

The Inspector's last interview with Scott that morning, immediately before the suave Apperley had called at Harlingham Police Headquarters, had robbed the young man of the final vestige of hope. She had been a swimmer, but the time had long ago passed for realisation of the fact that, if the best of swimmers had not turned up by then, she would not be turning up at all. The coastguard search had become so desultory by now that it had practically been called off. If the body of the girl was not to be found fairly recently after the "fatality" then it seemed a fair supposition that it might not be found in the future. Or, if it were—maybe out in mid-Channel, for instance, although that seemed a slender chance—it might be a comparatively long time after.

So that Scott was despairing. It seemed utterly useless to go on longer, hoping against hope. If truth were told, there was a good reason why he had not gone back to London before now, instead of putting through a trunk-call and urging upon his employers the advisability of letting him stay on at Harlingham for a few more days. Not only was it that he might be available if some further opportunity were presented him of negotiating for Castleton House. He was also praying desperately, even at that late stage, that Marjorie Castleton might yet be found somewhere. Discovered perhaps exhausted and injured at some remote spot on or along the shore, but nevertheless found.

The odds against that miracle had grown longer and longer as the time had passed. And if it had ever faintly entered Tony Scott's mind that all was "not on the up and up"—that it might *not* have been "drowned by accident"—then there were reasons to militate against such half-formed suspicions. Principal of these was that he knew Detective-Inspector Croft of Scotland Yard to be astute, naturally suspicious, zealous, conscientious. And Croft had been able to do nothing. What was good enough for the Inspector might, then, be presumed to be certainly good enough for Scott.

Scott had had a minor brush with Apperley twice, now. Once in that ghastly period at Castleton House when he had rushed back to the place following news that the headstrong girl might have met with some accident in the storm, and once, the next morning, that was now today. His bitter stiffness towards Apperley, outside Croft's office, might obviously be interpreted as not only suspicion of Apperley's movements and motives but—more probably—resentment against him, in that Apperley had not acted even more vigorously in trying to prevent Marjorie Castleton from going to her supposed "death."

If those suspicions had been couched in a different direction—that there might have been deliberate foul play in connection with the girl's disappearance—then Scott would have thrown all discretion to the winds and would have made it his business to investigate the houseboat long before now.

As it was, he could do nothing. Croft could do nothing. Apperley had taken good care to put in an early appearance and Croft knew only too well just how far the law allowed him to go. Since the interview with Apperley, coupled with the finding of the smashed motor-boat, any latent suspicions that the Inspector might have had about Apperley and White seemed to be completely unreasonable.

Croft had been genuinely frank in his conversation with Apperley. Most decidedly was he in the hands of the Chief Constable and the coroner of Harlingham, for all the latitude allowed him.

Therefore he could leave the dying search to the coastguards, let Apperley go as he pleased for the time, and concentrate on the job that he had come to Harlingham to undertake. He must find out who had killed the yet unidentified man just after midnight on Saturday, at Castleton House. That was a little item that Scott and others were inclined to overlook in their excitement over the missing girl and the news of her supposed death by drowning. Understandable, perhaps, but there it was.

The killing at Castleton House was primary to Croft of the Yard. Unless the "death" of Marjorie Castleton could be proved to have a practical and distinct bearing on a solution of the case, then the killing came first and Croft was bound to concentrate all his energy and powers upon it. So it was that he stayed on at Harlingham Police Headquarters and did his best to get on with the job. And there was little enough he could do.

While awaiting results of the parallel inquiries being made by his colleagues in London, he could only indulge in local inquiries as far as possible in Harlingham. But to those inquiries he brought all the best that was in him. That meant that he could devote little or no time to Tony Scott. He was willing to keep him posted with news, as far as lay in his own discretion, but there was nothing on which he could usefully employ him, in an unofficial capacity. Scott must kick his heels, must try to possess himself in patience for any possible news of the girl he now realised he loved more than anything else in life.

Otherwise, he would be merely in Croft's way, and he had sense enough to realise that without being told. The Inspector had said: "Drop in again, my son, this afternoon and I'll keep you posted." And Scott had gone away dejectedly, but in obedience.

At half-past four he could stand it no longer, and again sought Croft in the temporary office that had been granted him in the red-brick building in Marine Drive. In compassion, the bluff Inspector realised that he could not refuse Scott. And, anyway, he was breaking for a cup of tea and might as well share it with the young man he had come to like so much. So he came out of his office and clapped Scott on the shoulder, and as he did so realised that it might be just as well that he *had* put in a second appearance. No harm in dropping a hint or two of news that had recently been flashed to him over the teleprinter from the Metropolitan Police Headquarters at Scotland Yard. It had to do with the murder at Castleton House, and Castleton House meant, among other people, the poor girl whom Scott was eating his heart out or.

"Let's find a nice quiet little café somewhere or other, away from the holidaymakers," Croft suggested. "I'm darned sure that, like myself, you can do with some tea."

"Suits me," Scott said, trying to smile. "But I'm rather a stranger to the place."

"I think I have a little advantage over you there," Croft said. "Remember that I was born and bred in these parts and that I've been in them quite a few times since then. This way."

He led Scott out into the coolness of Marine Drive, and turned away from the direction of "the front." They walked in silence, Scott busy with gloomy thoughts. He was telling himself that if the miracle *had* been accomplished and that some news, however slight, had come to hand about the actual finding of Marjorie Castleton, then Croft would have told him at once. That much seemed to be obvious.

"The Misses Radley," Croft said with an attempt to cheer him up, "keep an olde worlde tea shoppe affair in Clifton Road. They've had it since I was a lad and I've always patronised them. They do you a damned good sardine-on-toast, if you care for that sort of thing."

"It'll suit me," Scott said, glad of the delicacy exhibited by the Inspector in retraining from mentioning the girl and any sympathy he might have felt for Scott because of that. It had already been expressed that morning, and further reference to the unhappy affair seemed to be now out of place. "I'm not too hungry, but—"

"But we can talk," Croft answered as they went around a corner. "Cross over here."

He opened the lace-curtained door of a quiet little restaurant and they went inside. The room was fairly large and there was a good sprinkling of customers, yet the atmosphere was one of peace and seclusion. Croft said: "Damn' good. There's my favourite table in the window-recess," and made a bee-line for it, Scott following on dutifully.

The elder of the Misses Radley spotted the presence of one of her favourites who, however, put in but rare appearances, and came over to their table at once. "Why, Inspector, how nice to see you again!"

"You're looking younger than ever." Croft smiled at her. "This is my friend, Mr. Scott of London. I've been telling him how nicely you look after me here."

Croft looked across at his companion. "Did you say that you'll try the sardines? Good!"

"My sister's out," Miss Radley said. "She'd have liked a word with you. Your order won't be long. I'll see to the toast myself."

"A good old warrior," Croft said reflectively, as she moved away. "Well, Mr. Scott?"

"My friends call me Tony," Scott answered in a valiant attempt to appear cheerful.

"You honour me—Tony. I'm glad that you're still keeping up that chin of yours."

Scott laughed a little feebly. "Don't think that I'm a fat-headed hero, Inspector."

And you're doing your best to keep off the subject of poor Marjorie Castleton, Croft thought. Good for you.

His stubby fingers beat a tattoo on the table cover. A difficult situation, with conversation not easy to maintain. "Tony," eh? Yes, it fitted well with Scott's frank, youthful appearance. There was no denying that he liked the fellow enormously. And they seemed to work well together.

"Look—Tony," he said. "I know that I can rely on you to keep this under your hat. It's really official, but—hang it all—perhaps I'm just trying to find something to talk about. There is a little something I can tell you."

Scott had put out a hand to play idly with the menu in its neat holder and suddenly his fingers began to almost tremble. He seemed about to speak, then thought better of it.

"Nothing to do with that poor kid, Marjorie Castleton," Croft said gently.

Scott did not reply. He put the holder straight and ran a finger around the collar of his white shirt. "I appreciate your confidence and co-operation, Inspector. You've got a line on the killing at Castleton House—is that it?"

"I don't know." Croft was guarded. "But it certainly looks as though *something's* breaking, at last."

Their tea arrived, and Croft eyed it with pleasure. Clearly sardines-on-toast, as served by the Misses Radley, was his favourite tea-time dish. Scott tried to humour him by tackling the contents of the plate laid before him.

He was patient for Croft to begin what he had to tell him, and Croft talked as he ate. He told Scott about as much as he knew himself of the mysterious affray in Shannon Street, London.

Scott listened in absorbed fashion. This was news, red-hot news that interested him keenly. He put in a swift question now and again and grasped the facts intelligently and well. Croft stirred his second cup of tea and brought out his pipe. "So there you are. We're really no nearer when it comes to a solid lead in this business, but we do know that it's wider than we might have expected. This name given to the old woman of the house at the Elephant and Castle— Thomas Caley—might well be an alias. It doesn't help us, because even if it's the true name of the man murdered at Castleton House, we still don't know what he does, where he comes from, or anything about him."

"So you're not really any forrader, as regards *him*," Tony Scott answered. "And how about this big thug with the scar? Do you think you'll find him?"

"We've found better men," Croft said in his quiet, determined fashion. "It may take time. London's a big place, and if he decides to leave it, well—" He lit up, and puffed blue smoke out contentedly. "Somehow I don't think he will. He strikes me as being of the quick-thinking type; and he might decide that it's better to lay low in Town rather than making a break for it. I dunno."

"You've given me a most concise description of him," Scott said. "Fat chance there is of my ever meeting him. Still, you've honoured me by your confidence, Inspector, and I appreciate it."

"I've taken you out of yourself for a bit, at all events." Croft grinned at him. "We'll all get over it, I suppose. We might be hellishly lucky and pick this unknown Scarface up. Then I can go to work on him. And I certainly will; I can promise you that. Ah, well—I'll have to be getting back to the office. Go out for a nice walk."

"And keep in touch with you, Inspector. I know."

"It's a good old formula," Croft answered, "and the best I can give you at the moment." He got up, brushed aside Scott's protestations and laid money on the table in payment of the check. "By the way," he said, as they made their good-byes and regained the street, "don't think badly of me in this. I can't help mentioning it, although you'll probably think it superfluous. But—if . . ."

Scott's face was grim as they halted on the pavement. "Thanks. But I don't expect to hear anything about that. I'd like to say how very grateful I am for everything."

"You're more than welcome." Croft turned away. "I go back this way. Take an airing on the promenade. It'll help a little." His strong hand closed over the right hand of Scott. "Don't hesitate to call in on me if this damned town becomes unbearable to you, or you think that I can help in any way. Cheerio."

He went off at a brisk but heavy walk, and Scott turned away with something perilously near to a sinking heart. Then he straightened up. No sense in being a sentimental idiot.

Croft's advice was homely and sound.

Certainly there seemed so little he could do in the matter of Marjorie Castleton. Before all else he was down here to solve a murder case, and he seemed to have his hands full enough with that.

Here in the spaciousness of Marine Drive, life seemed to be pleasant enough. A sleek, well-ordered place that seemed remote from tragedy. But the oppression of it still plucked at Tony Scott's heart. If only she had listened to him. If only he had been daring enough to presume further than he had done upon their short acquaintance and risked offending the head-strong girl even further in his efforts to ensure her well-being!

And he couldn't really blame her, he supposed. He tried to put himself, mentally, in the same position in which the girl had found herself a few hours ago. How would he have reacted or behaved? Marjorie Castleton had a fighting spirit —wrong or right.

It seemed that the past couldn't be mended now. Life for Scott had become tasteless, almost morbid. He was obsessed by memories of the vital personality of the girl he now knew that he had loved deeply, but in an unspoken way. Would he have been a fool to have declared that love, perhaps as a last desperate resort to stop her from running herself into danger and complication? Back came the answer to him from the depths of his own thoughts. If only he had done so!

But he hadn't done so. Snap out of it now, he told himself. There's nothing you can do. Nothing but to keep going, mentally and physically. The force of a subtle analogy came to him then. In front of him lay the busy Promenade of Harlingham, a place that didn't care for his troubles, and couldn't be expected to care. He must stop being a sentimental fool afflicted with memories and join that world. His feet must surely take him out of Marine Drive and on to the broad sea-frontage.

And he couldn't stay mentally in the position that was distracting him so sorely. The world lay ahead and he must forget that such a person as Marjorie Castleton ever existed and must rejoin it.

Right, then! He put back his shoulders and quickened his pace a little. He turned the corner by a little sub-post office that also did a thriving outside trade. Racks of blatantly-coloured, frankly vulgar postcards, beach balls, spades and buckets, Cellophane-and-paper bonnets inscribed with invitations to "Come over here, honey," and "Cuddle me," sticks of rock, magazines, windmills. Here the full tide of the ever-growing Harlingham swept by. Cars, landaus, bicycles, motor-coaches. The place was on the way to soon becoming a second Brighton.

Three piers now, one erected only last year. On the left of Scott, as he faced the sea by the corner shop, lay the ill-fated

Castleton House, five miles away. Memories of the place plucked at his heart. He turned right to continue his walk in the direction of the station and the huge "Hotel Metropole" some distance away. Scott had told himself that he didn't care for such expensive luxury. When he had proposed the humbler "George Hotel," on the spur of the moment, he had wanted to be near Detective-Inspector Croft, a damned good man in trouble. And Croft had been glad to have him.

Memories again! The mere thought of the two hotels brought back a chain of associations that led to Marjorie Castleton. Scott groaned in agony of spirit. Why couldn't he forget the poor kid!

The curse of the Castletons!

Tony Scott checked in his stride. The implication of something he had almost forgotten came to him with stunning force. "Good God in heaven!" he whispered to himself. "Again!"

He *had* forgotten it. Forgotten it completely. But now the tragedy of Marjorie Castleton brought it back to his mind in a way that made him almost catch at his breath. For a desperate moment or two he fought for sanity, reasonableness, a sense of proportion in things. Rot! But . . . was it rot?

All very well for him to deride it previously. The Castletons at most had been just unlucky. The long line of descendants since the crazed girl, gripped by religious mania, had run into streak after streak of bad luck. Coincidence had had more than a fair share in their tangled lives. But a curse—no. He had insisted on that, had argued from his worldly-wise point of view with the girl he had since grown to love.

"Impossible!" he had said. "Fantastic! Just an old woman's story without the slightest basis in cold, hard fact!" Now . . .

Now it seemed that on this broad, sunlit promenade, where people were bent upon having a good time, where a prosaic world ran swiftly as antithesis to the slow, heavy, almost morbid atmosphere of Castleton House, the curse of the doomed family was reaching out to him—a stranger. Not in shattering, tragic incident, but in a ghostly plucking at his mind. It was forcing him into belief, paying him back for his light-hearted defiance of it.

Tony Scott had talked his way through the case at a great rate when trying to purge the minds of others. He had exhibited sympathy—genuine sympathy—and had been gentle in his refusal to believe. Marjorie's mother—how terrible it had been to lose her! But the accident that had caused that loss had been an understandable one. It had upheld a devilish coincidence, admitted; but it had still been an accident. Then her father, the Colonel. Another sad blow there. But still Tony Scott had refused to be shaken.

Amazing coincidence, amazing sheer bad luck yet again. But it had finished with that. He had assured the pretty Marjorie Castleton so. And she had listened to him and believed.

And then—good God!—*another* death! Admittedly, an unknown—an unfortunate who had come in from the deep summer night outside like a moth to a light. Blundering, desperate, probably bewildered. And, like a moth, a blind fate had reached out to crush and kill.

In that moment the busy promenade, the sun, the whipping breeze, the speeding traffic, were blotted temporarily out of Tony Scott's mind as he walked on automatically. He could understand, now; *could* sympathise with what the girl had insisted upon, in the mental regression that had been strong enough to force her to an unbreakable determination to be rid of the old house for ever. Childish? Unsophisticated? Foolish? By God, no!

No! The toughest, most practical woman in the world might well have pursued the same action as Marjorie Castleton in setting off, there and then, sink or swim, to try to break the chain of damning circumstances somehow, before it overwhelmed her. Get out of it—get out before it was too late!

Who *could* blame her—even in this "practical," down-to-earth, twentieth-century world? It the man who had craved for Castleton House were somehow evil, cunning, greedy, lustful, why—then he was the one to turn the hated old house over to, and without delay. Poor, poor, desperate, frightened child only just out of the seclusion of finishing school—how could he condemn her? How could he fail to understand now?

She had tried to get out, but the curse of the Castletons was not to be denied. Face it! Scott whispered to himself fiercely as he walked. Face it! Whatever she had done, however she had thought or struggled, there was no escape. The curse had dragged her down, the sea had dragged her down. She was lost to him; and the grey, tormented Castleton line that had stubbornly fought this thing throughout the years had been defeated.

The last of the Castletons had succumbed and the curse was triumphant.

Tony Scott stopped to ease the quickening in his breath. Stopped to get a grip of himself.

Then he went on, thoughts subjugated, head up.

He altered course slightly to avoid a couple arm in arm— the man strong-jawed, tanned, capable and well-dressed; the woman approaching middle-age, hard, distinctive, expensively arrayed in town wear. On that informal scene of slacks and linen skirts, she might have stepped out of a Bond Street salon.

Then a fatigued mother, dragging a petulant little boy by the hand. Then an old man with a stick being helped along by his teen-age daughter who was casting rebellious glances in the direction of a pier where open-air dancing was now in session. Then two cocky youths, all brilliantine and ogles. Then three small girls, marching along with arms linked.

And then—a man in a fine grey suit, eyes hidden by dark sunglasses. A big man with strong shoulders, resolute chin, determined stride. He passed Tony Scott and the latter was yards away before he pulled up suddenly at a second crashing, numbing shock to his thoughts.

Indecision.

Impossible to mistake what Detective-Inspector Croft had only just told him. Impossible not to recognise the careful description. And yet . . . coincidence—that elusive something that wove itself through the tragedy and tears of the Castleton affair?

Any man might have a scar, glimpsed beneath the tortoiseshell frame of the sun-glasses, hastily purchased and assumed in an effort to half obscure it, since whatever the risk the cream-coloured mackintosh could not be worn and hampered movement in the heat of the late afternoon. There were possibly hundreds of men in the country who, because of accident or surgical operation, were afflicted by such a facial disfigurement. But not in Harlingham. Hell, no. Not in Harlingham. Countrywide such scars might be.

But Harlingham was a link. If a man went by with a scar in this particular place then it could only mean one thing, because this particular place had known murder in its area, and an unknown scarred man was linked up in that murder.

Additional to which the clothing, the build of the man, tallied exactly with what Croft had just told his friend Scott.

Coincidence be damned. That was the man badly wanted by Scotland Yard for questioning! Scott wheeled around. No time to try to contact Croft, lest he lose the fellow. After him, then. In his present mood this was just what he wanted—action, and action with a capital "A."

CHAPTER XIII

HIDE AND SEEK

IF THE MAN whom Tony Scott was not yet to know as "Big Johnny" Kreig had any idea that he had been recognised, he gave no sign of it.

But that might be solely because he was too busy following someone else, in his turn. Inside the vestibule of the "Hotel Metropole," by the elevator, Kreig had been surprised to see Freda White and Ed Munroe, the crooked pair from "back home." To avoid recognition by them on the spot he had been taken up to his own room in wake of the "bellhop" with his solitary piece of luggage. He had tipped the page, shut the door after him, peeled off the mackintosh that had become an encumbrance to him in the heat, and then sat down to think again.

"Big Johnny" could not get things to line up properly, at this point. He could not be expected to, since he was not omniscient. But he knew enough of the game to realise, shrewdly, that where Ed and Freda were then Apperley and White might soon be expected to be found. From that point, he was only interested in the present and the immediate future.

Downstairs, then. He mustn't let them out of his sight. A fat lot of good it would be, he told himself, if he were to just barge in upon them now and try to force some sort of an issue. It would be fatally overplaying his hand.

The couple now below were of no use to him by themselves. He had no particular quarrel against them. They were only a means to an end. Disturb them before the two men he hated most on earth and was determined to liquidate came on the scene, and he might well lose everything. The quarry might be scared off, and he would be robbed.

On the other hand— On the other hand, "Big Johnny" realised that he must follow the man and woman from now on. Follow them carefully and unobtrusively. It seemed more than clear that they had not come to Harlingham for nothing. For some reason—as yet unspecified, fear, revenge, the making of a deal—he didn't know—they were bent on contacting his enemies.

No time to lose, then. Kreig went into the bathroom of the suite he had engaged and washed his hands and face, left the mackintosh lying on the bed, and went out, his case as yet unpacked. The elevator took him down, obedient to the press of his heavy forefinger upon a button. No sign of them in the vestibule, of course.

He smiled grimly to himself. He didn't think it would do to start making inquiries for the couple at the reception desk. That might give the show away to them—the last thing in the world that he wanted to happen. And, like as not, they would have registered here under yet another alias. This whole business seemed to be full of aliases.

Yet he hoped to God that he hadn't lost them altogether. The "Metropole" didn't care for non-residents, even in its public rooms, although outsiders were sometimes unavoidable. And, anyway, Kreig argued with himself, the damned pair had looked as though they were staying on here. Arm in arm, an automatic masking smile that was part of their stock-in-trade concealing any anxiety they might have felt.

Kreig looked across the vestibule to where an attendant stood outside handsome swing doors, flanked by pillars. He guessed it was the dining-room of this expensive place. Freda and Munroe had looked as though they might be coming in for tea. Sure enough, there they were. Kreig stood at the top of three steps leading down into the dining-room and spotted them almost immediately, in a corner alcove.

The head waiter came to him. He was obliging when Kreig gave his assumed name and the fact that he was resident to the place. He gave "Big Johnny" a table where he

wanted it—around the corner of the steps. From such van-
tage place he could see without being seen. He could look
across at the pair he was interested in and note how their
light meal progressed. He could time his own tea—that he
felt he needed—by theirs.

And they would have to pass him, going out. But they
would not be able to see him *en route*.

Kreig ordered, and was served. He got through the food
set before him, and got through it quietly. Then he was on
his feet, bill signed, and out through the swing doors in their
wake—still unsuspected. If Freda had any idea of slipping
upstairs for anything, or if they weren't going out again yet.
the vestibule was a pretty big place. Big enough to screen
him behind a newspaper, anyway.

But it seemed that they *were* going out, and immediately.

Kreig had his hat in his hand as they quitted the hotel. He
put it on and pulled the snap brim well down. Ahead of him
it seemed that Freda and Munroe were bent upon a stroll,
from their negligent, aimless way of walking. Probably a fill-
in before dinner, a killing of time. On the other hand, that
might be a blind, even though they had clearly not realised
that he was behind them. Even now they might be on their
way to contact Henry Apperley and his friend.

"Big Johnny's" first speculation was correct, if only he
had known it. The pair he was following were engaged upon
a lengthy and aimless stroll to occupy time. They preferred
such sedative to their nerves instead of moping in an hotel
room discussing endlessly a situation that had been forced
upon them and which both knew they could not hope to escape. After dinner, a drink or two at the bar, possibly a look-
in at the nightly dance in the grill room, and then back to the
bar to meet Apperley and White at ten. The deadlock that the
four faced must then be resolved, one way or the other.

Freda White and Ed Munroe turned left and began to
saunter along the Promenade. Kreig let a little distance
elapse before he followed them. He had not the mackintosh
to help hide him now, and began to think, a little worriedly,
about his scarred face. He was not concerned too much about

the law. He argued that time was still on his side and that miracles only went so far. It was a million to one that any cop was interested in him down here. But he was perturbed a little lest, by some mischance, he should slip up by getting near enough for the couple in front to turn around and recognise him. And certainly they *would* do so if he slipped up, if only by accident. And they knew him of old. There was only one Johnny Kreig, and he was unforgettable.

So, being in the wake of the pair on the shop and amusement arcade-lined pavement of the Promenade, rather than having been forced to cross the road to the actual sea-front with its shelters and railings, Kreig had the chance he sought a moment or two later and profited by it. A huge dress shop had an attractive arcade into which Freda as a woman must needs turn, although Munroe seemed to be a little reluctant. But it gave Kreig time to risk diving into a convenient chemist's shop, planking down a pound note and grabbing up the first respectable pair of sun glasses that he thought might fit him. He could scarcely wait for his change.

He got out to the pavement in time to see Freda and Munroe come out of the arcade and continue on their way. A few hundred yards farther on, two incidents occurred that Kreig had not bargained for, but they happened just the same. One was that Tony Scott passed him, went on his way for some distance and then suddenly wheeled around, incredulous. The second was that Freda and Munroe seemed to have had enough of walking, in face of a horse-drawn landau that had been cruising slowly along beside them, empty. The driver was persuasive—what seaside landau-driver is not? A nice three-mile drive, cheap. Munroe looked at the woman at his side and laughed unspoken inquiry; and she, totally unaware that they were being followed, agreed. With a celerity born of long practice the driver leaned over from his box, jerked open the door of the vehicle and slammed it to again as they climbed in. Then he shook his horse into a trot.

And all in the same identical moment that Tony Scott, not knowing who they were or that the man with the scar was following them, took his courage in both hands and started back to have a word with Kreig.

It was a snap decision. He might be wildly wrong. There *were* innocent men with scarred faces, even in Harlingham. But the rest of the description tallied so exactly with that given him by Detective-Inspector Croft that it would be a million to one that he, Scott, would be right. Worth trying, anyhow. There could always be apologies. Scott began to walk hurriedly, just as Kreig had the mortification of seeing the couple he was pursuing being whipped away before his eyes.

He was too far away to stop them. His own careful keeping of distance had ensured that. And, even in a landau, normally reserved for pure pleasure seeking, they might be now on their way to White and Apperley. At all cost he must follow. He paused and looked desperately around into the roadway. A taxi . . .

Not one in sight at the moment. Kreig swore fluently beneath his breath; and Scott put out a hand to his arm. He said: "Excuse me. I'd like a word with you."

Kreig spun round to face him. He did not know who he was. Certainly he was broad-shouldered and determined in manner enough to be a plainclothes detective. And following his own words, Scott began to wonder in his mind just what he should say next. What right had he after all, as a private citizen, to pursue an on-the-spot inquiry?

He knew all about the citizen's power of arrest in an emergency. If a felony were suspected as being committed, wasn't it? But—somehow this was different. One couldn't just go up to a fellow and say, "Look here, I think the police are looking for you."

Kreig was trying to bluff it out. He had not yet lost his head. He said, very dangerously: "Well?"

"I'd like a word with you," Scott said, conscious that he was repeating himself, and somehow doing it lamely. "Inquiries are being made about a man missing in London and answering your description."

It was out now, Kreig snarled: "And who the hell are you—a policeman?"

Good enough for Scott. This man's very attitude told him all he wanted to know; that he had not made a mistake. Now to get him to Inspector Croft. And what better way to do it than by acting a necessary white lie? "Right," he said, refusing to dissemble more than was necessary. "I'd like you to come along with me, please, to police headquarters for questioning."

"Hell!" Kreig shot back; and sprang into instant action. He would not be taken now by one man. Not after he had come so far and had already risked so much, and with so much to live for in the future. At any hazard, confronted by just one supposed police-officer, he was determined to make a break for it. He had never seen this man in his life before. He might hope yet to escape him.

To lay him out, if necessary. If not, to somehow get away without trace. That narrowed time down for him. If he succeeded in evading this "detective" then there would be a comb-out of the town, although that might take some little time to organise. Yet it might give him enough to somehow pick up Freda and Munroe again. He guessed that a meeting between them and the pair he had determined to destroy might not be so far away. Munroe was not the one to waste time unnecessarily in a dump like this place.

"Big Johnny" brought up a ham-like fist and pushed Scott away from him, by the shoulder. And as Scott reeled back, he turned away and began running. But he soon slowed down to a quick walk. Kreig realised that such running would undoubtedly excite comment. He might be taken for a pickpocket being pursued, or something like that. Dodge this man behind him, then. That seemed to be the only feasible way out. Dodge him unless he were lucky enough to be able to face him in some quiet place, alone.

But here there were crowds. The "front" was at its busiest, just after tea. Kreig came to a gap in the pavement, with a circular stall presided over by a hoarse, red-faced man, skilfully chivvying a crowd of holidaymakers to throw numbered balls into a revolving wheel. "Any prize on the stall, bless yer!" he shouted. Behind him was the cavern of a big amusement arcade.

Kreig hurried around the stall, with Scott perhaps twenty yards off. God knew, he told himself, why he was going inside, but *something* had to be done. He dodged behind a bank of tall "what-the-butler-saw" machines, and did it as naturally as possible. When he ventured to look around he saw the figure of Scott outlined in the entrance with the late afternoon sunlight behind him.

And Scott was coming forward, though it seemed a little uncertainly. Kreig saw stairs leading upwards, and took them two at a time. Why the hell hadn't he kept on, instead of coming into this place? Only that he thought that he might somehow lose Scott in the throng of penny-jerkers. At the top of the stairs were more amusements—a "dodgem" track, curtained side-shows, dart and hoop-là stalls, a rifle range, more slot machines. A wild idea occurred to Kreig that he might slip in somewhere up here; that he might be lucky in waiting until Scott had toured the ground floor. Perhaps, then, he might only give this upstairs place a superficial glance.

Anything to get away. Kreig turned to the dark recess of a side-show. "Girls! Girls! Girls!" the sign said, and he planked down a shilling and went inside. Curtains closed behind him. There was a hot, closed-in smell in here. There was a roped alley-way and "This way round" painted up on a sagging board.

No exit at the other side. Kreig had hoped for one, but saw that the alley-way led back to the curtained entrance. He went a few steps forward and saw a partition, on the other side of which was a brilliantly-lit exhibition. And he knew that Scott had spotted the slight subterfuge and was coming up behind him. He knew it as infallibly as though his unknown enemy were in full view.

The "beheaded" girl . . . She was blonde and brassy, heavily made up, with tired eyes and seductively-permed hair. The stale perfume she wore hit Kreig at twenty paces.

White light rained down and blazed back upwards from the expanse of plate-glass mirror around her, artfully contrived in the old, old way with a huge spider's web and artificial greenery to help the illusion. The silver dish she wore as illusory collar fitted snugly, but was exceedingly hot to her skin. Purple velvet curtains draped the front of the booth. The girl wearily rolled a wad of gum into the other cheek and spoke to the eight-hundredth customer that day. She said her party piece.

"Welcome to the palace of mystery. Here you see me without my body. My cruel master, the Sultan of Azaza, beheaded me five hundred years ago. Yet I still live on. Pass on to the next exhibit, please—the girl in the den of serpents." The gum was rolled back into place. The blonde closed her eyes in wearied disgust.

At the entrance, Tony Scott bellowed, "Hey, there!" And Kreig bent down, whipping up the purple draperies like a flash. The blonde said: "What the heck!" and felt the frenzied Johnny Kreig blunder under the mirrors, his head butting into her legs as she sat on a cane-seated chair. "Quiet, sister!" he ground out as he sought to extricate himself. "Damn you—be quiet! If you got into this thing from behind—"

Scott was on his knees, trying to grapple with the purple drapery that had swung back. The blonde was rocking on her chair and calling out for a mysterious "Jimmy," somewhere below. Kreig twisted to the right and cannoned into the captive of the "den of serpents," dust rising up to stifle him. Somehow he got to his feet and kicked out brutally at Scott's face as it emerged from the tangle. But his heel grazed the enemy's shoulder. He saw a murky, half-opened window and almost dived through it.

The surprised blonde couldn't get out. It seemed that the mysterious Jimmy had not yet heard the rumpus. The second girl was frantically clawing at the made-up plastic coils that surrounded her, so that she might help Scott to his feet.

"Thanks," he panted. "Where does that window lead to?"

"Don't know," she said. "Flat roof, I think. What's it all about, mister? You had a fight?"

"We're having one right now," Scott shot back. "Sorry for the disturbance." Then he was away. Through the window, and almost directly on to the flat roof that the girl had spoken of. But the distance to the ground was negligible.

No sign of the man he was following. A passageway between buildings leading to the left, as he swung himself to the ground. Two empty dustbins.

Scott took breath. Where now?

Obviously along the alley. At the farther end of it he saw Kreig lumbering away by some hoardings and into a fairground.

Scott broke into a trot in pursuit of him, lost him in the crowd. For a moment or two he stood completely baffled, chest heaving. Somewhere in this farrago of flaring stalls, roundabouts, helter-skelter, swings, people, was Scarface.

Then he saw him again and plunged forward. He bellowed at him in rage, across the intervening distance. The words were lost to all but Kreig in the general uproar. And the garishly-façaded "Fun House" was now before him. A mix-up of youths and girls suddenly surged forward to close him in, to surround him and give him the opportunity to go forward up the steps. To try to turn and break through the young people would bring him full tilt into Scott.

Up the steps, then. Another shilling, change from the pound note given at the chemist's. Kreig grabbed at a paper ticket, had it torn in two by a man dressed as a clown, was thrust inside a yawning doorway. A girl in front screamed in delight; a puff of compressed air caught at the American's trouser-bottoms, as Tony Scott dodged around the press at the bottom of the steps to gain admission. Kreig stepped on to a jolting "shake-up," his fingers clawing for the safety rails. Off it then, and into darkness.

Scott was negotiating the compressed air jet, as Kreig stumbled forward into the blackness. Behind Scott, a middle-aged woman shrieked and clutched at her skirts. He damned her innocence heartily but silently as she crashed against him in her excitement. On to the "shake-up." Kreig was cursing at an unexpected spray of cold water being dashed into his face from nowhere.

Jolting barrels, strung together as a trap for the unwary in the blackness. Scott risked breaking an ankle and felt for Kreig to crash out a blow and miss. The cold water, automatically sprayed at seconds' intervals, ran down his neck. If only he could *see* the man in front! Kreig saw a phosphorescent death's head come grinning at him in the angle of the twisted way that skilled showmen had laid out for the delectation of thrill-seekers. He turned there in the narrow corridor because he must, clutched at a steel bar, also gleaming in the darkness and temptingly placed as support, and swore violently as a mild electric shock ran up his arm.

Scott's fist grazed his cheek. A shallow trap opened and plunged him downwards. He was on his back, sliding helplessly while Tony Scott panted in his struggle with the live rail and the creaking wooden doors that came up to close at his feet. Then the trap swung open for him—again the engineered interval. Somewhere behind him the stout woman was battling with the pitching barrels, her position complicated by fresh arrivals at her back.

Kreig shot feet foremost into three girls and a youth who were in an abandonment of ecstasy in a huge revolving drum. But there was more light here. They were being drawn to the edge and from thence on to a big flat disc, spinning around at fair speed. Somehow he got to his feet, teeth bared to meet the raging Scott at the bottom of the chute. Then Kreig was knocked off balance again.

But he had his first solid satisfaction of the hectic scramble when he got his hands around Scott's windpipe and squeezed—squeezed . . . On his back, Scott shot up his own hands, elbows being scraped on the smooth sides of the contraption. He gripped Kreig's hairy wrists, sought to break his hold. His knee came up; there was no time here to respect the niceties. And "Big Johnny" grunted in pain and let go.

The drum pitched him on to the wheel in its own remorseless way. Spectators crowded at the bottom of the ride laughed heartily. Such a mix-up seemed, at a superficial glance, to be all part of the fun.

Kreig did not dally with centrifugal force. He had lost his sunglasses and his hat. Scott was pitched out of the drum, winded. He lay almost supine on the wheel while Kreig picked himself up at the exit of the Fun House. An alert attendant saw that Scott had had enough, although the fight had escaped his attention, and helped him off.

Scott suddenly clung to the man's arm, knees buckling beneath him. His throat felt raw. Red specks danced before his eyes. The world was distorted and mad. Kreig was away again in the crowd.

"You orlright, mate?" the man asked diffidently, and Scott nodded his head and felt for a handkerchief as he swayed on his feet. "Thanks—yes." He mopped sweat from his face and straightened up. "It's—tough going on that thing."

The man in front—where was he? People passed and re-passed across Scott's line of vision, blurred by the sudden blinding sunlight. Noise, confusion, raucous music. Where was he?

Where? A small boy with a balloon on the end of a long cane brushed it against Scott's face and he felt like swearing at him.

Should he cast around to try to find a policeman? Scott decided against it. Now, more than ever since he knew he was pursued, the man with the scar would make a break for it. And if Scott were not behind him, on the spot, he would be able to do it unchecked.

But somehow he must find him again in the midst of this bustle and confusion. A man in a gaudy shirt thrust a ride at Scott and implored him to "try a shot," but he ignored him. A little boy, busy with some "fairy floss," a mysterious con-coction of spun pink and white sugar, stumbled against Scott's legs. And there was the man with the scar once more.

Skirting a group of motor-caravans. Scott started for-ward. He saw the move that the other was up to. Behind the caravans was quietness and a way to slip out of the pleasure ground at the side, rather than to try to seek the main entrance and run into his pursuer in the light. Scott's head had cleared by now. Good enough for him. He would get around the same parked vans and meet the enemy from the other side.

Where Kreig went around by the right of the vans, Scott plunged around the corner of them to the left. There were eight of the substantial vehicles, and beyond a deserted expanse of cinders and dust, with a street-end plainly visible. Scott barked his shins against an empty bucket left there, and blundered into the surprised Kreig face to face.

Kreig wasted no time in words. He steadied himself in his mad rush and launched a pile-driver at Scott's chin that, had it connected, might have settled the hectic chase on the spot. But Scott saw it coming and sidestepped the blow, retaliating with another—a short-arm jab to the ribs. He heard the scarred man grunt at the shock, rather than the pain, of it; then Kreig had him around the body and brought him down.

Deliberately he kicked him, saw out of the corner of his eye two men coming around the corner of the van, attracted by the noise, and broke away yet again. Somehow he eluded the two fairground men, but they were now blocking a dash across the cinders that he had planned like lightning. Nothing for it but to get back into the fair itself again. Scott was on his feet by now, but one of the men gripped his arm.

"What's going on, chum?"

"Lemme go!" Scott raged. "That man—"

"Take yer blasted fight somewhere else, then. We don't want trouble—"

"Okay; okay," Scott babbled in desperation. "Sorry. But let me go. There he is!"

Kreig was looking back over his shoulder as he hurried away. It seemed impossible to shake this determined young man off, and the handicaps were great. If he could only ditch him temporarily, put him out—anything . . . If he could only elude him sufficiently to be able to gain the narrow end of that street he had glimpsed beyond the cinders—the street

with low-walled yards and the backs of houses abutting on to
it and with washing hung here and there.

Tony Scott was nearly up to him again. Yet another huge
"attraction" came up before Kreig, and his mind worked like
lightning—the "Ghost Train."

Darkness inside this place. Perhaps a chance to lay his
pursuer out in it, and somehow get out at the other side.
From the size of the enclosed building it seemed that the ride
would be long enough. Then a doubling back to the little
street and safety.

Kreig mounted to the wooden platform of the contrivance, almost hurled himself into an empty car. A man in oily
blue overalls and a red muffler boarded the car expertly as it
began to move and took the silver coin that Kreig thrust towards him. The American began to bless the amount of small
change that the chemist had unloaded upon him.

And then they were moving as Scott came pounding up
the steps. The man in the muffler put out an arm and said:
"Nex' time!" but Scott shoved him aside recklessly, jumped
and somehow clung to the four-seated car following Kreig's
and like his own fortunately empty. The attendant took a
chance, swung himself aboard, plucked half a crown from
the fingers of the quick-thinking Tony Scott, and dropped
off, unable to find change before the string of cars was rock-
eting along a narrow passage.

The promoters of "The Ghost Train" were enterprising,
inasmuch as they had seemed determined to combine the
mystery of that interesting contrivance with the thrill of a
miniature scenic railway. And all in the dark. Or mostly so.
Here and there was a brief intermission of light from an
opening in the canvas-and-wood partitions, but the greater
part of the three-minute journey was stygian.

The clatter of the wheels was interspersed by sundry
screams and shrieks from female patrons somewhere ahead.
Tony Scott realised that he and Scarface were occupants of
the last two cars. He was impatient of the usual distractions
flung at this load of clinging humanity—phosphorescent spi-
ders, skeletons, a crude white-sheeted affair that moved its

wooden arms stiffly and fell behind. Kreig reached into an inside breast-pocket and realised that he had left his slim automatic still packed in his case at the hotel.

The screaming wheels rocked upwards on the climbing rails. Then the cars dipped sharply. Scott was crouching in the front of his, hands gripping a short rail. Another patch of light from somewhere above, and he had thrown a leg over recklessly. Then another leg. He was straining himself back against the curved front of the car, and held on with hands behind him as there came another sickening dip. Then the rise, and mechanics came slightly to his aid. He was at the bottom of the slope, "Big Johnny" was in the back of his empty car at the foot of the following rise. The steel coupling between the two had its links bent like an S. Scott leaned forward and grabbed.

Grabbed and almost missed as the cars straightened out and roared upwards, the distance between them now too great to admit of passage one to the other. But Scott was inside with Kreig and fumbling for him in the darkness. He found him by means of fingers that clawed at his face; then had the American down and was pounding blows at his body. Kreig had the rear rail of the car biting into his back, wriggled to one side, rasped a sliding blow against Scott's chin and was pitched to his knees. He was conscious that the ride was slowing up.

They had topped the incline, but the descent on the other side was shorter, more gentle. Outside the attendant in the red muffler did his duty and jerked a string, so that a cacophony of sound, meant to represent a train-whistle, suddenly blasted at their ears. Kreig caught Tony Scott around the ankles in a bear-hug, whipped him off his precarious balance, swung him so that he was half-over the side.

"Ur!" he said as Scott clawed at his ear. "You blasted—"

Tony Scott felt himself going. He left the ear and tried to get a grip of the rail again. Kreig felt the obstacle in the darkness and bit his fingers savagely into his opponent's wrist. He broke his hold, lifted the weight of Scott, pushed.

Planking sagged beneath Scott's body as the car slowed down. He grabbed at nothing, fell farther—down into smelly blackness. Ahead of Kreig a tunnel-end of light appeared and grew. Scott hit the ground from a distance of thirty feet in a tangle of struts and canvas a little before the cars were braked at their starting-point and Kreig leaped out, resisting all questioning.

He was lucky in that. The mufflered one had felt the thud of Scott's fall and had already lowered himself into the bowels of the interior staging to investigate. He swung himself down expertly, somewhat like a grotesque and oversize ape, and came upon Scott bleeding from a cut on the temple and temporarily out.

People congregated. The two men left the parked vans by the cinder patch and came over to help. Kreig evaded them easily, brushed himself down, hid bleeding knuckles in a handkerchief at the street-end that he had marked as his objective. He thrust the bound knuckles into a trouser-pocket, smoothed back his rumpled hair with the other hand. He negotiated the two or three quiet streets that he came into, swung left, found himself again on the Promenade.

And this time there was a taxi when he wanted it. It was not far to the "Metropole"; and the driver profited by that fact to take a circuitous course, grinning to himself the while. Kreig got back his breath in the interior of the cab and was glad that hatless men at the seaside are by no means uncommon.

This had most decidedly put the fat in the fire. He might have killed that plainclothes dick. Damned good job if he had, he thought.

It meant a murder rap if he were caught—but that was nothing to him now. He meant to stage another murder before the night was out, somehow. A double murder of Apperley and White. Back to the hotel to pick up the trail of Freda and Ed Munroe again.

And to get his gun. That, above all else. With that he might have a chance.

"Big Johnny" Kreig brooded upon the situation. If that dumb plainclothes man was not dead, then surely the crash might have robbed him of consciousness. He might wake up some decent time after—and *then* all the ponderous machine of the law would have to be put in motion to start searching. Johnny had a hunch that, as far as Freda and Munroe went, things were about due to come to a head. They didn't, he repeated to himself, waste time unnecessarily in a dump like this.

Perhaps another few hours might resolve matters, and he himself might just squeeze by with that hour before the bulls at police headquarters got around to ceasing an argument that a man who would be riding the "Ghost Train" was scarcely the sort of person to be associated with the august "Hotel Metropole."

That was, if the plainclothes man either came around in time to talk or if the guy in the red muffler was smart enough to recognise that a man with a scarred face might have been the one to throw the other overboard. Either way, it seemed that he, "Big Johnny" Kreig, might somehow be granted the time to do what had now become an unquenchable obsession with him, and then making a dash for home.

CHAPTER XIV

A RIDE IN THE DARK

TONY SCOTT came to to find himself lying on someone's raincoat, and a constable bending over him. The noise of the pleasure-ground had grown to a confused roar. People were being pushed back to give him air. The constable was feeling his pulse in expert manner, and gently pressed him down again as he struggled to rise. "Take it easy now," he said.

Scott ignored the conventional "Where am I?" He knew well enough, and damned the luck to himself silently. This meant that Scarface, whoever he might be, had got away at last.

A searing pain shot through the still-bleeding temple and across his right eyebrow as he lifted his head. He was glad to lie back. For a time, at any rate. The policeman said: "There's an ambulance on the way, sir. Don't worry. We'll look after you."

Scott moistened dry lips. "The other fellow—"

"They tell me," the constable said, "that there appears to have been some sort of trouble between you and another man. Ah—here we are! Just keep still." He was brisk and authoritative, this man of the law, but gentle enough with it. Under his direction, Scott was expertly loaded on to a stretcher and put into the ambulance, and once more tried to get up as the doors were shut behind the constable. "Look here," he said. "I'm quite all right. I appreciate all this, but I assure you that it's quite unnecessary. I feel fine."

"May be so, sir," the constable insisted. "But I'm only doing the job laid down for me in these circumstances. I don't think so myself, but there may be unsuspected internal injuries. In any case, there's your head to be considered. And don't worry about the other fellow; we can straighten all that out at the other end when I make my report.

"I'd be glad, then, if you'd make it to a Detective-Inspector Croft," Scott groaned. "He's a friend of mine. I do feel that you should get on to him right away. Whew!"

The pain shot across his eyebrow again like a red-hot wire. The constable showed interest at sound of Croft's name.

"There, now. What did I tell you? You're in no condition to be up and about without at least a check at the hospital. Inspector Croft, you say? That's the officer from Scotland Yard."

The remark somehow seemed fatuous to the man on the stretcher. "Will you telephone him from the hospital? I tell you that he knows me."

"If you say so, sir."

The ambulance had no more than perhaps a quarter of a mile to go. It was unloaded at the entrance to the casualty department, the policeman by then having got Scott's name and address and the few other particulars that he deemed necessary, He insisted upon confining himself to such matter-of-fact details; the rest was a matter for Croft himself.

That gentleman arrived some few minutes later. He came briskly into the casualty department, went behind screens and saw Tony Scott between sterilised sheets. He said: "Hullo there, my boy. What's all this about?" And Scott, who was feeling very much better, breathed a sigh of relief at his appearance.

"Good job you've arrived, Inspector. They've taken all the clothes off me."

"What's the damage?" Croft asked a young house-surgeon with horn-rimmed spectacles and a lock of hair falling negligently across his forehead; and the doctor shrugged.

"Very little, if any. I'd like to keep the gentleman overnight for observation."

"Don't let them do it, Inspector," Scott said, a trifle hollowly. "They've already run the rule over me about six times. I want to be out and about."

"To go after a mysterious bloke who nearly put 'paid' to your account, eh?" Croft asked. "How about his head, doctor?"

"A bruise and a slight laceration. The rest would do him good, but I won't press it. If the gentleman insists on leaving, he'll be all right."

"Thanks," Scott said. "Can I have my clothes?"

He fingered the sticking plaster on his temple. "Bit of a headache, Inspector, but that'll go in time. Well?"

Detective-Inspector Croft nodded to the doctor. A nurse brought in Scott's neatly-folded clothing, on instructions. Inspector Croft stepped out of it as she pulled the screens fully around the leather couch whereon Scott lay, and found a convenient chair.

The constable came to him, fresh from formalities at the porter's office and saluted. Croft got up to hear the man's report carefully, then dismissed him.

Tony Scott emerged from behind the screens with his jacket over his arm and buttoning up his waistcoat. "Have I kept you waiting?"

"Not much," Croft smiled. "Better come back to the office with me. Okay?"

"Right!" Scott answered, and accompanied Croft to the police car. Back at Marine Drive he lowered himself into a chair with a little sigh.

"They do you proud in these parts, Inspector."

"We've got a good hospital," Croft said. "Or isn't that what you're meaning?"

"Not quite. I was referring to that unknown thug with the scarred face. Care to hear about it in detail?"

"That's why I've brought you here," Croft replied in his patient manner. "Give it to me carefully, now. There may be more in this than you think."

Scott took a deep breath. "Then this is what happened . . ." He went on to relate his amazing adventure of the late afternoon, and Detective-Inspector Croft listened patiently, pipe going strongly meanwhile. When Scott had finished, he sat silent for a while.

"This deepens the mystery, Tony. I thought I'd got around to understanding it—up to a point. But now—I don't know. I just don't know. Feeling all right?"

"Good enough to take another crack at this fellow, Inspector. But I don't suppose that I shall be meeting him again."

Croft knocked his pipe out. "You never know," he said. "I'm putting arrangements in hand immediately. Harlingham's a fair size and it's pretty well crowded now, at the height of the season, but that doesn't mean that it's an unmanageable task to try to locate this bird you've told me about. It might take a long time, that's all. I'll devote all my energies to it, I promise you that; so you might yet have the pleasure of meeting our scarred friend in this building."

"Than which nothing would suit me better, Inspector—"

Croft grinned. "I hope that we'll be able to accommodate you. Look, it's a quarter to ten now."

Scott was aghast. "Has all that time elapsed since they carted me off to the hospital? Why, it seems only an hour or so ago that we were discussing sardines on toast."

"It's amazing how time flies when you're busy," Croft said. "And you've certainly been busy. Well, you said that you'd drop in on me again for any further news, but I didn't think it'd be like this."

"Any—further news," Scott said slowly. "Hell, Inspector, I'd almost forgotten."

"You couldn't be expected to remember," Croft reminded him. "But there it is. I'll be brutal and say at once that there's still no news of Marjorie Castleton. The coastguard stations have been reporting back by telephone, every hour. But there's nothing turned up."

"And—?" Scott asked despairingly.

"The search goes on."

"I wish I could have done something for the poor kid, Inspector."

"You did your best," Croft said, taking him by the shoulders. "And you're in no condition to worry about it tonight, in spite of what the doctor said. I think that you must have scared him into submission. Back to the 'George' for you, my boy, and bed. You'll feel better in the morning."

"I can't promise you about the bed," Scott said, with an effort to be cheerful again. "But the 'George' strikes me as a good idea. What's the hours around here?—you should know, as a policeman."

"Eleven. Thinking of a drink before you turn in? I can't blame you, after what you've been through. You look as though you need it."

"And how about you, Inspector?" Scott wanted to know, as he prepared to depart under stress of the friendly little shove administered on his shoulders by Croft.

"I'd like to join you, but I can't. I fix my own hours of duty here; but you've tossed a nice little manhunt into my lap now. Now get out. 'Bye. I might drop into your room when I get back, if you're not asleep, and tell you how things are going."

Croft went back to his desk. "And look," he said, as Scott got to the door, "do me a favour in the future, will you? I forgive you the muddle up in this jam you've just got out of, because I don't think that in the circumstances you could have done much else. But the next time, call a cop, eh? Don't try to see things through all by yourself. I commend your spirit, but you've seen for yourself how liable you are to get hurt."

Scott smiled at the cloud of blue tobacco smoke now rising above the desk, and went out.

The streets were now cooler. The light was beginning to fade almost imperceptibly. Scott fingered the sticking plaster again as he walked in the direction of the Promenade. Certainly he'd take Croft's advice—if there was a next time.

But no doubt by this time Scarface would be busy packing.

To the "George," then. A good stiff drink and his pyjamas.

To get there, he had to pass the "Hotel Metropole," and he headed in this direction. Somehow he could not help scanning the faces of men who passed him, each intent on his own affairs. Perhaps it was that Tony Scott expected a minor miracle—that for a second time he would encounter the American on these pavements.

But "Big Johnny" Kreig was elsewhere. Upstairs in the same "Hotel Metropole," in fact. He had changed, more for his own comfort after his recent affray, rather than with any idea of altering his appearance on the grounds of being identified. And, by judicious tipping, he had discovered that the couple he sought as having occupied such and such a table at tea time, had reserved the table for dinner. Additional to this, he learned their aliases and the fact that they had only arrived the day before.

That meant at least that they were "at home." "Big Johnny" had dinner served in his room rather late. The issue was crucial now. He could not risk his scarred face in the dining-room again. The occasion would be more elaborate, the meal more protracted.

But, after he had dined himself, he went downstairs, although there plucked at his mind the thought that he might be taking a hell of a big risk in so doing. The police might, even now, be somehow getting around to the fact—though in cold logic he couldn't quite see why—that he might be in this place.

A risk. But to damnation with the risk. He was poised and "ready to go." The slim automatic was now in the inside pocket of his neat dark brown suit. So great was his smouldering resentment that he was willing to take *any* chance to be even with the pair he hated.

The well-tipped hall porter hadn't yet telephoned up to Kreig to say that Munroe and Freda had gone out. All right. Kreig himself would take over from there. Half-past nine; and he located the couple in the huge bar of the "Metropole," dallying with cocktails in a well-screened corner. Kreig got well out of sight in another convenient alcove on the opposite side of the room, opened an evening newspaper and was once again glad of the old, old dodge to shield his face.

He took his bourbon straight, but made it last. Kreig was no drinker from choice rather than convenience, when there was work like this afoot. Almost disinterestedly he read what little the local Press had to tell him on the affair of the missing Marjorie Castleton. Nothing doing yet.

While he waited, he tried to disentangle things for himself. He knew that the girl had lived at Castleton House. He knew that Selden had been found murdered at Castleton House. He knew that Seldon had been after Apperley and White, on his orders. But he couldn't be expected to know much more.

Rather was his attention occupied by the pair across the way from him. Their nervousness, that they were able to successfully hide from other occupants of the room, was only too apparent to one like himself who was deliberately keeping them under surveillance and knew what to look for. From their very manner it seemed to Kreig that they were expecting to meet Apperley and White here, in the bar of the "Metropole" itself.

What then? A deal of some sort? Once more, he didn't know and couldn't be expected to know. All that would doubtless come later when he moved in on the interesting party. And he would have a gun, and the advantage of surprise.

And an evening newspaper, as "Big Johnny" Kreig knew only too well in the past, has many unconventional uses, besides the one to which he was now putting it—the screening of his scarred face.

So the time crept on. It seemed that Freda White and her companion had no idea of his presence. But constantly the grim Munroe looked at his watch and then at the bar clock and tried to assuage the woman's nervousness. "Big Johnny" treated himself to a half-smile behind his newspaper at this. Let it run.

He would not interfere until Apperley and White showed up, however great his own impatience. He had waited so long. He could afford, in spite of the danger in which he was beset, to wait a little longer.

And outside, at the end of the Promenade, Tony Scott saw Henry Apperley and Arthur White leave the hotel parking place nearby and come into full view as they made for the "Metropole's" ornate entrance.

Something went click inside Scott's brain. Here was Apperley again, with his precious partner this time. What the hell were they doing here at ten o'clock at night?

Bent on business, evidently, from their appearance which included their not having time to see Scott, a yard or two away. Did they live here?

Celebrating? Celebrating what? The death of poor Marjorie Castleton? Why the devil wasn't Apperley back on the houseboat, helping to do something to find his unfortunate cousin's body? And a car, too? And a hired one at that.

Scott knew this very well, simply because he recognised the vehicle as one belonging to a local garage. The thought brought back a stab of mental pain. Marjorie Castleton again. She had gone to the trouble to hire it and send it to the station to meet Scott on Saturday morning, when he had arrived for the week-end at Castleton House that had ended so tragically.

Impossible to mistake the vehicle, Scott realised, as he slipped into the car-park for a look. But no driver provided this time.

Perhaps it was that Scott's suspicions of everyone and everything were inflamed on this hectic evening. He wanted a drink. All right—what was wrong with the swanky bar of the "Metropole," rather than the more humble one of the "George"? And if Henry Apperley desired, in such palatial premises, to take it up where he had left off and to "hang one" on Scott's jaw, well—it suited Scott himself. He was ripe and ready for trouble—smarting for it, in fact.

"Call a cop," Croft had said. But what for? Fruitful as the last encounter after inquiry had been, Scott now found himself in much the same dilemma.

He couldn't seek a policeman and tell him that Henry Apperley and Arthur White had gone into the hotel, that he disliked the pair of them and please, what about it? Neither could he ring Detective-Inspector Croft and break the glad tidings to him that Marjorie Castleton's cousin, and his precious pal, had just entered the "Metropole." Croft's obvious and justifiable answer would be: "So what? What do you expect me to do about it? Are you aware that they've just committed a blasted crime, or something?"

Nevertheless, Scott couldn't help thinking of the implications of this position. And, underneath it all, although he would not admit to it, was the fact that he was in fighting mood, that he wanted a word or two with the saturnine Apperley. If the latter wanted to make anything of the ingenious query that Scott was already shaping in his mind of whether anything had yet been heard about finding the girl's body, then Apperley was welcome to make it.

Scott followed inside. Apperley and his friend were nowhere in sight in this busy vestibule. On impulse, Scott located the bar and looked into it.

His eyes picked them up instantly. They had joined a man and a woman in the far corner.

Once again Scott hesitated. Here was further complication, and something that came to him as a complete surprise. He ordered a light ale and leaned an elbow on the highly-polished bar counter. At least he could watch them without appearing obtrusive himself. So engrossed was he in watching the four people at the secluded table inside the farthest of the chromium and frosted glass partitions, and doing it, as it were, "out of the corner of his eye," that he had no time for the occupants of the room.

Otherwise he might have seen a scarred-faced man looking furtively over the top of his newspaper and preparing for action. But even at that, the newspaper would have defeated Scott.

Apperley and White dropped into the two vacant chairs kept against their coming as nonchalantly as though they were meeting friends from whom they had quite recently parted. There were no greetings exchanged. Only Munroe's lean jaw tightened under the strain, and Freda paled a little beneath her make-up. All, it seemed, had decided to dispense with formalities or preliminaries. Straight down to business, but drinks as a matter of good form.

Munroe said: "What'll you have?"

"Whisky for both of us, I think," Arthur White answered; and his eyes went to the woman sitting opposite them. Apperley cursed under his breath as he noted the look in them. The infatuated fool!

"Pink gin," Freda said, in answer to Munroe's inquiry.

He called a waiter and gave him the order. Kreig raised the newspaper again and patted his breast pocket. The order was brought.

It seemed that the scared woman was content to let Munroe do the talking. He lifted his glass and hesitated. "Here's how, gentlemen."

White reached across the table and touched Freda's jewelled wrist softly with his fingertips. "To hell with all that," he said in a whisper. "Are you coming back to me?"

She shrank back from him. Munroe swallowed something. "So—you've caught up with us. We put in the ad. like you told us. We decided to act sensible. Now what?"

"We could," Apperley said smoothly, "just about flick you off the face of the earth, like flies. You know us, and the people we're in with."

White spoke as though almost in a dreamy ecstasy, eyes still on Freda's face. His own eyes were gleaming with fanaticism. "You ever hear of a guy called Seldon, Freda? Don't you read the newspapers?"

Munroe swallowed again. "I read of a killing in these parts."

"Over at a place called Castleton House," White murmured. "You must have heard of Seldon, back home. 'Big Johnny' Kreig's gorilla. We gave him his, a night or two back."

"And . . . we're just as liable to do the same to you," Apperley said.

Freda White almost tittered under the tightening nervous strain that had come to her. "But—but—Honest to God, Arthur, don't you know that 'Big Johnny's' gunning for you? That he'll get you? That—"

"Can it, Freda!" Munroe snapped, and looked White in the face again. "We try to be reasonable."

"You tried to be reasonable when you shopped me into Leavenworth, the pair of you," White retorted, but still in the same low voice. "Damn and blast it, you left me to rot. I always swore, Munroe, that I'd have the dirty hide of you for that. That I'd kill you and get away with it."

Munroe was white to the lips now. "But you hinted that we might come to some arrangement. I trusted you. That's why we came here at all."

Apperley laid a restraining hand on White's wrist. "Listen, now. We're trying to let you down lightly, although you both deserve a bellyful of lead for the magnificent cross staged. Some men take some understanding, don't they, Freda?"

She shrugged her shoulders. "Some men."

Apperley went on: "I risk offending my very good friend, Arthur, when I say that personally I wouldn't touch you with the traditional barge-pole, short of bumping you off, Freda my dear. You're just about my lowest idea of womanhood minus. Arthur, on the other hand, is worth knowing."

He paused to look around the bar. But Tony Scott had his head down, drinking. Away at the farther end "Big Johnny" Kreig lowered his newspaper and beckoned to a waiter.

Munroe's fingers were beating an impatient tattoo on the glass-topped table. "Cut the dramatics. We know all that, Apperley. Just what is it you want?"

"I'll try to put the position in a nutshell," Apperley answered, "if Arthur will try to keep quiet. Like you, I want to skip the superficialities, because it doesn't do an atom of good to go around in circles. Let's get to the meat of the matter. Quite apart from the fact that we've got heavy work of our own on hand—and I think you'll know what I mean—

Arthur would just about break his heart it he were forced to let Freda go."

Apperley took a thoughtful sip at his drink. Kreig whispered to the waiter who had come to him.

"Well?" Munroe said impatiently, and Apperley smiled at him.

"I don't mean let her go to you, you skunk. I mean to the undertakers. Look, I like to work with contented people. How can Arthur give of his best in turning out those delightful, soul-satisfying artistic creations that bring us in the big money, if he's constantly pining for a toy that might be damn' well worthless, but which he must have if he's to go on breathing?" Apperley was scowling. "Or I'll put it another way, and give it to you quick. Cracked or not, he can't live without that skin-and-hair that you've got with you. She goes back to him or we rub you both out. Get it? God knows what he sees in you, Freda, and God knows what he'll do with you, but that's not my affair. I've carried out my part of the show as I promised, in giving you this ultimatum."

Freda half-rose, but Munroe pulled her down to her seat again. He had opened his lips to speak when a waiter brought a chair, with a word of apology, and set it down at the table. Apperley said: "What the hell! We didn't order—"

And then "Big Johnny" Kreig stood before them, the scar twisted in a smile of venomous hate. He held a partially folded newspaper in his left hand and his right was under it, Apperley's eyes flicked downward to it.

"We-ll," Kreig said, and the words had the rasp of chilled steel about them. "All old pals together, eh? So nice to get me a seat so that I can join you, Apperley. Don't trouble to order me a highball. I've had a couple, over there, and this thing I'm holding might go off, if you start making signals."

He sat down. The newspaper was lifted aside for a second. They saw the slim automatic's muzzle slide on to the gleaming table-top. Kreig said: "Quiet, all of you, an' let me do the talking."

He was enjoying himself, but in a deadly quiet way. At the bar, Tony Scott set down his glass with a bang and gasped in utter astonishment. The man with the scar! And with Apperley!

"I don't profess to know what this is all about," Kreig said, his face a mask of hatred. "But I think I can guess. Something to do with bumping off, eh? Great; great. But cancel your arrangements, if you've damn' well made any. If there's any bumping off to do, then I'm here on the job."

In spite of the obvious peril of the position, Munroe's eyes showed his relief. The scarlet nails of Freda White went shakily up to her mouth.

"Cross an' double cross," Kreig rasped. "Wheels within wheels, ain't it? Lovely. You're the best collection of lousy, undersized rats that it's been my misfortune to meet since I was a kid."

Apperley moved, and the newspaper was shaken warningly. "Don't try anything smart," Kreig said. "Leave that to me. This rod has a silencer, and there's a lot of chatter in here. There's a full clip to the baby I'm holding, and I'd just as soon empty it here as anywhere else. I ain't choosey."

It was Apperley's turn to ask the inevitable question. "What d'ye want, Johnny?"

"Ain't *that* a honey?" Kreig said. "As if you didn't know? I've got things about weighed up by now. You and White are thirstin' for Freda and Ed's blood, but you seem to have overlooked the fact that I'm thirstin' for yours. I get first cut in this rubbing-out business. And there ain't a damned thing that you and White can do about it."

A man left the bar and moved in their direction—Tony Scott. He lingered behind the next partition, thankful that the pair who had occupied the table therein were just leaving. He could hear what was being said, but was blissfully unaware of the newspaper and the hidden gun.

Kreig said: "It's four to one, but I'm going through with this thing."

"Five to one now," Tony Scott said clearly, and stepped out to stand at Kreig's elbow. Kreig looked up with a start. Scott's fists were clenched by his sides, the light of battle in his eyes. He raised a hand.

Apperley spoke, if only in opposition to Kreig, the man he hated. "Don't try anything, Scott. He's heeled."

"Right," Kreig mocked, and lifted the paper again for an instant. "See it? I don't know what they call you, mister, and I ain't particularly bothered. But you make my evening complete—by heck, you do. This is a joyful occasion. I'd planned to send at least two to the gates of glory, but while I'm at it I might add to the number. Hell, I owe you that much for this afternoon."

Scott was unafraid. "But aren't you taking on terrific odds, you rat—whatever they call you?"

"Make it 'Johnny'." Kreig smiled menacingly. "All my pals call me that. 'Big Johnny' Kreig of New York and all points east. Can you find a chair behind you? Reach out a hand, son, and bring one forward. Then you can sit down and join in this interesting little party."

Scott did as he was ordered, eyes on the gun. Freda White was sobbing beneath her breath as she made room for him.

Kreig leaned back. "I ain't got time to either argue or explain, and I won't. What do they call you? Scott, did you say, Apperley?"

"You're likely to hear more of the name in the future." Scott's voice was curt and steady.

"Perhaps," Kreig mocked. "But to answer your question: I like long odds. I've gambled all my life. To business, now. I can handle five as easily as I can handle one. But I'm not averse to a little assistance, and I'll do a deal with you, Munroe. You surely know me and recognise me."

Munroe eyed him steadily. "You think that you've got us all dead to rights."

"I *know* I have. I've no particular quarrel with you and Freda, although I warn you that I'll blast you both down unless you go my way. For the benefit of the gentleman who's just joined us, I repeat that this gun has the latest in silencers, straight from the States. You should know that I mean business by now, since I've come all the way from there."

It seemed that Kreig must talk and talk, but perhaps un-understandably so, since he clearly held the whip hand. He said: "Don't any of you get foolish ideas that I'm unable to pull off this thing that I'm planning."

"Munroe," he went on, "you always were a louse, an' I'm giving you the opportunity to go on being one. Someone in this hotel who likes the feel of paper money told me that you came down here with Freda in a car. From London, wasn't it?"

"So what?" Munroe almost snarled at him.

"So I'm going to let you use it, on my behalf. I put it to you squarely: Will you take the opportunity of getting out of this thing with a whole skin, you and the doll you call Freda? Or do I have to save White and Apperley the trouble of kill-ing you? I believe that's what they originally had in mind."

Freda White sucked in her breath sharply. "What d'ye want us to do?" The scarlet nails were hovering near her lips again.

"Big Johnny." Kreig smiled at her. "Baby, you're being sensible. Reach over and see if your dear husband and his pal are heeled. And don't anyone else move," he added. "I might take to reading this newspaper again."

The woman hesitated, then did as she was told. Kreig jerked out to Apperley: "Get up, blast you, and let the lady do as I tell her!" And Apperley got malevolently to his feet so that she could reach his hip pocket.

Arthur White put a hand to the side of his coat, then froze as Kreig looked at him. "Big Johnny" motioned to the woman and she understood. As in the case of Apperley's weapon, she slid White's gun across the table to Kreig and the latter coolly stowed them away on his own person, secure in the complete seclusion of the corner booth. Then he cocked an eye at Munroe. "Yours?"

"I never carry a gat, Johnny. You know me."

Kreig reached over and patted Munroe's pockets. "Fine—fine. I couldn't really expect it in a con. man. Now you, sonny."

"If you're referring to me," Scott said, as calmly as he was able, "I've never carried a weapon in my life."

"An' you said that you were connected with the police department?"

"I know a man there, if that's what you mean. But I'm an ordinary civilian," Scott answered. "So you're bent on a killing, that it? And it includes me?"

"It includes you," Kreig bit off. "I owe you that much for this afternoon. I think I get it. You poked your ugly snout into my business because your pal, whoever he might be—"

"Name of Detective-Inspector Croft, of Scotland Yard," Apperley cut in mockingly.

"Shut up. Whoever he is, Mr. Clever Scott, he must have tipped you off that the police are out after me. All right. You recognised my description and thought that you'd do that pal a favour. Hell, I wish that I'd have broken your damn' neck. It'd save me so much trouble now."

"Just how do you propose to dispose of me?" Scott asked, still retaining his calmness. He was painfully aware that to the rest of the occupants of the vast, crowded bar it must surely seem that here was a normal party of five engaged in conversation. How adroitly Kreig had stage-managed things! "Permit me to say that you've got hold of a fat-headed idea that won't work. Indeed it won't."

"You're going to have the pleasure of seeing it in operation," Kreig assured him. "You're going to wish that you'd confined yourself to plain holidaymakin' before I'm through. It'll work, all right."

He looked at Munroe again. "You've always looked after your own skins, you and Freda. What about it now? That's the point I'd reached before the lady did me the little favour I asked of her. You've got a car, and somewhere close by, I take it."

"In the car-park here." Munroe was sullen.

"Couldn't be better. I put it to you, then. Will you take my word on the deal? You know me—'Big Johnny.' I'm classed as a crook but you know that I never let down a pal and I always keep my bargains. I've come thousands of miles to keep this one."

Munroe swallowed again as he hesitated. Then: "I'll— I'll play ball with you, Johnny. Me and Freda."

"Great," Kreig said. He turned his dark, vengeance-racked eyes on to White and Apperley. "How about you prize rats?"

It was Scott's turn to volunteer information, and to find in it the same little thrill of malevolence that had come to Apperley. "Our friends have a car in the park as well. A hired one."

"Couldn't be better," Kreig said. "Co-operative, ain't we? Just aching to help one another? The beautiful soft summer twilight has now come to this delightful place by the sea; in fact, I judge it to be damn' near dark. The same man on the staff here, whose palm I've been greasing liberally, tells me that there's a fairly quiet coast road running out of the town. I intend to make use of it."

"Big Johnny" brought his attention back to the treacherous Munroe. "Here's what we do, then. I take these three gents in Apperley's car. You follow on with Freda. No, dammit, you'll go ahead. Our Mr. Scott will drive me, Apperley and White; and I'll be in the back with Apperley beside me and White next to Scott. In that way I'll be able to cover all three. They know what to expect if there's any funny business. You'll stop when I make friend Scott toot his horn three times. That'll be when I've decided on a suitable spot having presented itself as I look outa the window."

Munroe nodded. "What then?"

"That's when you and Freda get busy. You've got a beautiful example in front of you now, and I want you to profit by it to the extent of seeing this through." Kreig set his teeth. "If you don't, I'll make it my business to engage on a second hunt for revenge, after I've put these rats to sleep. Don't think I can't do it. I'm giving you a chance that you don't deserve. I'm willing to call it quits between us if you help me to get the job over quickly and well. I'll trust you to the extent of a gun apiece when we stop. I'll get these three at the edge of the cliff, but I'll have to do it one by one. That means that you cover the rest. But, Munroe, if you value the lousy skin of yourself and Freda, don't forget that I shall have a gun in my hand, too. Understand?"

Freda spoke. She was quavering. "You force us into this . . . "

"I'm doing you both a big favour," Kreig rasped back. "I'm taking White and Apperley outa your hair. Something you want to say?"—to Scott, who was moving uneasily in his chair.

"Yes," Scott answered, unafraid. "You're determined to go through with this thing, then?"

Kreig's eyes held a devil of mocking cruelty. "You heard, brother. This is another ride—in the dark. Just as dangerous and hellish as the one you and I took this afternoon. But this time there'll be no getting out of it for you. I'll make a real job of it."

Scott tried to still the pounding of the grazed temple, though he sat passive. "Okay. I'll try to take what comes and I shan't complain. Only do me a favour before we get moving in this thing."

"A favour?" Kreig raised his eyebrows. "And that is?"

"Give me a few words with Apperley before we start."

Kreig pondered the request, "I don't know what's between you," he said at length. "I've been trying not to waste time. I haven't even gone into the point of which one of those two swine actually bumped off Seldon. All I'm concerned with is that they did me dirt. That they tried to get even with Munroe and Freda on the same grounds; and that I beat them to it. It's a plain issue with me. What more do you want?"

Tony Scott took a desperate plunge, right or wrong. It didn't much matter now, anyway. He looked at Apperley.

"Tell me," he said distinctly. "What have you done with Marjorie Castleton?"

Trapped as he was, Apperley jeered at him. "Ask our dear friend Johnny to lend you that paper he's holding. The latest news is that the poor girl's body has not yet been recovered from the cruel, cruel sea."

Scott had expected such an answer. Yet a faint spark of hope still lingered within him. Desperately he played his last card.

"Mr. White." And the sullen and silent artist looked up.

Scott said clearly: "According to this thug who sits among us, we're facing certain death. You're included. Forgive me for saying so, but you seem to be almighty interested in the lady with us."

White moistened hot lips. The words seemed to be dragged from him: "She's—my wife. I came a long way, dared a lot, to reclaim her. I . . . want her to know that, whatever she's done to me, I . . . forgive her. I still . . . love her."

Even the sarcastic Kreig was silent at the words. White looked down at his tapering fingers. He fought against honest sentiment, and could not resist it as a genuine heart-cry. "I'd damn' well die for her alone—and well she knows it."

"You'd die for a worthless woman," Scott said between his teeth. "Yet she's not worthless to you. I respect you for it. But the thing that I'm getting at is this. You seem to be booked to die, in any case. And you know what love is. So do I. That's why I'm asking your help. Apperley's incapable of love."

White raised his dull eyes. "It won't help you any," he whispered.

"But it'll put my mind at rest. Is Marjorie Castleton alive or dead?"

"This ain't my pigeon," Kreig said, glancing over his shoulder at the bar clock, "but I'll give you just two minutes to settle this sentimental mush, whatever it is, an' then we get moving."

Scott ignored him. Hope was knocking at his heart now. White's very manner . . . "Alive or dead?" he repeated steadfastly.

Once more Arthur White looked down at his locked fingers, then bowed his head in shame. "Alive."

The pounding in Scott's damaged temple increased. The world had become glorious, even in face of threatened death. "Alive! Good God in heaven—alive!"

"One minute," Kreig said, and pushed his chair back. "Understand, everybody. When we start out of here you walk in front. I'll have my baby tucked in my pocket with my finger round the trigger. I repeat that this is a silenced weapon; and the first one to try to make a break for it gets it right in the back. I don't care. I can empty the whole clip among you and then run for it."

"You've come so far in an effort to redeem yourself a little," Tony Scott persisted, still ignoring Kreig. "You can't leave me in total darkness now. Where is she?"

"There's a—fisherman's hut," White answered despairingly. "The coast road—But I've told you that it's no good. Apperley and myself had planned to take her back to Castleton House when we'd settled with Munroe and Freda."

"If we could get out of this, we'd pick her up just the same," Apperley snarled, in a clumsy effort to turn the knife in the wound for Scott. "But it seems that we're all booked for the long drop together. I'm glad to tell you because it gives me a certain amount of vicarious satisfaction to know that you'll be eating your heart out, and it won't do you a scrap of good. Not one damned iota."

Kreig stood up. "That concludes your interesting spot of private business, then, gents. On your feet, everybody, and try to act natural."

Whatever else he might be, Scott couldn't help but think that "Big Johnny" Kreig had an outstanding characteristic. He was amazing. Cool, confident, watchful, willing to gamble against long odds singlehanded.

And he seemed quite capable of getting away with it.

CHAPTER XV

THE LAST OF THE CASTLETONS

THROUGH THE BAR of the "Hotel Metropole" and into the vestibule, "Big Johnny" Kreig was behind the five of them, resolute, grim-lipped, his right hand sunk into the pocket of the smart brown suit.

None dared disobey him. Although there were many here, the menace of the unseen gun was too great to be denied. There was a commissionaire, people going in and out, light, activity. The party gained the pavement and turned to the left.

Johnny's eyes were wide-ranging and dangerous. Munroe's lean jaw was still tight and strained. Freda clung to his arm in mute supplication, as though urging him not to make trouble. "Stop here," Kreig said, almost in a whisper.

He spoke directly to Munroe. "Don't turn around. Which is your car?"

"Straight ahead," Munroe said, and felt in his waistcoat pocket for the parking check.

"Okay. Straight forward and get into it. And mind what I've told you. Three toots an' you stop. And, Munroe—"

The confidence trickster halted in his stride. "Well?"

"Remember I can always find you . . . "

"I'm not likely to forget. And I'm thinking of Freda," Munroe jerked back over his shoulder. He hesitated, then went forward, still arm in arm with the woman.

Kreig said to the three left with him: "Now we all go on to the rattletrap you've hired, Apperley. You ain't got as much chance as Ed, an' he's damned sensible."

Apperley walked slightly to the left, the others following. He nodded to an attendant, gave up his check, produced a key. "This is it."

"Almost right by Munroe, eh?" Kreig mocked him. "Couldn't be better. Come here, Ed."

He lifted his voice so that the words might be heard over a short intervening space. Munroe helped Freda into the car and came back sullenly. "Well?"

"You know the road I mean," Kreig said, and moved the gun a trifle in his pocket. "Do this job for me right an' there won't be a thing between us. The coast road lies dead in front of you. Straight along this stretch that I gather they call the Promenade, and outa the town. And we'll be right behind you."

"I've already told you," Munroe answered. "Freda counts with me. You'll have to trust us."

"That so?" Kreig asked. "Hell, Ed, I've got an idea that if it wasn't for her you might be tempted to act smart. I'll credit you with that amount of guts. On your way."

Tony Scott told himself that the situation was so bizarre as to be almost farcical. In this busy place, one determined man was ordering the lives, the actions and destinies of five others. If he were not a forced participant in this nightmare, he might have been inclined to scoff at such melodrama. But this wasn't funny; it was real. It was being accomplished, like it or not.

Apperley and White were tough enough to risk almost anything, but "Big Johnny" had them licked into prudence. As for Scott himself—

His heart was lightened, in spite of the danger that encompassed him and from which there might well be no escape. At least Marjorie Castleton was alive.

Alive, but—she might as well be dead. She might yet be left to rot in the hut, the whereabouts of which were unknown to him. That is, unless Scott might somehow hope to turn the tables. A pretty tall order, that. It meant not only overcoming the watchful Kreig, but also White and Apperley as well; meant forcing them to disclose the whereabouts of the place where the helpless girl was imprisoned.

And—Detective-Inspector Croft. Thoughts of him tugged at Scott's mind. Once again he thought of the Inspector's warning. If only he could "call a cop" now!

Kreig shouldered Scott forward, and he felt the bulge of the gripped automatic through Kreig's pocket. "You drive, sonny. And drive carefully. I'll be sitting right behind you."

Scott cursed him beneath his breath and got into the driver's seat. Kreig jerked his head at the silent Arthur White, who placed himself beside Scott. Then Kreig turned to Apperley—his arch-enemy.

"I always like my best pals sitting right next to me. C'mon."

"Big Johnny" lowered his head and got in first. He reached out to grip at the muttering Apperley's arm and pull him in. "Squat down here, an' keep on saying nothing. I notice that all of you are wise enough for that. Get her rolling, Scott, and keep close behind the others.

"And don't think," he added, as afterthought, "that I'm getting tired of repeating myself when I say that this rod of mine is still loaded and capable of blasting you all to hell as you sit."

Kreig brought the automatic out into full view, resting it on his knees. His hand was as steady as a rock.

They started off along the smooth, well-lit Promenade. Scott thought to himself that Kreig had never thought to query the fact if he could drive or not. But in these modern days, he reflected, almost every man was expected to number such an art among his accomplishments. Certainly he found this car easy enough to handle. In spite of Kreig's jeer about the "rattletrap" the car was fairly new, was roomy and comfortable. And it held Munroe's expensive Hispano effortlessly in view.

Traffic thinned out as they came to the edge of the town. The Promenade ended at a huge illuminated roundabout, but it was impossible for Monroe, stranger though he might be to these parts, to miss the beginning of the narrow coast road. The sea was on his right.

Dimly seen, as the overhead lights finished and were replaced by concrete lamp standards that grew wider apart as they sped on. Kreig was still watchful and menacing, although he kept darting a quick look out of the window to his right, ever and again. They had gone about three miles before he leaned over and spoke to Scott.

"Lean on that horn."

It was the first words that had been spoken since this mad ride had started. Scott pressed down smartly on the electric button set in the middle of the steering column—banged it three times. So this was it.

Ahead of them Munroe heard it and slowed down. This was where he waited for Kreig to come up. Thoughts were seething within him. This was planned murder.

Murder. Something that he had done his utmost to avoid in his chequered criminal career. He was being forced, with Freda, to become an active accessory to the killing of three men.

A bullet for himself and the woman with whom he had thrown in his life, if he didn't do it. But how about the consequences? Ed Munroe had a wholesome respect for the law, which was undoubtedly why he had survived so long as a quick-moving international crook. Keeping a move or two ahead of the police in his racket was one thing. Trying to evade a triple murder rap was another.

Munroe thought just as fast as Kreig himself had done. He planned as rapidly. His astuteness in fitting things together told him that the police already knew that Scott was interested in following Kreig, and, furthermore, that Scotland Yard also knew, or guessed, that Apperley and White were involved in the relationship as well.

So that to find the lot of them together in a wrecked car would, on the whole, seem to be perfectly natural.

Who would know? Scott had come upon Kreig, White and Apperley, had somehow got Kreig's gun, was on the point of bringing the wanted men back to Harlingham police headquarters single-handed. He had been foolish enough to drive, no doubt with the gun beside him. The other occupants of the car had made a break for it. The road here was completely deserted and most conveniently narrow, with a sheer drop over the cliff to the side of it.

All this in the second or two occupied by slowing down. Munroe made up his own mind, since the cowering Freda was incapable. He wouldn't stand for murder. Not because of any moral principle, but because he had himself and the woman to consider in the future. The law. And, perhaps, an over-cautious Johnny Kreig. Wasn't he capable of anything? Wasn't he capable of mowing *them* down and toppling them over the cliff after the others, just to make sure?

To hell with that! Munroe thought, and started up again. He brought the big car around skilfully. It was his own and he had long ago made it his business to know how to drive in an emergency. His well-being might depend on it. Already slowing up himself, Scott saw what was happening ahead, and swore violently. Munroe had negotiated the bend, was bearing down on the accelerator and was charging straight at them on their left.

Over Scott's shoulder, Kreig saw what was happening, but could not find words. Apperley saw it, too, and grabbed with every fibre of his being at the slimmest of chances thus presenting itself. He was reckless. He was marked to die, anyhow.

Tony Scott rose to the emergency, although he didn't quite know how. Munroe was savagely twisting the wheel of the Hispano over—over. Then back the other way, violently. His maneuvre was clear. He planned to force them off the narrow road strip, then go bouncing back to the centre of it himself. Perhaps a fraction of a second might have accomplished that.

But that fraction of a second was Tony Scott's. He accelerated savagely, almost without thinking, as Munroe roared down upon him. The bonnet of the Hispano did not catch his own car full in the middle. Had it done so there would have been no hope. He would infallibly have been over the grass verge. Instead, his rear wheel was grazed; and even as he felt the shock he spun his own wheel to the left so that he fought with the bucking demon of steel on the other side of the road. Munroe felt what had happened, straightened out, and slammed on speed as he shot by. Back to Harlingham, to pack. He might yet have a chance, even if he had misjudged the distance slightly. Kreig still had his hands full.

And, as he shot by and Scott fought for control, the vengeful Henry Apperley acted by flinging himself at the startled Kreig. Now or never. Kreig was off guard, the gun that he had had to perforce hold lightly lest the trigger be pulled, since the safety-catch was off, knocked from his fingers by the force of the impact. Apperley clawed at Kreig's throat, and White was as quick to follow his lead.

He took a chance with Scott, still fighting to bring the car to a standstill, knelt on the seat beside him and reached over, just as Kreig got in a short-arm jab to Apperley's heart that made the latter grunt. Then his hand plunged downwards. But Arthur White was too quick for him. The gun was easily discernible on the floor, in that well-lit interior. He brought it up against Kreig's big chest, and panted with the strain.

Half-kneeling Kreig slowly got back to a sitting position. Apperley snatched the automatic from his partner. "Thanks."

"Out," he snapped to Kreig. And White hauled at Scott's arm, as the latter became dismally aware of what had happened. "This is where the position is reversed, Johnny," Apperley went on, through his teeth. "I thought it was a dumb move to try to look after five of us, you big bonehead. You might have known that Munroe'd pull a fast one."

Kreig's eyes blazed, but he made no answer. White pulled Scott out to the roadway to stand beside him.

Apperley was exulting in the feel of the gun. "Silenced, eh, Johnny?"

Kreig swallowed twice before he could speak. "You— you can't—"

"But *you* could," Apperley said. "Now the bumping-off goes forward as planned, blast you. But this time there's a slight alteration. The positions are reversed." He glowered at

Scott in the darkness. "And I'm glad to include you in this arrangement. You've given me too much trouble already not to pass up this lovely chance presented now."

"And the girl?" Scott asked levelly.

"What do you think?" Apperley flung back. "We take this car and pick her up. Then straight back to Castleton House. Then a clean-up. Presses, photographic equipment. You've surely guessed by now what's behind the entrance to our neat little place in the study?" Apperley laughed.

"Then we blow. This is a killing, Scott—a double killing. You've forced us into this. We'd have liked a little more time to satisfy our associates and add to the profit, but all that'll have to go by the board now. Dear Mr. White and myself have enough salted away for a lifetime of ease in, say, South America, where the extradition laws aren't too strict and two good men can always find a use for their talents. Shut up, Arthur."

Kreig said: "You're determined to go through with this, Apperley?"

"I am," Apperley said. "We put you two skunks to sleep and then we add on to the total by another one. Three in all, Scott. What the heck! The girl's supposed to be dead already, anyway."

"I'll come back from hell to get you for this," Scott said quietly.

The gun jutted forward in Apperley's hand. "March—both of you."

They went forward the few paces to the cliff edge, just glimpsed in the darkness against the sheen of the sea. It seemed to be a long drop, all right. Kreig was sobbing in great racking breaths. And suddenly he bent, began to run almost double, so that his feet slithered among small stones and sand. And Henry Apperley cursed the darkness and pulled the trigger.

Flame stabbed into the blackness, twice, as the wary Scott launched himself full at White. Kreig screamed and went over the edge. White reeled back from an uppercut, came at Scott as he collected himself for a second blow, and went for his legs. Scott felt a bullet sing past his neck as he clawed desperately at nothing.

Over—nothing could stop him. He went down bumping, fighting, breath knocked from his body. Then a shallow ledge came up to meet him and displaced boulders hurtled from his path.

White and Apperley heard the splashes they made and stood panting, White said slowly: "All the way down. That's it."

"Saves us a lot of trouble," Apperley rasped. "For God's sake let's get moving."

Scott heard the car roar away as he lay there, fingers twining desperately in a tussock of coarse grass. There wasn't much room. It only needed a touch to yet go down.

There was something stirring and groaning a few inches away. As his head cleared a little, Scott dragged himself forward. "Big Johnny," jammed against a bush that bent outward beneath his weight—that threatened to snap and send him crashing.

Scott pulled his knees up, so that he might somehow drag Kreig farther back to safety. He found his hands wet with blood from the gaping shoulder wound that had shattered the American's arm so that it trailed down uselessly. But he would not die. Not unless he slipped forward and over from sheer exhaustion.

Scott investigated in groping fashion. The small ledge that had saved their lives went back, a little farther on, into a recess that formed a natural platform. How he managed it, he didn't know, but he got his hands beneath the groaning Johnny's armpits and dragged him inch by inch, until the gangster's back rested securely against the rock, feet stretched out. There was room to move here. Kreig's head drooped forward on his big chest.

Unconscious, and he might well stay that way for a short while. Scott realised that he now had a fighting chance. He used both their handkerchiefs to stanch the wound in Johnny's shoulder as best he could, then went scrabbling upwards.

It seemed that he could not pump air back into his lungs as he finally lay on the grass verge of the road. He got to his feet and glanced helplessly about him. Just the long row of widely-spaced lights, the wind, the sound of the sea. Was he to be licked now?

Then the miracle came along in the shape of the bus from Harlingham. Scott stood in the glare of its headlights, frantically waving it to a stop, and the driver saw him although he was not overpleased that this was not a regulation pull-up "By Request." Scott tried to straighten his clothes in face of the few curious passengers, gladly paid his fare and asked for direction, lest he miss his mark. Then he dropped off at the iron gates and deserted lodge of Castleton House.

The car stood at the end of the driveway, but there was no sign of Apperley or White, and the house seemed to be in darkness. This puzzled Scott for a moment, although he could not be expected to know the truth—that his two enemies had doubled over to the stables with the girl they had quickly liberated from the hut. She was untied completely now, and had been forced to run to the stables between them. From there into a huge semi-natural cave, somewhere under the famed Long Gallery of Castleton House, where they thrust her into a corner and went to work to destroy all they could against the ebb of the night tide.

There was always a spare dinghy kept in readiness, hauled up high and dry. When the lower cave that provided egress had its mouth revealed by the rapidly-lowering water the houseboat would be available to them. As the converted cabin cruiser Apperley had boasted it to be, it had good engines.

And Marjorie Castleton could then be conveniently knocked over the head and dumped overboard as they got up the anchor and slipped away in the darkness. She might yet be found a drifting corpse.

Elspeth McCracken was upstairs in her own room as Tony Scott threw discretion to the winds and pulled the antique iron bell-chain in the porch of the Castleton House that Apperley and White had determined to leave for ever. The sound went shattering through the ancient building. Apperley heard it, and dropped an armful of photographic gear. The housekeeper heard it and nerved herself to go downstairs.

Apperley lifted up a simple sliding panel in the oak of the "sacrosanct" study and came out into the Great Hall to investigate. Elspeth McCracken saw Scott charging to meet him as she opened the front door and he brushed past her. Over his shoulder Scott yelled to her: "The telephone! *Use* it this time! 999 . . . " Then Apperley met him toe to toe.

No need to find glasses now. The scared housekeeper conquered her revulsion of the "de'lish contraption" and somehow managed to dial the number. Detective-Inspector Croft himself heard her gabbled story, roared for Inspector Paynter and a squad car, and left the old Scotswoman hanging helplessly on to the instrument.

Scott jerked out: "I told you that I'd oblige you sometime in this little matter of beating the daylights out of me, and here we are, Apperley. Next time make sure that a cliff goes all the way down." Then the surprised Henry Apperley had rocked him backwards.

Scott rolled his head aside to break the full force of the blow and retaliated. Somewhere below them, Arthur White found himself fully occupied with the courageous girl who was again getting into action for herself.

The fight raged on. Miss McCracken sat down weakly; while Croft and Paynter tore up the intervening miles. The small wound in Scott's temple had been reopened, Apperley was pounding him on the floor near the great refectory table. Then he was up again to receive a smack that sent him flying.

Apperley seized such slight advantage and doubled back to the study. Croft now. Everything was slipping away from him. In the study, with the panel still raised, Scott launched a blow that missed, and Apperley tripped him expertly. But he was too late to get away and into the passage before Scott had scrambled to his feet and followed. He clawed at Apperley in semi-darkness in a narrow passage that seemed to be stifling.

Scott was undoubtedly too busy to note that the darkness stretched away to the left—the stables. But he got a confused impression of a small square of light somewhere over on his right. And he heard White struggling with the fighting Marjorie Castleton in that direction, but on a lower level.

Minutes had sped by unnoticed in the hectic fight that had raged throughout the Great Hall. A skilled police driver had established a record speed along the twisting coast road, somewhere along which the unconscious "Big Johnny" Kreig had been passed, because his existence there had been unknown to either Croft or the housekeeper. The Inspector flung himself out of the car and ran forward.

Apperley and Scott were now in the lighted cave, surrounded by apparatus. Close by, White had the girl down, trying to pinion her arms to the ground. Scott and his opponent went down yet again, and Apperley banged Scott's head ruthlessly against the hard stone. He heard the voices of Croft and men with him, struggled drunkenly to his feet a few paces away and groped for a recess in the rock wall.

Croft was in the study by the still-open panel as Henry Apperley pulled the iron lever that had not been disturbed for hundreds of years. In a flash of premonition, the Inspector stepped back and mighty chains securing the huge stone boulder that was poised over the passageway groaned and creaked. Then it moved in thunder and the whole house seemed to rock.

Croft wiped dust from his eyes and guessed what had happened. He found the quavering old Elspeth McCracken at his elbow. "That cuts them off frae ye, Inspector. An' I heard Miss Marjorie doon there. I tell you, she's no dead. I heard her!"

"But we've lost her for good," Croft snarled.

The skinny fingers of the old woman raked at his arm. "Let me—let me make amends a little. I—" She closed her eyes for very weariness and rocked where she stood.

Croft understood in that instant. "You know, but you've tried not to tell me," he whispered. "Out with it, woman!"

"I had my duty to the Colonel," she said. "I foun' oot, but he made me swear . . . "

"Never mind that," Croft insisted. "There's another way?"

Elspeth McCracken rocked herself in sorrow as she stood. "Ye once tellt me that you were frae these very parts, Inspector. Ye look guid enough to climb a cliff yet. Follow me. I ken where there's a rope in my kitchen cupboard."

It was perhaps three minutes later that the party of policemen stood on the verge of the private stretch of cliff belonging to Castleton House to the left of the strip of shingle. Men held on to one end of the rope while first Croft and then Paynter went over. It was not too far down to the cave.

Croft had a gun in his hand and did not scruple to use it in face of what he saw. White was trying to tie the girl up once again. Tony Scott was in a corner, being menaced by Apperley with a revolver kept on a shelf in the cave for just such an emergency. Croft barked: "Drop it!" received no response, and fired.

The gun spun away from Apperley as he clutched at his wrist; and the useful Inspector Paynter took the exhausted White by the scruff of the neck and lifted him clear of the girl.

But she was not clear for long. Tony Scott gripped the hand of Detective-Inspector Croft and then reeled over to Marjorie Castleton. Once more she found arms about her—but this time they were friendly ones.

Scott panted out the story of the cliff adventure, and Croft turned to Paynter. "Get up into the hall," he said, "and telephone for cars and an ambulance to be sent to the spot. You're bound to find this man called Kreig before long. From what Mr. Scott says, he can't have moved much."

Inspector Paynter grinned. "And while I'm at it, I'll have men move on the 'Metropole.' That's where you said, isn't it, Mr. Scott?"

"It is," Scott said happily. "Munroe and his woman can't have managed to check out yet. I'll bet, Inspector, that the Yard'll find something on *them*, all right."

"They seem to strike a responsive chord in my mind," Croft answered. "By the way, this 'Big Johnny' Kreig of yours seems to tie up with the forgery blocks in the suitcase he left behind in Shannon Street, in London. Yes, I think he'll have a pleasant future."

He turned away. Marjorie Castleton was crying in Scott's arms.

Croft said over his shoulder: "I think someone else should have one, as well. Eh, Miss Castleton?"

She knew what he meant. "But I don't deserve it, Mr. Scott—Tony—I've been wrong, silly, impulsive—"

"Hush!" Scott told her, as Croft moved in the direction of the cave mouth that led out to sea. "There are times when impulsiveness can become a virtue, my dear. Such as now, for instance. You can be impulsive enough, and I'd worship you for it, to—"

She smiled through her tears, "To come to some arrangement after all?"

Scott drew a torn coat sleeve across his blackened face. "Something like that. I could put through the deal as I originally intended and—"

"We could *both* live here," she said daringly. "Do you forgive me enough for that?"

Scott drew her closer to him. "Suits me. The office might well appoint me curator of this venerable pile. That upstairs wing would still be large enough." And she snuggled against him.

"You very nearly lost the—last of the Castletons," she whispered, and he laid his lips against her hair. His eyes were sparkling.

"The last of the Castletons? How very right you are, my darling! The line's finished and done with. And from now on—"

"You'll be Mrs. Marjorie Scott," said Detective-Inspector Croft, as he turned away from the shimmering waters and felt for his pipe.

THE END

RAMBLE HOUSE's

HARRY STEPHEN KEELER WEBWORK MYSTERIES

(RH) indicates the title is available ONLY in the RAMBLE HOUSE edition

The Ace of Spades Murder
The Affair of the Bottled Deuce (RH)
The Amazing Web
The Barking Clock
Behind That Mask
The Book with the Orange Leaves
The Bottle with the Green Wax Seal
The Box from Japan
The Case of the Canny Killer
The Case of the Crazy Corpse (RH)
The Case of the Flying Hands (RH)
The Case of the Ivory Arrow
The Case of the Jeweled Ragpicker
The Case of the Lavender Gripsack
The Case of the Mysterious Moll
The Case of the 16 Beans
The Case of the Transparent Nude (RH)
The Case of the Transposed Legs
The Case of the Two-Headed Idiot (RH)
The Case of the Two Strange Ladies
The Circus Stealers (RH)
Cleopatra's Tears
A Copy of Beowulf (RH)
The Crimson Cube (RH)
The Face of the Man From Saturn
Find the Clock
The Five Silver Buddhas
The 4th King
The Gallows Waits, My Lord! (RH)
The Green Jade Hand
Finger! Finger!
Hangman's Nights (RH)
I, Chameleon (RH)
I Killed Lincoln at 10:13! (RH)
The Iron Ring
The Man Who Changed His Skin (RH)
The Man with the Crimson Box
The Man with the Magic Eardrums
The Man with the Wooden Spectacles
The Marceau Case
The Matilda Hunter Murder

The Monocled Monster
The Murder of London Lew
The Murdered Mathematician
The Mysterious Card (RH)
The Mysterious Ivory Ball of Wong Shing
 Li (RH)
The Mystery of the Fiddling Cracksman
The Peacock Fan
The Photo of Lady X (RH)
The Portrait of Jirjohn Cobb
Report on Vanessa Hewstone (RH)
Riddle of the Travelling Skull
Riddle of the Wooden Parrakeet (RH)
The Scarlet Mummy (RH)
The Search for X-Y-Z
The Sharkskin Book
Sing Sing Nights
The Six From Nowhere (RH)
The Skull of the Waltzing Clown
The Spectacles of Mr. Cagliostro
Stand By—London Calling!
The Steeltown Strangler
The Stolen Gravestone (RH)
Strange Journey (RH)
The Strange Will
The Straw Hat Murders (RH)
The Street of 1000 Eyes (RH)
Thieves' Nights
Three Novellos (RH)
The Tiger Snake
The Trap (RH)
Vagabond Nights (Defrauded Yeggman)
Vagabond Nights 2 (10 Hours)
The Vanishing Gold Truck
The Voice of the Seven Sparrows
The Washington Square Enigma
When Thief Meets Thief
The White Circle (RH)
The Wonderful Scheme of Mr. Christo-
 pher Thorne
X. Jones—of Scotland Yard
Y. Cheung, Business Detective

Keeler Related Works

A To Izzard: A Harry Stephen Keeler Companion by Fender Tucker — Articles and stories about Harry, by Harry, and in his style. Included is a compleat bibliography.

Wild About Harry: Reviews of Keeler Novels — Edited by Richard Polt & Fender Tucker — 22 reviews of works by Harry Stephen Keeler from *Keeler News*. A perfect introduction to the author.

The Keeler Keyhole Collection: Annotated newsletter rants from Harry Stephen Keeler, edited by Francis M. Nevins. Over 400 pages of incredibly personal Keeleriana.

Fakealoo — Pastiches of the style of Harry Stephen Keeler by selected demented members of the HSK Society. Updated every year with the new winner.

Strands of the Web: Short Stories of Harry Stephen Keeler — 29 stories, just about all that Keeler wrote, are edited and introduced by Fred Cleaver.

RAMBLE HOUSE's LOON SANCTUARY

A Clear Path to Cross — Sharon Knowles short mystery stories by Ed Lynskey.

A Corpse Walks in Brooklyn and Other Stories — Volume 5 in the Day Keene in the Detective Pulps series.

A Jimmy Starr Omnibus — Three 40s novels by Jimmy Starr.

A Niche in Time and Other Stories — Classic SF by William F. Temple

A Roland Daniel Double: The Signal and The Return of Wu Fang — Classic thrillers from the 30s.

A Shot Rang Out — Three decades of reviews and articles by today's Anthony Boucher, Jon Breen. An essential book for any mystery lover's library.

A Smell of Smoke — A 1951 English countryside thriller by Miles Burton.

A Snark Selection — Lewis Carroll's *The Hunting of the Snark* with two Snarkian chapters by Harry Stephen Keeler — Illustrated by Gavin L. O'Keefe.

A Young Man's Heart — A forgotten early classic by Cornell Woolrich.

Alexander Laing Novels — *The Motives of Nicholas Holtz* and *Dr. Scarlett*, stories of medical mayhem and intrigue from the 30s.

An Angel in the Street — Modern hardboiled noir by Peter Genovese.

Automaton — Brilliant treatise on robotics: 1928-style! By H. Stafford Hatfield.

Away From the Here and Now — Clare Winger Harris stories, collected by Richard A. Lupoff

Beast or Man? — A 1930 novel of racism and horror by Sean M'Guire. Introduced by John Pelan.

Black Beadle — A 1939 thriller by E.C.R. Lorac.

Black Hogan Strikes Again — Australia's Peter Renwick pens a tale of the 30s outback.

Black River Falls — Suspense from the master, Ed Gorman.

Blondy's Boy Friend — A snappy 1930 story by Philip Wylie, writing as Leatrice Homesley.

Blood in a Snap — The *Finnegan's Wake* of the 21st century, by Jim Weiler.

Blood Moon — The first of the Robert Payne series by Ed Gorman.

Bogart '48 — Hollywood action with Bogie by John Stanley and Kenn Davis

Calling Lou Largo! — Two Lou Largo novels by William Ard.

Cornucopia of Crime — Francis M. Nevins assembled this huge collection of his writings about crime literature and the people who write it. Essential for any serious mystery library.

Corpse Without Flesh — Strange novel of forensics by George Bruce

Crimson Clown Novels — By Johnston McCulley, author of the Zorro novels, *The Crimson Clown* and *The Crimson Clown Again*.

Dago Red — 22 tales of dark suspense by Bill Pronzini.

Dark Sanctuary — Weird Menace story by H. B. Gregory

David Hume Novels — *Corpses Never Argue, Cemetery First Stop, Make Way for the Mourners, Eternity Here I Come*. 1930s British hardboiled fiction with an attitude.

Dead Man Talks Too Much — Hollywood boozer by Weed Dickenson.

Death Leaves No Card — One of the most unusual murdered-in-the-tub mysteries you'll ever read. By Miles Burton.

Death March of the Dancing Dolls and Other Stories — Volume Three in the Day Keene in the Detective Pulps series. Introduced by Bill Crider.

Deep Space and other Stories — A collection of SF gems by Richard A. Lupoff.

Detective Duff Unravels It — Episodic mysteries by Harvey O'Higgins.

Diabolic Candelabra — Classic 30s mystery by E.R. Punshon.

Dictator's Way — Another D.S. Bobby Owen mystery from E.R. Punshon

Dime Novels: Ramble House's 10-Cent Books — *Knife in the Dark* by Robert Leslie Bellem, *Hot Lead* and *Song of Death* by Ed Earl Repp, *A Hashish House in New York* by H.H. Kane, and five more.

Doctor Arnoldi — Tiffany Thayer's story of the death of death.

Don Diablo: Book of a Lost Film — Two-volume treatment of a western by Paul Landres, with diagrams. Intro by Francis M. Nevins.

Dope and Swastikas — Two strange novels from 1922 by Edmund Snell

Dope Tales #1 — Two dope-riddled classics; *Dope Runners* by Gerald Grantham and *Death Takes the Joystick* by Phillip Condé.

Dope Tales #2 — Two more narco-classics; *The Invisible Hand* by Rex Dark and *The Smokers of Hashish* by Norman Berrow.

Dope Tales #3 — Two enchanting novels of opium by the master, Sax Rohmer. *Dope* and *The Yellow Claw.*

Double Hot — Two 60s softcore sex novels by Morris Hershman.

Double Sex — Yet two more panting thrillers from Morris Hershman.

Dr. Odin — Douglas Newton's 1933 racial potboiler comes back to life.

Evangelical Cockroach — Jack Woodford writes about writing.

Evidence in Blue — 1938 mystery by E. Charles Vivian.

Fatal Accident — Murder by automobile, a 1936 mystery by Cecil M. Wills**.**

Fighting Mad — Todd Robbins' 1922 novel about boxing and life

Finger-prints Never Lie — A 1939 classic detective novel by John G. Brandon.

Freaks and Fantasies — Eerie tales by Tod Robbins, collaborator of Tod Browning on the film FREAKS.

Gadsby — A lipogram (a novel without the letter E). Ernest Vincent Wright's last work, published in 1939 right before his death.

Gelett Burgess Novels — *The Master of Mysteries, The White Cat, Two O'Clock Courage, Ladies in Boxes, Find the Woman, The Heart Line, The Picaroons* and *Lady Mechante.* Recently added is A Gelett Burgess Sampler, edited by Alfred Jan. All are introduced by Richard A. Lupoff.

Geronimo — S. M. Barrett's 1905 autobiography of a noble American.

Hake Talbot Novels — *Rim of the Pit, The Hangman's Handyman.* Classic locked room mysteries, with mapback covers by Gavin O'Keefe.

Hands Out of Hell and Other Stories — John H. Knox's eerie hallucinations

Hell is a City — William Ard's masterpiece.

Hollywood Dreams — A novel of Tinsel Town and the Depression by Richard O'Brien.

Hostesses in Hell and Other Stories — Russell Gray's most graphic stories

House of the Restless Dead — Strange and ominous tales by Hugh B. Cave.

I Stole $16,000,000 — A true story by cracksman Herbert E. Wilson.

Inclination to Murder — 1966 thriller by New Zealand's Harriet Hunter.

Invaders from the Dark — Classic werewolf tale from Greye La Spina.

J. Poindexter, Colored — Classic satirical black novel by Irvin S. Cobb.

Jack Mann Novels — Strange murder in the English countryside. *Gees' First Case, Nightmare Farm, Grey Shapes, The Ninth Life, The Glass Too Many, Her Ways Are Death, The Kleinert Case* and *Maker of Shadows.*

Jake Hardy — A lusty western tale from Wesley Tallant.

Jim Harmon Double Novels — *Vixen Hollow/Celluloid Scandal, The Man Who Made Maniacs/Silent Siren, Ape Rape/Wanton Witch, Sex Burns Like Fire/Twist Session, Sudden Lust/Passion Strip, Sin Unlimited/Harlot Master, Twilight Girls/Sex Institution.* Written in the early 60s and never reprinted until now.

Joel Townsley Rogers Novels and Short Stories — By the author of *The Red Right Hand: Once In a Red Moon, Lady With the Dice, The Stopped Clock, Never Leave My Bed.* Also two short story collections: *Night of Horror* and *Killing Time.*

John Carstairs, Space Detective — Arboreal Sci-fi by Frank Belknap Long

Joseph Shallit Novels — *The Case of the Billion Dollar Body, Lady Don't Die on My Doorstep, Kiss the Killer, Yell Bloody Murder, Take Your Last Look.* One of America's best 50's authors and a favorite of author Bill Pronzini.

Keller Memento — 45 short stories of the amazing and weird by Dr. David Keller.

Killer's Caress — Cary Moran's 1936 hardboiled thriller.

Lady of the Yellow Death and Other Stories — More stories by Wyatt Blassingame.

League of the Grateful Dead and Other Stories — Volume One in the Day Keene in the Detective Pulps series.

Library of Death — Ghastly tale by Ronald S. L. Harding, introduced by John Pelan.

Malcolm Jameson Novels and Short Stories — *Astonishing! Astounding!, Tarnished Bomb, The Alien Envoy and Other Stories* and *The Chariots of San Fernando and Other Stories.* All introduced and edited by John Pelan or Richard A. Lupoff.

Man Out of Hell and Other Stories — Volume II of the John H. Knox weird pulps collection.

Marblehead: A Novel of H.P. Lovecraft — A long-lost masterpiece from Richard A. Lupoff. This is the "director's cut", the long version that has never been published before.

Mark of the Laughing Death and Other Stories — Shockers from the pulps by Francis James, introduced by John Pelan.

Master of Souls — Mark Hansom's 1937 shocker is introduced by weirdologist John Pelan.

Max Afford Novels — *Owl of Darkness, Death's Mannikins, Blood on His Hands, The Dead Are Blind, The Sheep and the Wolves, Sinners in Paradise* and *Two Locked Room Mysteries and a Ripping Yarn* by one of Australia's finest mystery novelists.

Money Brawl — Two books about the writing business by Jack Woodford and H. Bedford-Jones. Introduced by Richard A. Lupoff.

More Secret Adventures of Sherlock Holmes — Gary Lovisi's second collection of tales about the unknown sides of the great detective.

Muddled Mind: Complete Works of Ed Wood, Jr. — David Hayes and Hayden Davis deconstruct the life and works of the mad, but canny, genius.

Murder among the Nudists — A mystery from 1934 by Peter Hunt, featuring a naked Detective-Inspector going undercover in a nudist colony.

Murder in Black and White — 1931 classic tennis whodunit by Evelyn Elder.

Murder in Shawnee — Two novels of the Alleghenies by John Douglas: *Shawnee Alley Fire* and *Haunts.*

Murder in Silk — A 1937 Yellow Peril novel of the silk trade by Ralph Trevor.

My Deadly Angel — 1955 Cold War drama by John Chelton.

My First Time: The One Experience You Never Forget — Michael Birchwood — 64 true first-person narratives of how they lost it.

Mysterious Martin, the Master of Murder — Two versions of a strange 1912 novel by Tod Robbins about a man who writes books that can kill.

Norman Berrow Novels — *The Bishop's Sword, Ghost House, Don't Go Out After Dark, Claws of the Cougar, The Smokers of Hashish, The Secret Dancer, Don't Jump Mr. Boland!, The Footprints of Satan, Fingers for Ransom, The Three Tiers of Fantasy, The Spaniard's Thumb, The Eleventh Plague, Words Have Wings, One Thrilling Night, The Lady's in Danger, It Howls at Night, The Terror in the Fog, Oil Under the Window, Murder in the Melody, The Singing Room.* This is the complete Norman Berrow library of locked-room mysteries, several of which are masterpieces.

Old Faithful and Other Stories — SF classic tales by Raymond Z. Gallun.

Old Times' Sake — Short stories by James Reasoner from Mike Shayne Magazine.

One Dreadful Night — A classic mystery by Ronald S. L. Harding

Pair O' Jacks — A mystery novel and a diatribe about publishing by Jack Woodford

Perfect .38 — Two early Timothy Dane novels by William Ard. More to come.

Prince Pax — Devilish intrigue by George Sylvester Viereck and Philip Eldridge

Prose Bowl — Futuristic satire of a world where hack writing has replaced football as our national obsession, by Bill Pronzini and Barry N. Malzberg.

Red Light — The history of legal prostitution in Shreveport Louisiana by Eric Brock. Includes wonderful photos of the houses and the ladies.

Researching American-Made Toy Soldiers — A 276-page collection of a lifetime of articles by toy soldier expert Richard O'Brien.

Reunion in Hell — Volume One of the John H. Knox series of weird stories from the pulps. Introduced by horror expert John Pelan.

Ripped from the Headlines! — The Jack the Ripper story as told in the newspaper articles in the *New York* and *London Times.*

Rough Cut & New, Improved Murder — Ed Gorman's first two novels.

R.R. Ryan Novels — Freak Museum and The Subjugated Beast, two horror classics.

Ruby of a Thousand Dreams — The villain Wu Fang returns in this Roland Daniel novel.

Ruled By Radio — 1925 futuristic novel by Robert L. Hadfield & Frank E. Farncombe.

Rupert Penny Novels — *Policeman's Holiday, Policeman's Evidence, Lucky Policeman, Policeman in Armour, Sealed Room Murder, Sweet Poison, The Talkative Policeman, She had to Have Gas* and *Cut and Run* (by Martin Tanner.) Rupert Penny is the pseudonym of Australian Charles Thornett, a master of the locked room, impossible crime plot.

Sacred Locomotive Flies — Richard A. Lupoff's psychedelic SF story.

Sam — Early gay novel by Lonnie Coleman.

The Curse of Cantire — Classic 1939 novel of a family curse by Walter S. Masterman.

The Devil and the C.I.D. — Odd diabolic mystery by E.C.R. Lorac

The Devil Drives — An odd prison and lost treasure novel from 1932 by Virgil Markham.

The Devil of Pei-Ling — Herbert Asbury's 1929 tale of the occult.

The Devil's Mistress — A 1915 Scottish gothic tale by J. W. Brodie-Innes, a member of Aleister Crowley's Golden Dawn.

The Devil's Nightclub and Other Stories — John Pelan introduces some gruesome tales by Nat Schachner.

The Disentanglers — Episodic intrigue at the turn of last century by Andrew Lang

The Dog Poker Code — A spoof of *The Da Vinci Code* by D.B. Smithee.

The Dumpling — Political murder from 1907 by Coulson Kernahan.

The End of It All and Other Stories — Ed Gorman selected his favorite short stories for this huge collection.

The Fangs of Suet Pudding — A 1944 novel of the German invasion by Adams Farr

The Finger of Destiny and Other Stories — Edmund Snell's superb collection of weird stories of Borneo.

The Ghost of Gaston Revere — From 1935, a novel of life and beyond by Mark Hansom, introduced by John Pelan.

The Girl in the Dark — A thriller from Roland Daniel

The Gold Star Line — Seaboard adventure from L.T. Reade and Robert Eustace.

The Golden Dagger — 1951 Scotland Yard yarn by E. R. Punshon.

The Great Orme Terror — Horror stories by Garnett Radcliffe from the pulps

The Hairbreadth Escapes of Major Mendax — Francis Blake Crofton's 1889 boys' book.

The House That Time Forgot and Other Stories — Insane pulpitude by Robert F. Young

The House of the Vampire — 1907 poetic thriller by George S. Viereck.

The Illustrious Corpse — Murder hijinx from Tiffany Thayer

The Incredible Adventures of Rowland Hern — Intriguing 1928 impossible crimes by Nicholas Olde.

The Julius Caesar Murder Case — A classic 1935 re-telling of the assassination by Wallace Irwin that's much more fun than the Shakespeare version.

The Koky Comics — A collection of all of the 1978-1981 Sunday and daily comic strips by Richard O'Brien and Mort Gerberg, in two volumes.

The Lady of the Terraces — 1925 missing race adventure by E. Charles Vivian.

The Lord of Terror — 1925 mystery with master-criminal, Fantômas.

The Melamare Mystery — A classic 1929 Arsene Lupin mystery by Maurice Leblanc

The Man Who Was Secrett — Epic SF stories from John Brunner

The Man Without a Planet — Science fiction tales by Richard Wilson

The N. R. De Mexico Novels — Robert Bragg, the real N.R. de Mexico, presents *Marijuana Girl, Madman on a Drum, Private Chauffeur* in one volume.

The Night Remembers — A 1991 Jack Walsh mystery from Ed Gorman.

The One After Snelling — Kickass modern noir from Richard O'Brien.

The Organ Reader — A huge compilation of just about everything published in the 1971-1972 radical bay-area newspaper, *THE ORGAN*. A coffee table book that points out the shallowness of the coffee table mindset.

The Poker Club — Three in one! Ed Gorman's ground-breaking novel, the short story it was based upon, and the screenplay of the film made from it.

The Private Journal & Diary of John H. Surratt — The memoirs of the man who conspired to assassinate President Lincoln.

The Ramble House Mapbacks — Recently revised book by Gavin L. O'Keefe with color pictures of all the Ramble House books with mapbacks.

The Secret Adventures of Sherlock Holmes — Three Sherlockian pastiches by the Brooklyn author/publisher, Gary Lovisi.

The Shadow on the House — Mark Hansom's 1934 masterpiece of horror is introduced by John Pelan.

The Sign of the Scorpion — A 1935 Edmund Snell tale of oriental evil.

The Singular Problem of the Stygian House-Boat — Two classic tales by John Kendrick Bangs about the denizens of Hades.

The Smiling Corpse — Philip Wylie and Bernard Bergman's odd 1935 novel.

The Spider: Satan's Murder Machines — A thesis about Iron Man

The Stench of Death: An Odoriferous Omnibus by Jack Moskovitz — Two complete novels and two novellas from 60's sleaze author, Jack Moskovitz.

The Story Writer and Other Stories — Classic SF from Richard Wilson

The Strange Case of the Antlered Man — 1935 dementia from Edwy Searles Brooks

The Strange Thirteen — Richard B. Gamon's odd stories about Raj India.

The Technique of the Mystery Story — Carolyn Wells' tips about writing.

The Threat of Nostalgia — A collection of his most obscure stories by Jon Breen

The Time Armada — Fox B. Holden's 1953 SF gem.

The Tongueless Horror and Other Stories — Volume One of the series of short stories from the weird pulps by Wyatt Blassingame.

The Town from Planet Five — From Richard Wilson, two SF classics, *And Then the Town Took Off* and *The Girls from Planet 5*

The Tracer of Lost Persons — From 1906, an episodic novel that became a hit radio series in the 30s. Introduced by Richard A. Lupoff.

The Trail of the Cloven Hoof — Diabolical horror from 1935 by Arlton Eadie. Introduced by John Pelan.

The Triune Man — Mindscrambling science fiction from Richard A. Lupoff.

The Unholy Goddess and Other Stories — Wyatt Blassingame's first DTP compilation

The Universal Holmes — Richard A. Lupoff's 2007 collection of five Holmesian pastiches and a recipe for giant rat stew.

The Werewolf vs the Vampire Woman — Hard to believe ultraviolence by either Arthur M. Scarm or Arthur M. Scram.

The Whistling Ancestors — A 1936 classic of weirdness by Richard E. Goddard and introduced by John Pelan.

The White Owl — A vintage thriller from Edmund Snell

The White Peril in the Far East — Sidney Lewis Gulick's 1905 indictment of the West and assurance that Japan would never attack the U.S.

The Wizard of Berner's Abbey — A 1935 horror gem written by Mark Hansom and introduced by John Pelan.

The Wonderful Wizard of Oz — by L. Frank Baum and illustrated by Gavin L. O'Keefe

Through the Looking Glass — Lewis Carroll wrote it; Gavin L. O'Keefe illustrated it.

Time Line — Ramble House artist Gavin O'Keefe selects his most evocative art inspired by the twisted literature he reads and designs.

Tiresias — Psychotic modern horror novel by Jonathan M. Sweet.

Tortures and Towers — Two novellas of terror by Dexter Dayle.

Totah Six-Pack — Fender Tucker's six tales about Farmington in one sleek volume.

Tree of Life, Book of Death — Grania Davis' book of her life.

Triple Quest — An arty mystery from the 30s by E.R. Punshon.

Trail of the Spirit Warrior — Roger Haley's saga of life in the Indian Territories.

Two Kinds of Bad — Two 50s novels by William Ard about Danny Fontaine

Two Suns of Morcali and Other Stories — Evelyn E. Smith's SF tour-de-force

Ultra-Boiled — 23 gut-wrenching tales by our Man in Brooklyn, Gary Lovisi.

Up Front From Behind — A 2011 satire of Wall Street by James B. Kobak.

Victims & Villains — Intriguing Sherlockiana from Derham Groves.

Wade Wright Novels — *Echo of Fear, Death At Nostalgia Street, It Leads to Murder* and *Shadows' Edge*, a double book featuring *Shadows Don't Bleed* and *The Sharp Edge.*

Walter S. Masterman Novels — *The Green Toad, The Flying Beast, The Yellow Mistletoe, The Wrong Verdict, The Perjured Alibi, The Border Line, The Bloodhounds Bay, The Curse of Cantire* and *The Baddington Horror.* Masterman wrote horror and mystery, some introduced by John Pelan.

We Are the Dead and Other Stories — Volume Two in the Day Keene in the Detective Pulps series, introduced by Ed Gorman. When done, there may be 11 in the series. ·

Welsh Rarebit Tales — Charming stories from 1902 by Harle Oren Cummins

West Texas War and Other Western Stories — by Gary Lovisi.

What If? Volume 1, 2 and 3 — Richard A. Lupoff introduces three decades worth of SF short stories that should have won a Hugo, but didn't.

When the Batman Thirsts and Other Stories — Weird tales from Frederick C. Davis.

Whip Dodge: Man Hunter — Wesley Tallant's saga of a bounty hunter of the old West.

Win, Place and Die! — The first new mystery by Milt Ozaki in decades. The ultimate novel of 70s Reno.

Writer 1 and 2 — A magnus opus from Richard A. Lupoff summing up his life as writer.

You'll Die Laughing — Bruce Elliott's 1945 novel of murder at a practical joker's English countryside manor.

RAMBLE HOUSE

Fender Tucker, Prop. Gavin L. O'Keefe, Graphics
www.ramblehouse.com   fender@ramblehouse.com
228-826-1783   10329 Sheephead Drive, Vancleave MS 39565